'Welcome to my valley.'

There went her nerves again. Cassandra couldn't get enough of looking at the new Jack. Goodness. Wasn't he handsome? Perhaps he knew it. Perhaps this new confidence she sensed in him came from being aware of how he was perceived by the women around him. And those women...they had such fine features and beautiful skin.

It hurt to remember that she'd once looked like that. That she'd once turned heads and garnered male attention.

She composed herself and tried to remain positive. Jack hadn't asked anyone else to marry him; he had asked her. So Cassandra focused on what the future with him might bring, and gave him a cheerful nod.

'Nice to be here

'Yes, finally,' h   ng about something

She swooped d   of the roses, hoping the colour heating up her cheeks didn't show.

Finally, after all these years, Jack McColton would be taking her virginity.

RANCHER
WANTS A WIFE

Kate Bridges

Published in Great Britain 2014
by Mills & Boon, an imprint of Harlequin (UK) Limited,
Eton House, 18-24 Paradise Road, Richmond, Surrey, TW9 1SR

© 2014 Katherine Haupt

ISBN: 978 0 263 90936 4

Harlequin (UK) Limited's policy is to use papers that are natural, renewable and recyclable products and made from wood grown in sustainable forests. The logging and manufacturing processes conform to the legal environmental regulations of the country of origin.

Printed and bound in Spain
by Blackprint CPI, Barcelona

Award-winning and multi-published author **Kate Bridges** was raised in rural Canada, and her stories reflect her love for wide-open spaces, country sunshine and the Rocky Mountains. She loves writing adventurous tales of the men and women who tamed the West. Prior to becoming a full-time writer, Kate worked as a paediatric intensive care nurse. She often includes compelling medical situations in her novels. Later in her education she studied architecture, and worked as a researcher on a television design programme. She has taken postgraduate studies in comedy screenwriting, and in her spare time writes screenplays. Kate's novels have been translated into nine languages, studied in over a dozen colleges on their commercial fiction courses, and are sold worldwide. She lives in the beautiful cosmopolitan city of Toronto with her family. To find out more about Kate's books and to sign up for her free online newsletter please visit www.katebridges.com

This book is dedicated to my family
for their loving support and for always
coming through with their sense of humour.

In writing this story I owe many thanks to
my fabulous editor, Carly Byrne, for her talented
editorial input and advice. I'd also like to thank
Linda Fildew for her support, and the entire team
in the UK offices for their friendliness when I came
to visit and their dedication behind the scenes.
I would like to thank my marvellous agent,
Erica Spellman Silverman, for her enthusiasm
and guidance, and the whole team
at the Trident Media Group.
It's a great pleasure to work with all of you.

Chapter One

Chicago, February 1873
Mrs. Pepik's Boardinghouse
for Desolate Women

"What if my husband doesn't like me? What if I don't like him?" Cassandra Hamilton leaned forward at the crowded dining table. Her blond braid dipped over her shoulder as she lifted a stack of letters from her would-be grooms.

A dozen other chattering young women jostled around her to read the names and notes.

All these men, thought Cassandra, interested in her?

"Don't worry so much, my dear. Wedding jitters are normal. Especially since you'll be our first mail-order bride." The landlady, plump

Mrs. Pepik, peered down her spectacles at Cassandra and patted her hand.

A nearby fireplace sizzled with the last of the ice-covered logs they had rationed for this evening. The warmth penetrated Cassandra's cracked leather boots.

"You're pleasant and...and wholesome." The landlady's eyes flickered over the scar on Cassandra's cheek before she politely gazed away from it. "He'll like you."

Cassandra ran her hand along her right cheek, wondering if she'd ever be comfortable again with her own looks. Sometimes when she was alone and immersed in a task, she blissfully forgot about the burn injury, but in the presence of others, their curiosity and sympathy rarely allowed her that freedom.

"And as for you liking him," the landlady continued on a cheery note, "fortunately, *you* get to make the selection."

Giggles of excitement erupted at the table. The sound was much nicer to listen to than the sadness and despair when Cassandra had first arrived.

They were all survivors of what everyone now, nearly a year and a half later, was calling the Great Chicago Fire. A catastrophe that had caused over three hundred deaths and had left a hundred thousand people homeless. The fire had stolen the only two people Cassandra had loved—her beautiful younger sister, Mary, and their fearless father—and had made Cassandra silently question in the horrible months that followed whether she wished to go on without them.

Once, on what would've been Mary's nineteenth birthday, Cassandra had walked quietly to the railroad depot and had almost leaped onto the tracks before an oncoming locomotive. The only thing that had stopped her were the nearby voices of two children—a brother and sister arguing over a hopscotch game they were chalking on the pavement. It was then that Cassandra had realized what her little sister would desire, more than anything: for her to live a full life.

And so ever since Mrs. Pepik had come upon the idea of advertising "her young ladies" as mail-order brides in the Western newspapers, the boardinghouse had become a sanctuary of laughter and amicable debates.

Cassandra, good with geography, logically minded and possessing a surprisingly natural skill with investigation, had helped track down some missing persons in the aftermath of the fire. She'd found intervals of employment for herself and some of the other women, and she'd gone to the records office to follow up on lost documents for others. She had comfortably and voluntarily dealt with lawyers, bankers and jailers. Due to her meticulous uncovering of lost people and papers, some of the workingmen she'd encountered had jokingly nicknamed her "That Lady Detective."

Now, Mrs. Pepik stretched closer, eager to hear of the decision at hand. "Cassandra, which man will it be?"

A slender young woman in the corner spoke up. "I'd take the jeweler in Saint Louis."

"Oh, no," said another, "My vote is on the reverend in Wyoming Territory."

Cassandra's dearest friend and roommate, dark-haired Natasha O'Sullivan, offered her perspective. "Which man stands out for you, Cassandra? Which one does your heart point to?"

Cassandra took a moment, pressed back against her chair and decided. "The man from California."

She shuffled through the letters till she found his again. The one she'd been rereading ever since she'd received it three days ago.

"But he sounds as if he works too hard," someone said.

"California," Cassandra repeated. Of all the

replies to her carefully worded advertisement, his clearly stood out.

"Because of all the sunshine," Mrs. Pepik assumed.

"Because you'd like to find employment as a detective," said Natasha. "And California would allow you that as a woman."

"That is true," said Cassandra. "But mostly it's because I know him."

Feet stopped shuffling. Women stopped talking. Hands froze on correspondence.

Cassandra peered down at his signature. Jack McColton. She was besieged with a torrent of emotions. How could she express to her friends all that she felt? Jack was a link to the loving past, a tender link to Mary and Father, a link to pleasurable times and heart-thrilling memories. Yet, he was also a link to painful times, to an explosive night and accusations she never should have made, to a time when her skin had been perfect and her looks had been whole. She'd behaved so shamefully when she was younger, assuming her good fortune would last forever.

Mrs. Pepik glanced at his name and cleared her throat. "How is it that you know this man, Jack McColton?"

Trying to ignore another wave of apprehension, Cassandra proceeded to explain.

Four Months Later
Napa Valley, California

"I urge you to reconsider."

"Is this why you called me to your office? It's too late. She'll be here any moment." Jack McColton removed his Stetson. He ran a hand through his black hair as he stood by the door, exasperated at the contrary advice he was receiving from his attorney.

June sunshine and summer-fresh air poured in from the window, rustling the gauze drapes.

"Don't throw it all away, Jack." Hugh Logan was more than an attorney; he was slated to be best man at the wedding. Jack had come to trust him as a dependable friend in the three years he'd been living and working in the valley.

Hugh, in his mid-thirties and a few years older than Jack, rose from behind his mahogany desk to allow his tailor to mark his new suit. The tailor, a rotund man from eastern Europe who didn't speak or understand English well, quietly pinned the gray sleeves.

"I'm not throwing anything away," Jack insisted.

"A new ranch. Two dozen horses. A veterinarian practice. Neighbors who would like nothing more than for you to marry one of *their* daughters." Hugh's red hair glistened from a recent cut at the barber's.

"I *was* intending to find a suitable wife in Napa Valley, but things don't always work out the way you plan."

"Doesn't mean it's time to throw away the plan."

"I know this girl."

"You mean you knew her five years ago."

Jack, many inches taller with broader shoulders than his friend, disagreed. "I've got to go."

"Reconsider, Jack. Take your time with this. Court her all over again. Then get married if you still want to. Maybe what she's truly attracted to is that big ranch of yours."

Jack scoffed.

"That's the attorney in me speaking." Hugh's gaze flashed down to the tailor, who was kneeling and making his way round the edge of the waistcoat, giving no indication that he was intrigued by the conversation. Even so, Hugh lowered his voice. "You know it's fair advice, Jack. Hell, last night in the saloon you told me yourself she spurned you when you were livin' in Chicago. Now that my head has cleared, I'd like to bring it to your attention, for the record, that the only thing that's changed since her rejection then and her acceptance now is your net worth."

Jack frowned. "It's not the only thing." Yet the comments cut deep into his pride. Cassandra had never been the easiest woman to deal with; in fact, she'd been downright spoiled by her father. But she'd suffered through a hell of a lot since Jack had last seen her. Both physically and emotionally.

And five years ago, he hadn't proposed marriage to her. Damn, at the time when he'd approached her, she was engaged to someone else. It had all been so complicated and convoluted.

Yet, he did recall that her rejection hadn't been a gentle one.

Jack rubbed his jaw.

The tailor asked Hugh to turn, then continued pinning.

Mail-order brides weren't uncommon in these parts. Jack didn't know any personally, but he'd heard tales. There were so few women in the West that many men used any means necessary to procure a bride and start a family. Jack imagined that some of the women were desperate— as were the men—but some of the ladies were adventurous and wished to travel West. It was less restrictive here than in the East, for lots of women owned their own property and ran businesses, or worked just as long and hard on the ranches and vineyards as their husbands. At least, that's what Cassandra had written—that in addition to the compatible marriage, she was looking forward to the freedom in choosing her own occupations to fill her time.

She'd always been ladylike and restrained, and had listened quietly to her father's advice. Jack imagined she'd be just as respectful of his opinions, and that she likely only wished to start up a library, perhaps, here in town. Or a knitting group, or work with him in some capacity on the ranch.

The ground outside rumbled. A team of horses pulling a stagecoach suddenly thundered past the window. She was here.

Jack took a deep breath.

"See you at the wedding, Hugh." He planted his Stetson back on his head and strode out of the office, trying not to let on that the words still bothered him.

Sitting in the cramped stagecoach, Cassandra peered up from the book she was discreetly reading, *Tales of Bounty Hunters and Criminals*. Through the dusty windowpane, she observed vineyards on the slopes and palm trees among the town's buildings, and worried again how very late they were. She tried to suppress her rush of nerves. It was Wednesday afternoon at fifteen minutes past two—more than two hours behind schedule.

Would her soon-to-be groom still be here, waiting for her, or had Jack tired of it and left?

She opened her large satchel and slid the book in among her other things. There was a Chicago newspaper, another text entitled *California Courts and the Legal Code*, a silver-inlaid derringer pistol and a small box of .41 Rimfire cartridges.

The driver pulled the team of horses into a green valley and the pretty town called Sundial, and careened to a stop. The three other passengers with her—an elderly couple and a young cowboy—gathered their belongings as she quickly disembarked.

"Good traveling with you, miss," said the old gent, blinking at Cassandra's scarred cheek.

"Enjoy the last leg of your journey," she replied, turning her injured side away.

The young cowboy nodded goodbye. Although she and he were roughly the same age—mid-twenties—in all the hours they'd spent together, he'd never once gazed at her with any masculine interest in his eyes. Not that she wished him to; only that she noticed self-consciously that since her injury, most men silently dismissed her in that way.

Wearing a wide-brimmed sun hat with a chiffon scarf pushed through the top and hanging at her temples as ties, Cassandra instinctively pulled the dangling fabric over her marred cheek. She slid into the awaiting crowd and searched the faces.

What would Jack think when he saw her? She'd explained the injury to him in her letters. He'd responded that it was irrelevant to him, that he simply wished her good health and was relieved that she hadn't been seriously injured.

Of course, he had written those words thousands of miles away. Things might be different up close. He was about to marry her, and what man didn't wish to be sexually attracted to his bride?

Normally, being outdoors under the blue sky and sun calmed her, but not today. She searched the assortment of faces for someone who might resemble the man who'd walked out of her world five years ago. Back then their relationship had been strained, for it was a time when she had been engaged to someone else.

No Jack McColton.

Cassandra twirled around to study more faces. She was looking for someone tall, on the skinny side, with black hair. He was a veterinarian now, he'd written, working with horses in the vineyards, lumber mills and ranches of Napa Valley. He'd studied veterinary science in Chicago and she'd often seen him with a textbook in his hands. He'd always had a love of animals, she recalled, more interested in the livestock people owned than who might be knocking at the front door.

Searching the eager faces looking back at her, Cassandra dusted her threadbare skirts and adjusted her plumed hat to shield herself from the gleaming California sun.

So much hotter and drier than Chicago.

So much more hopeful and filled with promise.

So much more anxiety-inducing than she'd thought possible when she'd agreed to become a mail-order bride at Mrs. Pepik's Boarding House for Desolate Women. In the return address she'd given Jack, she'd left off the desolate part.

No need to tell him how far she'd fallen.

Besides, he'd see it in one glance, wouldn't he?

Stop that, she told herself, and straightened her posture with dignity and pride.

She was here to start a new life with a man she had known to be hardworking and law-abiding. In choosing Jack over the other prospects, she was at least going with a known quantity. She knew his flaws as well as his strengths. Surely that was an advantage, wasn't it?

But perhaps she'd been hasty, rushing to marry him because of past memories and his recollections of her late sister and father. Five years had passed. For all she knew, he might now be reckless and unfeeling. And back then, she hadn't spent that much time alone with him. Sometimes a person's behavior was totally different in private than in public.

"Cassandra?" said a deep male voice behind her.

Feeling a stab of terror mixed with excitement, she wheeled around and nearly bumped into him.

She got an eyeful of a very broad chest wearing a neatly pressed white shirt and leather vest. Holding on to her hat, she craned her neck and peered way, way up. Her scarf draped against her scar.

Those familiar deep brown eyes flashed at her with curiosity. Her first impression was that everything about Jack McColton was incredibly dark. Tanned skin, black hair, black eyebrows, black leather vest, black cowboy hat. And no longer thin. His shoulders were as wide as forever. Obviously, his work in the vineyards had seasoned his physique.

He reminded her of a Thoroughbred race-horse, muscled and built for speed. Her pulse tripped over itself in response to his powerful presence. Wavy hair, longer than the men wore in Chicago, touched his collar. A sheen of moisture from the heat of the sun dampened his brow. He was clean-shaven, but already a dark shadow underlined his firm jaw and cast shadows in the dimple of his chin.

"Cassandra," he repeated in a rich baritone. "Good to see you." And then her scarf came away from her cheek, exposing the ugly ripple of flesh four inches in diameter, and his studious eyes flickered over it.

The burning heat of embarrassment and shame, and an overriding wish to flee, overtook her. *This is what you ordered,* she thought. *How terribly disappointed you must be.*

He fumbled for barely a moment, almost imperceptibly, then glanced back up into her eyes with a smile. "You look lovely."

She took in a deep breath, touched by his kindness.

Why did the rhythm of her breathing still break when she was around him? Why had it always been like this? She nodded and smiled in a confusion of emotions.

She hadn't realized how parched her mouth

was. "Well, I...Jack...this climate certainly agrees with you." Clumsily, she reached out to shake his hand at the same instant he held out a bouquet of pink wild roses.

She took the flowers, mumbled a thank-you that got muffled when he leaned forward, planted a large warm hand on her wrist and pulled her forward over the roses in an awkward semihug that two distant relations might share. It was a wonderful display of strain and discomfort, the same awkwardness that had existed between them when she'd been engaged to his cousin, Troy.

Only now she was engaged to Jack, and all the witty and charming things she'd practiced to say on their first meeting flew out of her head.

"Sorry you got delayed," he said. "The coach is never on time."

"Thank you for waiting," she replied, still flustered.

"May I take your bag?" He extended his hand, and before she could stop him, took her woven satchel. Due to the weight of her books and gun, it thudded against his side. "What on earth are you carrying? Cannonballs?"

She smiled at his quip. She hadn't written to him about her desire to be a detective. She wanted to prepare herself first, to scope out the town and its facilities, and break the news to him gently, in the event he had any objections.

"How was your trip?"

"Long and dusty. But it is exciting to see this part of the country."

He gave her another one of those sweeping glances that seemed to sum her up. "I almost didn't recognize you."

Because of the massive scar?

He awkwardly tried to make it right. "I mean because you used to be a touch heavier, remember?" Then he groaned. Perhaps that wasn't quite what he'd meant to vocalize, either.

In her efforts to recall what he might look like, she'd forgotten that she herself had been on the plump side, last time they'd seen each other on the night of their ripping argument.

But if he'd had any decency at all, if he'd truly cared for her as he'd confessed that evening, why had he packed his things and left in the middle of the night?

Not a word goodbye.

He had tried to kiss her, but how on earth could he have expected her to react, when she was engaged to his cousin? What more could any decent man expect but a slap on the face?

Anger flashed through her. She was surprised by it and tried to hide it. She thought she'd feel a hundred different things when she saw him again, but never suspected she still hadn't gotten over the callous way he'd left. Those buried feelings of betrayal surged up and stung her. She didn't wish to be resentful. What she'd hoped to be when she arrived, had fantasized being, was a pleasant and optimistic bride.

Perhaps what she was truly indignant about were the circumstances she had found herself in, in Chicago—no way to support herself immediately after the fire, no family to help, relying on the mercy of a man to marry her.

"I guess we've both been through a lot of change." She smiled faintly, trying to overcome her emotions.

The artery at the base of his dark throat pulsed. He seemed to sense her discomfort as he watched her. "And how is Troy?"

Her lashes flicked as she averted her gaze. "Fine, I suppose. In England somewhere, last I heard."

She hadn't spoken to that turncoat for five years, either, but how would Jack know that? All she'd told him in her letters, when he'd asked, was that their engagement had been over for quite some time. The truth was, after that huge row with Jack, she'd gone to Troy and had discovered that all the terrible things Jack had said about him—his drinking and his carousing with painted ladies—were true. Cassandra had severed her engagement that very night. Yet when she'd gone to tell Jack that he was right about his cousin, he'd been nowhere to be found.

Over the course of the next few days and weeks, she had realized that she hadn't really loved either man.

And then out of the blue had come Jack's response to her ad as a bride.

He frowned, as if trying to read her expression, and any residue of sentiment she might still have for Troy. She pressed her lips together and tried to express nothing.

My, how good she'd become at that game.

The moment stretched and stretched. Then two young ladies walked by, whispering something about him with admiration in their tone. Jack didn't pay them attention; his dark eyebrows flickered at Cassandra. He rubbed the tense muscles in his jaw and tilted his mouth in an expression of friendliness.

"Welcome to my valley."

There went her nerves again. She couldn't get enough of looking at the new Jack. Goodness. Wasn't he handsome? Perhaps he knew it. Perhaps this new confidence she sensed in him came from being aware of how he was perceived

by the women around him. And those women…
they had such fine features and beautiful skin.

It hurt to remember that she'd once looked
like that. That she'd once turned heads and garnered male attention.

She composed herself and tried to remain
positive. Jack hadn't asked anyone else to marry
him; he had asked her. So Cassandra focused on
what the future with him might bring, and gave
him a cheerful nod. "Nice to be here, finally."

"Yes, finally," he said, as if he were thinking
about something more.

She swooped down to inhale the perfume of
the roses, hoping the color heating up her cheeks
didn't show.

Finally, after all these years, Jack McColton
would be taking her virginity.

Chapter Two

"My horse and buggy's up this way," Jack said to Cassandra as he found her larger piece of luggage and led her away from the crowd.

He tried to restrain the sorrow he felt when he gazed at her and the injury to her face. God. It had nearly felled him when he'd first seen her.

He took a deep breath, but his muscles were still tense.

The pocked flesh covered her entire right cheek. It wasn't that her beauty was affected, for he saw the lovely woman she was and always would be. It was that he felt such guilt in seeing the scar. If he had been there in Chicago, he damn well could've prevented her injury. He likely would've been living nearby, could've helped her and her family escape the fire, could've removed Cassandra from the burning timbers of her home.

But he hadn't been there for her, and not only had she lost her family, she had to live with the scar and the turning heads wherever she walked. Even now, men and women caught sight of her and followed her with inquisitive eyes. He tried to ignore them, and the ones shouting their hellos at him to give Cassandra time to adjust. He was ashamed at how much they were staring, and just wanted to get her the hell out of there.

He placed her suitcase and satchel in his shiny buggy and held out his hand to help her onto the seat.

She slid her palm into his. Was he imagining it, or was her touch slightly shaky? She hopped up onto the polished leather and quickly released her grip, before he could tell for sure.

"I thought we'd get married tomorrow evening," he said, trying to break the strain between them.

"Tomorrow? My, oh my." Her soft expression flashed with surprise.

Something flickered past her shoulder. When he looked to the two-story frame building across the street, he saw the white curtains shift in his attorney's office. Cassandra followed his gaze and peered at the office, too, then to the courthouse and the land registry building, as if orienting herself to the town.

Jack tried to ignore Hugh's warning all over again. He knew what he was doing. There were good solid reasons for doing this.

Lots of men got married. He was of the age. A wife would enhance his life, not detract from it.

"Is tomorrow too soon? Would you like more time to get to know...to get to know the place?" Standing on the street, Jack peered at her bunched-up skirts, over the lacy blouse peeking through her bodice, to the side of her left pretty pink cheek. A few strands of blond hair had trapped some beads of perspiration. The hot sun had already gotten to her face. Luckily, she was shaded now by the roof of the buggy. She was still wearing her hat with the billowing scarf ends covering her injury, and his heart buckled with tenderness and regret that she felt the need to hide behind it.

She inhaled, the tug of her breath making the feminine curves of her throat stand out. Her blue eyes shone. "Tomorrow's fine."

"Good. Reverend Darcy said he'd be available at six."

"Six o'clock, then." She rested her roses in her lap, as cool and unattached as if they were strangers.

He supposed so much time had passed, they *were* strangers.

"Just a simple ceremony, Cassandra. Then back to the ranch for a few days of...of rest before I get back to work."

"Yes, that's fine."

They had agreed in their letters that simple arrangements were best. She preferred a small ceremony. There would be no reception, since she didn't know anyone here and the arrangements would've been too difficult for her to schedule from Chicago. He had offered to do it but she had declined, and to tell the truth, he was relieved. The only thing she had asked for was a church wedding, and he was pleased to oblige.

The mare harnessed to his buggy craned her neck at him as if to say, "Hurry up. What's taking you so long?"

Cassandra, perched on the edge of her seat, seemed disarmed by the animal's antics and smiled.

He gave the mare a pat as he walked around to his side of the buggy. "Easy, there, River, we're going."

In Chicago, Cassandra had been full of life and energy, bouncing everywhere with her younger sister, Mary, in tow. Her eyes had sparkled with vitality, and she'd had a constant smile

on her face. Cassandra was much quieter here.
Less carefree. He couldn't blame her, considering the sorrow she'd been through. Her clothes
were much more drab, too, but they covered a
curvy new figure that intrigued him.

Dark blond silky hair, pretty blue eyes. But
she still had that thing about her, that way she
had of putting up her guard. If she hadn't recently accepted his marriage proposal, he'd
swear by looking at her that she wanted nothing to do with him.

Would he ever be enough for her? Would this
life in California come anywhere close to what
she'd dreamed her life would be like in Chicago?

The last time they'd spoken in person, he'd
tried to kiss her, and she'd been point-blank honest that she wanted nothing to do with him.

How could he ever erase those stinging words
from his memory?

It hadn't been the first time he'd tried to tell
her that he had cared for her, but she'd always
pushed him away. Black sheep of the family
was what he'd been then, and no one would've
been more against him as a possible suitor than
her father.

And now, sadly, it was just the two of them
trying to work things out on their own.

And still he couldn't trust her.

Oh, he felt plenty for her, physically, but what surprised him most in seeing her was the guarded feeling that sprang up, the knowledge that he might be just as hurt by her now as he'd always been.

He stole another glance at her as he reached his side of the buggy. The contradiction in her demeanor—the almost-smile and the heated flush, contrasting with the reserve in her stiff posture, made him ache to touch her. In fact, he wouldn't mind driving the buggy to the church right now, then taking her straight to the Valley Hotel, where they could *share* that room he intended on renting for her alone tonight. Where he'd strip her naked, starting with that silly hat, and that prim bodice, with its dozen little buttons, which was trying its best to hide the lovely profile of her breasts.

To hell with the polished politeness of Chicago society. He could teach her a thing or two about how men were supposed to behave around their women. But would he ever be enough for her?

"Howdy, Dr. McColton," said one of the Birkstrom brothers as he walked by on the boardwalk. "Wanted to thank you for tending to that calf last week. She's up and about like nothing happened."

"Glad to hear it," said Jack.

"Say, Dr. McColton," shouted another rancher from across the street. "Could you drop by to inspect that new stallion I got yesterday? He's jittery. I think the train ride shook him up. And he scratched himself on some barb wire this morning."

With hesitation, Jack glanced in Cassandra's direction, feeling guilty about the time he'd be taking away from her. But he couldn't let an animal suffer. "I'll squeeze in a visit later tonight."

"Much obliged." The rancher looked curiously at Cassandra, then nodded goodbye.

More folks nodded in greeting, but Jack turned his attention back to his bride. *Bride.* He swallowed hard at the reality. He'd never given marriage much thought. Since Chicago, he'd enjoyed his time with various women and saw no reason to change. Occasionally, he'd thought of marriage in the far future, something that he might do, perhaps *should* do if he wanted to pass down his land to an heir. Then, when he'd seen Cassandra's ad, the feelings had come rushing at him like a thundering buffalo.

He climbed aboard the buggy, settled beside Cassandra and flicked the reins. The vehicle rolled smoothly down the main street, its bolts and springs newly greased for the occasion. He became extremely aware of the woman beside him, the proximity of her elbow next to his, the lilt of her chest, the shifting of her thighs beneath her skirts.

"This is incredible." She craned her neck to take in the view.

Gently sloped hills rolled toward them, terraced with rows of grapevines. Orchards sat on other slopes, filled with peach and plum trees. Raspberry bushes sprang from another acreage. A stream gushed through the valley and on behind the cluster of stores and shops in Sundial, otherwise the place would be as dry as dust. In the distance, saws from the lumber mill echoed in the hills.

"Where's your ranch?"

He pointed to a sprawling house halfway up the slopes, built of stone and fresh-sawed lumber from the mills. "The white one in the middle of the trees."

"All that?"

He nodded with pride.

"You've worked hard, Jack."

"And from the sound of it, so have you. You must've come to know some of the women at the boarding house quite well." She'd done odd jobs to help support herself, she'd written in her letters.

She turned away and peered up at two soaring hawks. "Lovely people, all of them, trying to overcome such tragedy."

He wanted to offer his condolences again on the loss of her sister and father, out in the open this time and not simply through written correspondence. How did one convey the depth of compassion after such a catastrophe? The Great Fire had occurred nearly two years ago, in October of '71, but the loss was still raw. He shook his head at the thought that one-third of the city's population had lost their homes. And many had buried loved ones.

"I was so sorry to hear the news about your father and sister. If I had known...I would have been there to pay my respects, and to help if I could." As for comforting Cassandra, he had mistakenly assumed Troy would be there to do that. How wrong Jack had been. The cousin—the one whose parents had taken Jack in as a boy when his own had passed away from consumption—had offered no support to her at all, because he wasn't even *in* Chicago at the time of the fire.

She swallowed and clasped a pink rose on her lap. "Thank you. You mentioned you were in the new lands of Alaska and didn't hear about the fire till six months later. How did the news finally reach you?"

"I was on a ship traveling down the coast, heading to California. There was an old newspaper stuck inside one of the animal cages. When I opened it, there was a photograph of your street. Burned to ashes."

He swallowed hard at the memory of pulling out those pages, and the horror of not only seeing it, but being trapped on a ship and unable to do anything, not knowing what had become of Cassandra and her family. "It took another two weeks for the ship to land, and for me to get more information on the fire."

"That explains why I didn't hear from you."

"I tried sending a telegram to locate you. No luck. I wrote to the police. No reply. I wrote letters, two of them, addressed to your father. They came back to me with...with 'Deceased' written on them."

She murmured, "How awful to hear it that way."

"I tried sending one to Troy, but it was returned, too, with 'Address Unknown.' I could only hope you and he had married and you had moved away to another city before the fire started. Perhaps to New York to join his parents." Only his parents weren't in New York, according to the private detective Jack had hired, but had gone to Europe somewhere. As had Troy, it turned out.

"There was such chaos after the fire. The police were overwhelmed. All the mail got redirected. There was so much of it, the post offices didn't know what to do with it all, or how to locate anyone. One hundred thousand people with no address."

Jack shook his head in wonder that she'd survived all she had.

"I miss them." Her eyes glimmered with tears, her nostrils flared, her chin trembled. The depth of her loss left him speechless.

Then she took a deep breath and her sorrow shifted. "They would like it here. Mary loved sunshine, and my father would pick your brain on how many other lawyers are in town and whether he could make a fine living here himself."

"Gordon always did like a good argument."

She could have taken the statement badly, considering how often Jack had debated with the old gent, disagreeing on everything from city planning to job opportunities. Instead, she smiled softly and nodded.

"What newspaper did you see my advertisement in?"

"San Francisco Chronicle."

He'd been shocked as hell when he'd seen her ad as a mail-order bride. First, that she'd survived the fire alone, and was still in Chicago. Second, that she and Troy were not married.

Jack nodded in greeting to two older folks walking toward the mercantile that sat beside the post office.

Horses clomped along the rutted grooves of the wide road. Riders on horseback, and other wagons sped along the busy shops.

Cassandra craned her neck to look at the sheriff's office and jailhouse when they passed it, and another law office.

"So after the fire, Cassandra…who took care of you?"

She pivoted sharply to look at him, her manner cautious. "I took care of myself. I got a room at the boardinghouse, and made my own way."

There was a lot she wasn't telling him about that boardinghouse. Jack had received a report three months ago from the private detective he'd hired for a few days, as soon as he'd discovered where she was. This time in dealing with Cassandra Hamilton, he would go into the relationship with eyes wide open. But there was no reason to upset her with his knowledge. She was obviously trying to forget that she had wound up at a home for desolate women.

Desolate women. What a blow to her pride that must've been. She'd come from a wealthy family, having a new dress for every occasion, servants who said yes to everything she'd asked. The property had been lost in the fire, the land itself used to pay off debts her father had. Damn. If Jack had known, he would have done something to help her.

The one thing the detective couldn't clarify for Jack was when, exactly, she and Troy had ended their relationship. No one the detective had interviewed had firsthand knowledge of any fiancé, only rumors that she'd been engaged years earlier. So the thing Jack was most curious about was the thing still left up in the air.

"I hope you don't mind my asking, but when did you call off your engagement?"

She paused. "Five years ago."

"*Five?*" He flicked the reins and the mare turned the corner, past the two banks in town. A handful of people wove in and out of the bakery, and farther along, the smoke shop where a man could buy a good cigar. A stagecoach creaked by in the other direction and Jack tipped his hat in greeting to the driver. "I've been gone five years. So when, precisely, did you part company?"

Color crept into her cheeks. "The night you left."

Jack tried to piece together the timeline. It meant after his argument with Cassandra, Troy must've come to her, as well.

"Why didn't you tell me?"

Her arms stiffened at her sides. "You didn't leave a forwarding address. I didn't even know what country you were living in."

"Ah, hell." Another wave of guilt washed over him.

If she had known where he was living, would she have reached out for help? Something told him the answer would still have been no.

He directed the horse and buggy around the town square and the large granite sundial that sat in the center. Spaniards had built the structure more than a century ago, and it was how the town got its name.

Cassandra craned her neck to see it, intrigued. "Can you truly read the time from it?"

"Of course. I'll show you how next time, when we're on foot."

"Jack, now that we're face-to-face…and seeing that the date is planned for tomorrow, I'm wondering about a few things." She swung her knees slightly in his direction.

Questions? But there was much more he

wanted to ask her about Troy. Such as why they'd severed their plans for marriage, and who had been the one to walk away. Jack doubted it had been her, considering how much she'd defended Troy on that night.

Jack relented to her curiosity. "By all means, ask away."

He pulled in beside the Valley Hotel, a board and batten, two-story building with a large veranda encircling the main floor. He dropped the reins and looked at Cassandra. Her face was in shade, but a sharp shadow line from the hot sun sliced across her lap.

She struggled to find the right words. "There were at least two dozen people at the stage depot when you picked me up. You spoke to several of them, and we passed another half dozen on the way here. Yet you haven't introduced me to one person." The crest of her cheek flickered. "Didn't you tell anyone about me?"

He muttered under his breath, castigating himself. He'd handled her arrival all wrong.

"I'm glad you're here, Cassandra." He exhaled, wishing he'd thought things through in a different way. "The fact is I did tell some folks you were coming. Not the whole world, though. I'm not sure why I kept it to myself. It certainly wasn't to make you feel slighted. Maybe it was because I wasn't sure you'd *be* on that stage-coach."

"You thought I might not show up?"

"That's right."

She blinked. "I'm here."

He slid down from the buggy, strolled around to her side and lifted her by the waist with all the careful enthusiasm he used to have around her in Chicago, when they were younger and heading out for an evening with a group of friends.

It must've taken her by surprise. The wind caught her skirts and she yelped in laughter, sailing over the boardwalk. When he planted her feet square in front of the Valley Hotel, beneath a palm tree, he noticed they were being watched from two doors down.

Four young women were coming out of a hat shop, smiling and chattering, all holding several packages. One of the taller ones, Elise Beacon, peered over at him and Cassandra and, apparently startled by the sight, dropped one of her purchases.

Not now, thought Jack.

One of Elise's friends fumbled to retrieve the package for her, while the others whispered, and nudged her to continue walking.

Jack removed his hat in greeting. "Ladies."

Then he turned to Cassandra, who'd briefly glanced in their direction, and held out his elbow. "Shall we go inside?"

Chapter Three

Cassandra wondered who the women were who had stared at her and Jack. There was a taller one with brunette hair fastened up beneath a stylish hat, whose eyes had met hers. The woman had whispered something to a friend, and they'd both seemed to be stifling amusement.

Did they find something humorous about Cassandra? Surely they wouldn't be laughing at her scar.

She decided she was being foolish. They obviously knew Jack, and were giving him female attention—which seemed to be a common pastime in Sundial. And why not? He was a charming, hardworking bachelor. But soon-to-be-married, she hoped they realized.

Jack held out his arm and she took it. Soon

she was registering at the front desk, her bags were being whisked upstairs and she was exchanging pleasantries with the young man behind the counter. If he noticed her cheek, he didn't let on that anything was amiss.

"Take care of her," said Jack. "We're getting married tomorrow."

"Are you now, Dr. McColton? Congratulations to you both." The boyish clerk swung the registry back toward himself, read her name and addressed her. "Miss Hamilton, welcome to the Valley Hotel. Will you be needing any amenities shortly? Something from the dining hall, or perhaps a bathtub filled?"

Jack interjected, "Cassandra, I'm hoping you'll come with me to the ranch for dinner. Won't you?" When he turned his handsome face toward her, her qualms subsided about the women she'd seen outside. There was no need to get stirred up about what might or might not happen in this town now that she'd arrived. She was here, and determined to make the best of it.

"I'd love to see it. But I do need time to get back this evening, soak in a hot tub and prepare for tomorrow."

A smile tugged at the corner of Jack's mouth. Heat flashed in his penetrating eyes, and she got the distinct impression he was imagining her *in* that tub.

She tried to squelch the flutter she felt, wondering what the marriage night would be like, and nervously brushed back strands of wispy hair. "Please give me ten minutes to freshen up. I'll be right down."

"Take twenty," he said, strolling through the large, cool foyer.

The desk clerk tapped a bell on the counter. A porter appeared. Carrying her satchel, Cassandra marched up the wide wooden staircase behind him. The hotel wasn't as grand as some in Chicago, but its Californian flavor—with rustic timber, a stone fireplace in the front entry and plenty of windows—was appealing.

She knew there'd be no time for a honeymoon. Jack had explained it in his letters. She wouldn't be disappointed, she told herself. He enjoyed working hard in his profession, and made no excuses for it. She preferred that over someone sitting idle.

Besides, what other man who'd written to her asking for her hand in marriage had promised her an easy life? Not one.

The porter unlocked a door, handed her the key, set her large suitcase inside and politely left. Cassandra walked into the airy room. The furnishings were sparse, but a large window overlooked the street below. She pulled aside the curtain and noted again the buildings she would likely visit soon in her quest to become a detective—the sheriff's office, land registry, courthouse, the two banks on the corner. She peeked to see if that brunette woman was still at the hat shop, but saw no sign of her.

Cassandra looked down at her faded clothes. Her well-worn jacket and long skirt appeared so paltry compared to the freshly tailored suit the other woman had been wearing. She came from money, no question. And judging by the daring expression on her face, she definitely knew Jack. Did the woman know he'd be married tomorrow? Cassandra removed the derringer and box of bullets from her satchel, and hid them in the dresser. She tucked the newspaper and books in, too. One other question burned in her mind as she prepared for the afternoon with Jack.

Who was that woman?

To Jack, it seemed almost like a regular outing with a regular woman, except this one would soon be his wife. He stretched out his legs in the buggy, repositioned his silver-tipped cowboy boots and grasped the reins in his callused hand. Warm winds enveloped him and Cassandra as they drew closer to his ranch.

She'd changed from her traveling clothes into something plainer—long brown skirts, an ivory blouse and patched shawl. She'd let her blond hair fly free, and he enjoyed seeing it spill over her shoulders. However, she was still wearing that damn hat with the dangling scarf she was obviously using to shield her scarred cheek.

He wished she'd chuck the blasted thing. She didn't need it. But saying so might only embarrass her.

How many nights in the past month had he thought of what it might be like to bring Cassandra home?

He felt more awkward than he had imagined he would. When their knees brushed, when he pointed out his neighbors' ranches on surrounding hills, indicated the train tracks that ran through the valley to reach the lumber mills, even when they simply sat and said nothing, a mountain of tension rippled between them.

It was as if they each didn't trust the other. But why would she mistrust him? She was the one who'd turned him away in Chicago, more than once!

He was relieved when they finally approached the house. Red-colored dogwood lined the perimeter of the quarter-mile laneway. The buggy whisked into the shade of the big oaks as they neared the wide, two-story house. Sunlight danced off the clay roof, bounced on the walls of white-painted timber, and sparkled against blue shutters. A stone chimney dominated the north wall.

To the other side, one of his gardeners was painting the fence, his ranch hands were busy working at the two stables, and splendid horses galloped across the fields.

Cassandra turned her head to view the pretty sight. "How many horses do you keep?"

"Twenty-six at the moment. It's gone as high as thirty-six. I rent them to neighbors, whenever they're needed in the vineyards, or at harvest season, or sometimes for traveling. It works out well. My neighbors get the use of fine horses, and my animals get exercised."

"And you get to buy and trade livestock. Impressive. What you've always wanted."

He grinned at her perceptiveness.

The two sheepdogs came dashing out from the stables and circled around them, tails wagging.

Jack parked the buggy, signaled to one of the hands to come get it, and went to help Cassandra down from her seat. She didn't need assistance this time. She managed to slide out before he got to her, skirts billowing in the wind, scarf flapping against her face.

She didn't look well. Rather pale and shaken. "Are you feeling all right?"

She nodded. "It's been a long journey."

"I hope you'll like it here."

"It's breathtaking, Jack."

Her comment filled him with pride.

She smiled nervously, and when some of the men working in the vicinity cast their curious eyes her way, she stepped closer to Jack. The dogs swished their orange tails and panted at her. With a laugh, Cassandra bent down to say hello.

"Meet Caesar and Queenie," he told her.

She gave them a pat and a rub behind the ears. "By your names, it sounds as though you rule this place."

"Jack!" called his hefty foreman. "Sorry to bother you, sir. Got a scheduling problem with two of the mares."

"Excuse me." Jack left Cassandra's side for a moment, conversed with his foreman, ironed out the dilemma and returned to her side.

His housekeeper and butler greeted Cassandra warmly when she entered the oak double doors. They were a married couple from England, Mr. and Mrs. Dunleigh. Although conservative in their ways, underneath their formal exterior, and once folks got to know them, they were very friendly. Jack had already explained to them the nature of Cassandra's scar, that she'd been trapped in her burning home and that a timber had fallen across her face. She had dashed in after her father, to locate her sister upstairs. The other two hadn't made it out alive, but Cassandra had been rescued by a volunteer fireman.

The Dunleighs discreetly ignored the visual marking.

"Miss Hamilton," said the very tall housekeeper, whose gray hair was impeccably groomed. "Welcome to California." Her gold-rimmed spectacles slid down her nose.

"Very nice to be here."

"May I take your shawl?" asked her husband. He was six inches shorter than his wife and slightly hunched.

"Please."

"And your hat?" asked Mrs. Dunleigh.

Cassandra hesitated, then slowly slid it off. No one paid her any mind. Jack hadn't realized how tense he was about the whole hat thing until she finally gave it up, and he breathed out a sigh of relief.

He peered toward the table by the door, and the overflowing letter holder there.

"The mail came this morning, sir," said Dunleigh. "Some correspondence appears to need your attention immediately. One letter is from the auction house in San Francisco."

"I'll get to it shortly." There seemed to be a never-ending pile of paperwork from his suppliers and customers.

"Dr. McColton," chirped the housekeeper, "I've set some refreshments on the terrace."

"Very good." Jack ushered Cassandra through the house.

He wished they would warm up to each other, but there was only strain. She took in the view as their boots tapped on the clay-tiled floors. Colorful rugs lay scattered in the sitting room between the horsehair sofas and chairs and fieldstone fireplace. Mexican artwork adorned the plaster walls. Twenty feet up, timber rafters crisscrossed the ceiling.

The kitchen, with two fireplaces, butcher-block counters, sideboards lining two walls, and a wide pine table, overlooked one of the terraces. The dining table could easily accommodate fourteen.

"My, Jack," Cassandra said. "I had no idea your house was this huge. Why didn't you tell me?"

"Everything in California's big. I didn't notice."

She tilted her head, eyes sparkling as if she didn't quite believe him, and he noticed with a quickening of his pulse that there was some tenderness in her gaze.

"Shall we sit outside?" he asked.

She nodded. They made their way to the bamboo chairs beneath a trellis. Thankfully, the color had returned to her face, which was shaded by the lush fronds of the palm trees above. "What a gorgeous spot."

Jack adored the view, too. It was why he'd decided to buy this piece of property. Land as far as the eye could see. Rolling vales and sloped vineyards that blended into a big blue sky. The scent of earth and wind, and a feeling that Mother Nature had taken extra care when she'd created Napa Valley.

"Sir," interrupted the butler. "Two gentlemen to see you from San Diego."

"Today? But they weren't supposed to arrive till next week."

"They mentioned they had business this way, sir, and wished to call on you today. Shall I—" Dunleigh glanced at Cassandra, who seemed to withdraw "—ask them to return next week?"

"Please go ahead, Jack." Cassandra lifted a cool drink to her lips and sipped.

This wasn't what he'd had in mind for her

visit. He'd hoped to spend the whole day with her. However, the rest of the afternoon continued in the same manner. Every time they'd begin to talk, there'd be an interruption, and he was called away. Every time he'd try to lean over and say something more intimate than "Help yourself to another bite of cheese and grapes and walnuts," one of the Dunleighs walked in with another announcement.

He found Cassandra outside two hours later, steps from the terrace, gazing at the colorful flowers and shrubs he and his gardeners took such pride in. She bent lower and sniffed a wild rose, a pink one, and her hair tumbled over her shoulder. She pushed it back with pretty fingers.

"Now I know where you got that beautiful bouquet."

"Sorry for all the interruptions."

"I think I'd better get back. There's much I have to do for tomorrow."

"Won't you stay for dinner?"

"There's something very charming about the tradition of being separated from the groom the night before the wedding. Don't worry about me eating, I'll order from the hotel. Sorry, I'm not very hungry now."

He was concerned. "Are you feeling any better?"

"Yes, much." Her eyes were brighter, her lips fuller and pinker.

"Do you need help with anything at the hotel? I'm sure Mrs. Dunleigh would be pleased to lend a hand. With your wardrobe, for instance."

"I'll be fine."

He felt suddenly shut out of her life.

He understood she was a bride needing her privacy, but back in Chicago, she'd always shut him out of her thoughts and feelings. He shoved his hands into his pockets, brought back to their days there, when he'd been much younger and much more nervous around the fairer sex. Hell, he was a lot more experienced than he used to be, and being with Cassandra shouldn't affect him. But the five years he'd spent carousing in saloons with entertaining women didn't seem to help him now.

"I hope you'll consider this a fine home, Cassandra," he said.

"I look forward to it very much."

He wondered whether he should show her the second floor, where the bedrooms were located—his, soon to be theirs—but decided not to. It would be awkward to press something so personal upon her, in full view of the staff, when he and Cassandra weren't yet married.

"Tomorrow at six," he reminded her. "I'll

have the Dunleighs come to your hotel at quarter to the hour to escort you to the church."

She nodded and kept her distance.

He stayed at arm's length, too. He wanted to kiss her, but his staff persisted in intervening. Cassandra didn't seem to expect, nor did she appear to miss the fact that he didn't approach her. When he was called away again by his foreman to check on a sluggish colt, Jack said goodbye to her and asked Mr. and Mrs. Dunleigh to accompany her to the hotel.

"We'll see each other tomorrow," Jack said.

"Have a good evening," she replied, as cool as a moonbeam. She pulled her shawl around her slender shoulders and was gone.

He hadn't kissed her!

Hours later, alone in her hotel room with a towel wrapped around her newly washed hair, Cassandra still couldn't believe the slight. It was all she'd thought of since the moment they'd parted, during her ride back to town with Mr. and Mrs. Dunleigh, and during her bath on the lower floor of the hotel.

She stared at his pink roses on the nightstand. She'd placed them in a vase beside the lone lantern, which cast a dim glow. Why hadn't Jack tried to kiss her? Had he found her repulsive?

She didn't think so, for he was about to marry her. Most men wouldn't wed a woman unless they found her appealing in some way. Besides, the way his burning gaze sometimes raked over her, she knew with a rush to her pulse that he sometimes found her attractive.

Perhaps he'd wanted to be affectionate, but the sight of her marred cheek had stopped him.

She couldn't imagine how their wedding night would go. Was that promise of sexual excitement in his dark brown eyes deceiving? Or would his physical skills match the apparent appetite in his hungry gaze? If he was a passionate man, then why in blazes hadn't he kissed her?

Some men put up a good act, pretending to be what they weren't. Troy Wainsborough had been a prime example. On the surface, he'd been a successful attorney, a protégé of her father's at his law offices. She'd been coaxed and prodded for years in his direction by her father. Beneath the surface, however, Troy had a darker side that involved drinking and loose women. He'd been belligerent to her, not a family man at all.

His cousin, Jack, who was taken in by Troy's family at a young age upon the death of his parents, had always been labeled the black sheep. Her father had believed it, emphatically pointing out the young man's disobedience to his aunt and uncle, his frequent brawls and his argumentative nature.

Cassandra's misjudgment of Jack had come to light the night he'd left Chicago. Hours too late to apologize to him.

But here they had a second chance.

Dressed in her tattered nightgown, Cassandra lifted the hot iron she'd ordered from the front desk, and pressed it upon the limp lace of her wedding gown. Although the dress was third-hand, passed down to her from Mrs. Pepik at the boarding house, Cassandra adored it. She gingerly ironed the collar and tended to the small creases beneath the bust.

At the thought of all her dear friends in Chicago, her chest ached with emptiness.

Everything here seemed so solitary.

She wished her sister were here to help her prepare for the wedding. She wished her father would be here tomorrow to walk her down the aisle. She wished she had a single friend in this town. Most fervently of all, she wished that Jack McColton had swept her up in his arms and kissed her as if she meant something to him.

With a catch in her throat, she set the iron aside. It was getting cool, and the ironing was finished. As practical as she was, Cassandra knew she'd better get some sleep tonight.

But if she did have a true friend in this town, they would have spent the night talking, sharing thoughts about Chicago and what this new community was all about.

Instead, Cassandra finished the sandwiches she'd ordered from the kitchen, packed her luggage, gave her faded leather shoes a polish, and said a prayer for tomorrow.

When the sun beamed through her windows in the morning, she was awake and ready. She dressed in her casual clothes, dined by herself for breakfast and took a stroll down the boardwalk, ignoring the curious glances of strangers. Eventually she bought a newspaper and brought it back to the room.

In the afternoon, she read every article and advertisement. She paid particular attention to the Help Wanted section, news of a robbery on the San Francisco rail line, ads for the law offices, and properties for sale. There were lots of things people could hire her for—including searching for lost relatives, preparing documents to present to lawyers, helping to recover stolen property, and possibly uncovering criminal activity.

When the time neared, she brushed her hair, twisted ribbons through the blond strands and braided it to one side. She donned her corset, slipped into her stockings and garter, and stepped into her wedding gown.

There was only a tiny oval mirror nailed to the wall, just big enough to see her face, so she wasn't able to get a full view of herself in her wedding finery.

Perhaps she should have procured a veil of some sort to drape across her face. She sighed, hoping Jack would overlook her imperfections. Not many men would accept her as a bride. She respected Jack McColton for his strong sense of honor and his desire to marry her despite her flaws, and prayed that it would be enough when it came time to spend the night together.

She looked down at the white fabric cascading over her hips. Everything seemed to be in order.

The gown had a high waistline, cinched beneath her breasts, a plunging neckline offset by a half collar at the back, puffy sleeves and a very long train. Cassandra carefully picked up the swirly back end and slipped the elegant loop over her finger to hold the train off the ground. Her shoes weren't new—black stiletto boots with tiny leather buttons, the only good pair she owned—but they gave her a nice height.

She twirled with pleasure, and her hemlines brushed nicely over her ankles.

The knock on her door came at precisely quarter to the hour of six. When she opened it, Mr. and Mrs. Dunleigh were standing there in formal attire.

"My dear, you look beautiful." Mrs. Dunleigh gave her a tender smile, and Cassandra felt more appreciated in that one simple act of kindness than she had all day.

"Thank you."

The heavyset Mr. Dunleigh, more reserved than his wife, nodded at her scuffed luggage. "May I take your bags? There's a man outside waiting to take them to the ranch."

"Yes, please." Cassandra had repacked her pistol, bullets and books, and now welcomed the help. She looked at her wild roses. "I nearly forgot about a bridal bouquet. These will do." She picked up the bundle of roses, dried off the stems and wrapped the moist ends in a blue lace handkerchief. She wondered if Jack had imagined when he'd given them to her that she'd be carrying them down the aisle.

Ten minutes later, they were walking to the church. It was only a few blocks from the hotel, but even so, Cassandra attracted lots of attention. Shop owners peered out of their windows, a man sweeping the boardwalk stopped to stare, people on horseback craned their necks and a small child grabbed at her mother's skirts and pointed.

The church on the corner was covered with clapboard. A tall steeple rose above it, shaded by redwoods.

"There has to be some mistake," said Cassandra, drawing nearer and noticing all sorts of buggies lined up along the street. "We're having a small ceremony. Just a few people. Maybe this is the wrong church."

"No mistake." Mr. Dunleigh said matter-of-factly. "This is the correct location."

Mrs. Dunleigh leaned over to whisper, "I don't know what's gotten into Dr. McColton today. I heard him inviting everyone, whatever friends happened by the ranch. Said he should've announced the wedding weeks ago...."

Cassandra moaned softly. Had Jack assumed that she wanted a large ceremony because of her comment yesterday that he hadn't told many people about their impending nuptials? It was kind of him to think of her...but this wasn't what she'd meant. These were strangers to her, and would only increase her jitteriness.

"Come along, miss," Mr. Dunleigh urged. "We'll go through the side door and leave you with Reverend Darcy."

"Leave me? Oh, no, please," said Cassandra.

Husband and wife turned to her. The housekeeper's spectacles slid to the bottom of her nose as she peered down at Cassandra. "Yes, what is it?"

"Mrs. Dunleigh, surely you'll understand, but may I borrow your husband, please? My father's not here, and I feel awkward asking a stranger. But it would mean the world to me if Mr. Dunleigh could stand beside me and walk me down the aisle." Cassandra's mouth went dry as she peered at the gentleman. "Please, Mr. Dunleigh."

His wife pulled a hanky from her long sleeve and sniffled into it. "Of course, my dear, we wouldn't have it any other way." She gave a pointed look to her husband, who didn't appear to be convinced.

His eyebrows were raised as he deliberated. When he hesitated too long, he was reprimanded by his wife. "Yes, of course," she prodded, "he'd cherish the moment. Wouldn't you, dear?"

"Absolutely," he said with a simple nod. He wasn't enthusiastic, but was gentlemanly about the matter.

Mrs. Dunleigh entered the front of the church. Cassandra and Mr. Dunleigh took the side stairs and stepped into the alcove at the back. Reverend Darcy, with short gray hair and a long black robe and collar, greeted her kindly. "Good evening. Welcome, welcome, lass."

He gave her instructions on how they'd begin, then quickly departed. Cassandra stood nervously beside Mr. Dunleigh in the alcove. Judging by the shuffling of feet and amount of murmuring behind the wall, it sounded like a packed congregation.

When the pianist began "Here Comes the Bride," Cassandra placed her hand on Mr. Dunleigh's elbow and came out of hiding.

Up at the altar, Jack turned.

He looked splendidly handsome in a formal black tailcoat and blue cravat. His black hair caught the light cascading from an arched window, and the corners of his mouth lifted upward in what appeared to be approval. He glanced briefly at her burned cheek. His jaw tightened and she saw regret in his eyes.

What was he thinking?

Mr. Dunleigh marched her down the aisle. They fumbled a bit because their paces didn't match. Cassandra, light-headed, felt the strain of tension and worry that had been building for months.

The pews were jammed with a hundred bodies, all turned in her direction and staring. Some looked curious, some aloof; some were smiling.

Cassandra focused ahead, gripping her flowers as though they were a lifeline.

Jack's best man was standing to his side, a dapper-looking fellow in a gray suit, with slicked-back red hair. Because of his cool expression, he was harder to read than Jack. On the other side, as Reverend Darcy had explained to her, his elderly wife was waiting to be a witness for Cassandra.

They reached the altar. Mr. Dunleigh faded away, and Cassandra stepped up beside Jack. His eyes flickered over her, then down to her roses.

"This is it," he murmured. "Are you ready?"

She nodded and smiled, but couldn't help but wish he'd said something more personal. She bowed her head as the minister began.

"Dearly beloved, we are gathered here together on this beautiful summer day to join this man and this woman."

The rest was a blur to Cassandra. She was feeling queasy and started to rock. The next thing she knew, they were nearly at the end. Her head swam. Only a few more minutes...

"If there is any man who can show just cause why they may not be lawfully joined together, let him speak now or forever hold his peace."

"I object!" a woman's voice called from the back.

Cassandra snapped to attention.

People gasped. Jack swung around sharply.

Dismayed, Cassandra swiveled in her wedding gown, peering past all the faces to the stylish woman in a plum-colored suit who'd stepped out to voice her objections. She was the brunette who'd dropped her package coming out of the hat shop yesterday when she'd spotted Jack and Cassandra together.

Bouts of nervous coughing and shuffling ran through the congregation. Did everyone else know about this woman and this potential problem?

Had Jack seen this coming?

Chapter Four

Chaos broke out as Jack looked on, feeling powerless at his own wedding.

Reverend Darcy tried to take control of the situation in a calm, clear voice. "Miss Elise Beacon, please say what's on your mind."

Murmurings and exclamations turned into dead silence.

Elise stood in a pew next to the aisle, surrounded by female friends. She grasped the railing in front of her and glanced at Jack with what seemed like apology in her eyes.

He steeled himself. How could she do this? What gave her the right? He tried to restrain himself, but burned with fury.

"Reverend, I'm sure the whole town knows that Jack has been courting me, with expectations of…of… I feel he's being disingenuous to arrange a marriage to someone else."

"Our courtship ended months ago," Jack replied. He glanced at Cassandra, whose pretty mouth had fallen into a grim line. She'd lost her color, and his indignation flared at what this outburst was doing to her. "Reverend, I'm afraid Miss Beacon exaggerates the extent of our involvement."

Elise appeared crestfallen. She'd always been overly emotional, overly wrought when things didn't go well, and she certainly had no right to place blame at his feet. She was the one who'd flirted with other men when she'd been with Jack. But to say so here would be to smear her honor. No matter how unreasonable she was to voice her objections at his wedding, he would not stoop to her level.

Cassandra would have to trust him on this.

But dammit! He took a deep breath and tried to calm down.

Hugh, his best man, stepped out to try to smooth the difficulties. "Elise, everyone here knows and respects your forthright nature."

The reverend latched on to Hugh's train of thought. "Yes, Miss Beacon, it is always best to clear the air, and I do appreciate your communicating your thoughts on the matter. However, that is not a lawful reason to stop this wedding. Unless he formally proposed to you?"

Elise's color heightened as she slowly shook her head.

"Now, are there any just causes why this marriage cannot lawfully take place?" The gray-haired gent scanned the crowd.

When Jack looked again at Cassandra, she seemed to be swaying. He leaped to catch her and her bouquet before both could collapse to the floor.

Other people rushed to their aid.

The front pew was cleared and Jack helped her sit. He knelt at her feet, the white folds of her gown billowing around them. "Cassandra," he said gently.

"I'll be all right," she said. "So sorry. I think it's the heat and lack of sleep."

"There's no need to apologize. It's me who's sorry." And extremely concerned at her pale color. "Would you like to rest? Or would you like to leave?"

Cassandra didn't immediately respond. Hugh, however, slid in next to Jack, in the new gray suit he'd had fitted in his office yesterday. "Can I do anything?" His words sounded genuine, despite his earlier warnings to Jack to steer clear of marrying a mail-order bride.

Jack shook his head.

"Seriously, Jack," said Hugh, "maybe I can help by talking with Elise."

Mr. and Mrs. Dunleigh appeared beside them and fussed over Cassandra. Jack stood up in the swarm of people and searched for Elise, but she was no longer there. Neither were her friends. Hugh shrugged his shoulders in frustration.

The crowd hushed and watched. Jack held out his hand and Cassandra grasped it with renewed strength. He helped her to her feet. Whatever had happened, she had recovered. The warm white color of her gown accentuated the fresh glow in her cheeks. Dammit, every time he looked at her burn, he felt a flash of guilt. Especially today. No bride should have to feel self-conscious on her wedding day. He sensed the tension between them, as if they were more like strangers than a couple who'd once known each other and were happy to be standing before the altar.

"I would like you to be my wife, Cassandra," he said clearly, so there was no mistaking it in the crowd. "Would you do me the honor?"

"I would like to, very much."

With relief, they turned to face the minister, and were wed.

* * *

She waited, but still there was no seductive kiss.

"I now pronounce you man and wife," said the minister.

Jack briefly brushed his lips against hers. Cassandra wished for more, but gathered that he must be as apprehensive as she was, considering what they'd just been through with that combative woman. Why had she waited until that moment to speak out? She must have been seated in the congregation at least several minutes before Cassandra had arrived. Why not speak to Jack privately before the ceremony?

It was as though she had wished to be as dramatic and confrontational as possible. Jack's explanation seemed plausible to Cassandra, and when she'd known him in Chicago, he hadn't been one to string along any women. Plus there hadn't been one person in the congregation who'd corroborated the woman's story.

Cassandra was still trying to make sense of it when Jack whisked her outside and seated her in the buggy. To her disappointment, Mr. and Mrs. Dunleigh traveled with them. The butler took the reins, his wife sat in front with him, and Cassandra and Jack shared the rear seat. Cassandra desperately wanted to talk to Jack alone about what had happened, but considering that the Dunleighs were within earshot, she decided to keep her private thoughts to herself.

A few people hollered in good cheer as they left the church, and Cassandra wished she knew some of the friendlier ones.

The twenty-minute ride to the ranch was discouraging. She clenched her bouquet of wilting roses in her lap, looked out at the pastures and greenery, and wished that there wasn't two feet of space between herself and her new husband. She wished he would at least touch her.

"I've made you dinner," Mrs. Dunleigh said when they pulled up to the big house. "It's warming in the oven. If you'd like me to join you and serve it—"

"That's fine," Jack interrupted. "We'll manage from here."

"Congratulations to you both," said Mr. Dunleigh. "Sheila and I wish you many happy years together. And we look forward to many more years of service in this household."

"Thank you," said Jack, and Cassandra smiled in appreciation.

The gent tipped his bowler hat, then he and his wife headed toward a side entrance.

Cassandra looked after them. "They have their own wing of the house?"

Jack nodded. "They definitely won't be joining us on our honeymoon eve."

Flustered at the thought of finally being alone, Cassandra accepted his assistance from the buggy. His hands spanned her waist and she slid down beside him, so very conscious of his nearness.

"We were surrounded by other people for so long," she said, "I thought we'd never be alone."

Jack's grin was a welcome relief from the tension of the past few days.

"I've let all the staff know we're not to be disturbed. The Dunleighs have retired to their quarters, and the ranch hands and their cook are in the bunkhouse."

He took Cassandra's hand and pulled her around the house to the private entrance and terrace near the dining area. After opening the French doors, he turned, and before she realized his intent, swung her up in his arms.

"Over the threshold, right, Mrs. McColton?"

Hearing her new name spoken aloud made her shiver. She was his wife.

He set her on her feet inside the kitchen, where tantalizing aromas wafted from the brick wall ovens. And there were cut flowers everywhere—white and yellow roses, mountain orchids and pristine lilies of the valley.

When Jack set her down, he didn't let her go. He allowed his palm to linger on her shoulder blade, the warmth of his touch seeping into her flesh.

Breathless, she looked up at him. His dark hair, newly washed, tumbled to the sharp line of his eyebrows. His skin was tanned from the sun and the wind, and a muscle rippled in his cheek. Those eyes, those dark brown eyes the color of moist earth and swirling clay, swept over her. Not in such a detached manner as when she'd first arrived, but more pulsating, controlling, tempting.

Yet the two of them were still ill at ease with each other. He reached down and brushed a strand of hair from her left cheek, her good side, and stroked it. His touch caressed her skin.

Then he dropped his hand and glanced around the kitchen, as if scoping out what the housekeeper had arranged for them.

Cassandra took the moment to try to compose herself.

She'd lost her heart once to another man, with dire consequences, and didn't wish to risk it again. Though she and Jack were now married, the peril she felt in possibly having her heart ripped out a second time, only to be replaced with a painful emptiness, made her cautious. Perhaps more so now that they were wed.

There was so much more to lose.

Maybe it was the heartless ruin of everyone she'd lost over the last five years that struck her with such force. First, learning the truth about Troy, his uncontrolled fits of temper when he drank, his dalliances with prostitutes, his words, "I always found you too prim and proper," the last time they'd spoken. How could his pronouncement still hurt so much?

And then the second aching loss that would never be filled—the missing presence of her sister, Mary, and the loving protectiveness of her father. Cassandra would forever feel that pain.

It seemed that life's sorrows didn't stop at just one heartache. They kept coming and coming... and all she could do was try to protect herself the best she could.

Cassandra had tried her hardest to remain optimistic—especially in the boardinghouse, with the other women. Some had lost children in the fire, and that pain had to be indescribable.

Being here with Jack, she felt so terribly vulnerable and fragile.

He had the power to destroy her.

If she let him. If she let him into her heart, into her soul, into her very life.

It would be much simpler, much less damaging to her, if she kept him at a distance. If anything, the outburst by Elise Beacon today had forewarned Cassandra of how much she could still hurt. She wanted to ask Jack about that other woman, but now that they were alone, she was reluctant to bring it up and spoil their moment.

He turned around again, a smile lingering on his lips.

"You're a very beautiful woman," he murmured.

Beautiful? Really? Her?

Her breath tripped in her throat. It was the first sensual thing any man had said to her since the fire. But…would Jack be terribly disappointed, as Troy had been, when they became more intimate? Not that she had ever slept with Troy, but their relationship had been physical enough on one occasion that it still brought shame to her cheeks. He'd partially disrobed her.

How could she have been so deceived into believing he had loved her?

Stop it, she told herself. This was nonsense, thinking like this when she had another man, a more honorable man, standing before her, trying to express some gentle words.

"You look very dashing in your suit. I had a lovely day."

"It's not over," he said, and indicated that she should look around the room.

To their right, the dining table had been set with a lovely assortment of fine china, sparkling goblets and silverware. A feast was about to be consumed. Candles about to be lit.

Yet what she noticed most was that Jack had removed his hand from her back moments ago. A cold shadow, a phantom of his masculine touch, lay there instead.

"A toast to us?" He offered her the choice between a white chardonnay and a red pinot noir. "They're both superb wines from the area." They settled on the red, and he poured.

"It's very nice," she said, upon tasting it.

There was something very romantic, yet also very much missing, when the two of them sat down to eat, both in their wedding attire. Jack was attentive to her needs, serving her the finest cut of roast beef she'd ever tasted, potatoes pulled that day, green beans mixed with a walnut sauce, and savory desserts of raspberry custard and lime pie.

If they had been in love, the dinner might have been incredibly sentimental and romantic. Instead, without family and dear friends to share it, it seemed lonely. And awkward, with the two of them trying to pretend they were totally at ease with one another, that there was nothing but food on their minds, that they weren't both thinking apprehensively of the wedding night ahead.

Jack was trapped in a primitive urge of desire as he led Cassandra up the winding staircase to his wing of rooms. What red-blooded male wouldn't be anticipating a night with such a woman? She appeared so innocent and demure on the outside—always had—and that made him imagine all the more what lay beneath that shield of white lace and scrubbed skin.

There'd been some problems today at the ceremony that he needed to explain, but not now. The talk he wasn't too thrilled about having with her could wait a bit longer.

"This way," he said, leading her by candlelight to the far room with the best view of the valley. "Your luggage should be right inside."

"There." She spotted the bags on the right side of the bed—her side—and blushed.

Was there anything she didn't blush at?

"I'll show you to the bath."

"You've arranged a hot bath?" She followed him into his private dressing room.

"Of course."

"Well, then, you've thought of everything."

The massive room was lined in oak cabinets and armoires. Clay tiles covered the floor, along with a colorful Oriental rug he'd purchased on the docks of San Francisco, coming in from Hong Kong. Matching tapestries clung to the high walls. A freestanding pewter mirror stood in one corner, along with a basin and pitcher of water.

He took her down a private flight of stairs to a private bathing room. It was easier to have the tub on the main floor so that he or his staff could haul the water outside to drain.

Logs in the fireplace crackled softly. He walked to the cauldrons of steaming water hanging above the fire, lifted one and carried it to the claw-footed porcelain tub. He added its contents to the fresh cool water already there, prepared by his staff.

"You'll find everything you need here. Soaps, lotions, towels."

"It's the most incredible bathtub I've seen in a very long while."

When Cassandra turned to face him, the train of her wedding gown snagged on his cowboy boots. Her pretty blond braid nestled against her breast. Her eyes, as clear a blue as the sky in June, looked at him directly. Lord, she did wonders to his equilibrium when she gazed so boldly at him. Her nearness aroused him. All he wanted was to see her out of those stays and laces and whatever else she was wearing underneath that feminine cover, and to see her golden skin beneath him in bed.

"Take your time. But if you wait too long, I'll come looking for you."

She raised her eyebrows.

"Fair warning," he replied with humor.

Her full lips softened.

He set the candle on the side of the tub and went up the stairs to the bedroom to retrieve her suitcase.

While he was there, he thought he should light a lantern for the bedroom, and another to provide her more light in the bath. He slid out of his boots, removed his formal jacket, tugged off his cravat and lifted the luggage and lantern. Quietly, in sock feet, he headed back down the stairs to the bathing room.

He hadn't meant to startle her.

In his own state of pleasant shock, he stumbled upon her undressing.

"Sorry, I didn't mean… I thought I'd bring you these…."

She was completely naked, with her luscious back turned toward him. Candlelight rippled over the beautiful curve of her spine, down the golden swell of her buttocks, and shimmered along the smooth length of her legs.

Dismayed by his sudden presence, she clutched her wedding gown to her front and whirled around, concealing herself. "Jack." Her mouth puckered in dismay.

"More light," he murmured in explanation, indicating that he'd brought the lantern. "And your clothes." He set them down nearby, but couldn't get his eyes off her beauty.

Her blond braid hung loosely over her bare shoulder. The soft curve of her collarbones swelled with every breath she took. She pressed the lace of her gown over her bosom and he couldn't help but wonder how she might look if that dropped lower....

"Would you like me to leave?" he asked, restraining himself by every means he knew, but barely finding it possible due to the roaring of his blood.

Soft orange light glimmered over her cheeks. Every muscle in his body contracted, waiting for her answer.

"No," she finally answered, and dropped her gown.

He was hypnotized as if by some magical trance. His eyes slowly raked over her body, starting with the lovely line of her throat, to the luscious swell of her jutting breasts and pointed pink nipples.

Her rib cage was remarkably slender, curving down to a flattened waist. His gaze hungrily sought the lower curves, following the rise of her belly to the triangle of blond curls, and her long, firm thighs.

Her voice was provocative. "Would you like to slip into the water with me, Jack?"

Chapter Five

Cassandra dipped her foot into the steamy liquid, loving the sensation of heat over her toes, then calves, then hips and breasts, then full nakedness. She felt more secure about herself beneath a layer of water; she was unaccustomed to any man gazing at her fully exposed, even if he was her husband.

It was her turn to gaze at Jack as he undressed.

Revealed by the lamplight, his expression was at first disquieted, as though he was unsure what to say. Then it was gone, his dashing face awash in a wicked glimmer of arousal and expectation. There were the mischievous dark eyes, the sensual mouth, the dimple in his chiseled jaw and the primal need she detected in the hurried pace of his breathing.

He draped his trousers on the back of a chair, followed by his gray waistcoat, then crisp linen shirt. She barely had the nerve to watch him, but then could barely turn away.

Stripped naked for a brief, glorious moment, he epitomized sexuality and rough strength. His chest rippled with muscles, his waist tapered to his hips, and his erection was so hard and upright she wondered how on earth they were supposed to fit together.

She stared, trying to fulfill her curiosity. So that's what it looked like, the male part of him....

Embarrassed that she *was* staring, she reached for a cake of soap and slid it over her arm. How did a woman jump from being a virgin and shielding her most private parts from the eyes of men, to gain full acceptance and awareness of herself?

How was she supposed to be comfortable with this?

"Are you all right?" he asked, slipping one muscled leg into the tub, then the other. The hot water sloshed around them, nearly splashing over the top edge.

"It's just that I'm not used to this." She pretended to scrub dirt from her forearm.

"May I?" He took the soap from her, letting

the bar slide between their fingers, ever so slippery and wet. "Relax," he coaxed. "I won't hurt you."

He rubbed the cake up and down her arms, then the top of her shoulders, then down one breast. The cool soap slid over her areola, the sensation making the bud of her nipple swell. He moved the soap to her other side, then used his bare hands to lather her breasts. She inhaled in pleasure, leaned back and allowed him to caress her. She closed her eyes a moment, then felt the warmth of his mouth on her breasts.

The heat was incredible, the pull of wanton desire throbbing from her breasts to her stomach, making the center of her quiver with anticipation.

He teased her for a long time with his fingers, swirling them over her, down her arm, up the other one, across her collarbone and down her cleavage. He created a slowly building heat, until she was ready for so much more.

She opened her eyes and he approached, sliding on top of her, his large body on her slender one, splashing water over the tub edge and barely noticing. His mouth came down on hers.

Finally, a kiss.

It was soft and gentle. She'd gone too long

without this, without a man in her life, without someone who wanted her.

The kiss didn't last nearly long enough before he dragged his mouth along her left jaw and kissed her there, and down her neck. She gasped when he came back up the other side, over her jaw and pressed his rough cheek against her scarred one. It felt so intimate that she stopped breathing for a moment.

Then he ran his large hand along her waist and trailed down her hip and leg, making her burn with a splendorous promise that more was coming, soon to be hers.

The yearning. That shivery race of gooseflesh that rose and heaved. His hand was gliding farther down and over, and soon would reach...

Oh, he was there. That magnificent spot. He slid and stroked and pressed, slid and stroked and pressed, and just as she was ready, he lifted her out of the tub so her hips were raised up to his mouth, and he pressed his lips upon her.

It was exhilarating, the pleasure he brought. She was too alarmed, too surprised to fight it. His expert maneuvers were daunting. How did he know what she liked, what she wanted?

His hot breath, the excitement of his tongue, his fervor. His moaning, "I've waited so patiently all day, Cassandra...."

She exploded beneath the hot sensations of his mouth, his expert tongue and expert kisses. Then as the spasms waned, he lowered her back into the water and pressed himself closer.

He slid his shaft inside her, causing a sharp pang of pain. When she retreated slightly, he stopped, then pressed his forehead to hers and, staring into her eyes, began to pump deeper, then shallower, then deeper, then shallower again. The pain ripped, then subsided, ripped, then subsided, until he finally gripped her ankle and raised her leg, and she realized he was fully inside.

She could barely comprehend his size, but she tried to relax, and allowed him full control in guiding himself in and out. She imagined that allowing her to climax first had unwound her tense body and made it easier for him to enter, even though he was incredibly large.

He moved slowly and assuredly inside her, water slapping around them, steam rising over their bodies, a hush in the air, and glimmering candlelight making droplets of water look like liquid gold on his bronzed flesh.

Jack's breathing grew rough, his fingers clenched, his muscles heaved. When he climaxed into her, she marveled at the union that their marriage had brought, and how she'd never imagined five years ago, on the night of their stormy argument, that she'd ever see him again, let alone that they'd be doing this.

It was over much too soon.

Cassandra was left wanting. The sex itself had been very satisfying, more than she'd imagined possible for a first time, but the intimacy was lacking.

"Cassandra?" Jack leaned back in the tub and watched her from beneath his dark lashes. "Did it hurt so much?"

"At first...but I've recovered." The pain had been searing, but she'd expected it.

"I'll let you finish your bath in private." Jack stepped out of the tub.

She saw his backside—solid and muscled as he reached for a towel.

Stay, she wanted to say. *There should be more to this. To us.*

But he rubbed the towel over his skin, wrapped it around his waist, padded out over the clay tiles up the stairs, and left her. She inhaled and looked about the room. Everything seemed so foreign to her. The woods, the scents, the lighting. Most of all, Jack.

He was a stranger.

How could making love to her husband leave her so aching for more?

* * *

His new wife and their wedding night had surprised Jack more than he'd expected. Such incredible sex.

Contented, he grabbed hold of the towel wrapped around his hips and tossed it to the chair beside their massive four-poster, canopied bed.

While Cassandra finished her bath, he walked naked past the sizzling heat of the stone fireplace to the slightly opened bedroom windows. He inhaled an invigorating breath of fresh air tumbling in, and looked out over the valley.

He'd built the ranch house on a hill so no one could look into his bedroom, yet he'd be surrounded by things he loved—the dark sky dotted with a million stars, rambling redwoods, owls soaring into the night, insects chirping their songs, acres of prime land tinged with the spirit of California freedom.

The great sex he and Cassandra had just enjoyed would be the beginning of a great life. Or so he hoped.

Would it be possible to trust her again, as he had in earlier years in Chicago, when they were both young and innocent? To wipe the slate clean between them, let down his guard and say and do whatever he pleased, without feeling as though he was being judged? Sometimes he saw her watching him, as if she was always gauging what he'd do next. That kind of scrutiny would be unbearable.

But the day hadn't gone as smoothly as he'd hoped. He would have to explain some things about Elise Beacon, and trust Cassandra would understand.

With a sigh, he turned and headed back to the brand-new bed. He lifted the covers and slid into the silky new sheets.

They had ample pillows. He punched a couple, tossed them to the headboard and tried to get his shoulders comfortable. He'd worked hard and long for the ability to provide for himself and his new wife, and was grateful that he had the staff to take care of their needs. Heating water for the bathtub tonight and draining it in the morning, for example.

He could hear Cassandra in the adjacent room now, moving items on the shelves, which meant she was out of the tub. He imagined what she'd look like, breezing in.

He hoped she'd be sleeping naked, as he was, so they could enjoy each other in bed. Or at least if not bare, that she'd have on a pretty little gown made of thin silk or cotton, something that maybe revealed those mesmerizing breasts.

Her footsteps got louder, then Cassandra appeared—in a head-to-toe flannel nightgown. The collar was extra high, with a dozen buttons, the overly puffed sleeves fell below her knuckles, and a tent of fabric hid the outline of her gorgeous body.

It was like a huge potato sack.

He strained his eyes, but there wasn't one damn place in the fabric where he could see through it. Had she raided some granny's wardrobe?

"You might be too hot in that," he said, as politely as he could.

"My shoulders always get cold."

"You've got me to keep you warm."

"I move around a lot. I—I need some space. Sometimes I kick."

"Hmm." He paused, wanting to make her comfortable. "Should I put more logs on the fire?"

"No need. This'll be fine."

Cassandra lifted the covers and slid in. She didn't adjust a pillow, didn't yank up a corner of the covers. Just lay on her back, looking at the rafters. Her body scarcely made a dent in mattress.

At this rate, he might as well be sleeping alone. He had imagined that having a wife meant he could reach over and touch her any time he pleased. But maybe she was nervous, and would lighten up when she grew accustomed to her new home.

"Do you like the bed, Cassandra?"

"The bed?" She peered at the carved mahogany pillars, then the matching armoire in the corner. "Yes, of course."

"I ordered it specially for us, from San Francisco."

She turned her face toward him, her perfect cheek upward, her blond features soft in the glow of the lantern. The high tilt of her cheekbones and smoothness of her skin made her look years too young for that blasted old lady's gown.

"You've been very generous, Jack. The bed is beautiful. I thought only fairy princesses slept under canopies." And then, perhaps because they were both so relaxed, she asked a question that pierced his heart. "Jack," she said gently, "why didn't you stay in Chicago and fight for me?"

He sighed and leaned back against the pillows.

So she'd finally said it. And who could blame her? Her argument with Troy had come on the heels of his own argument with her. The timing had been so off... What would've happened, had he stayed a few more days in Chicago?

"Maybe I needed some perspective," he mur-

mured. "Maybe leaving was my way of simpli-
fying your life."

"I wish you would have complicated it."

It was a blow to his heart—and his damn
pride—to hear her criticize how he'd handled
that night. But he took his time to respond, tried
to temper his feelings, his immediate need to
defend himself against what he knew were his
flaws.

"You made it clear how you felt about me,
Cassandra. You slapped me, remember?"

"I was engaged to someone else when you
tried to kiss me!"

"But you wouldn't even hear me out. It wasn't
the first time I'd approached you."

"I wasn't sure how you felt about me, Jack.
Physically, yes, but you never talked about…
about the meaning behind the kiss. You sent
out mixed signals, sometimes trying to sit next
to me when we went out in a group, other times
ignoring me for weeks."

"I was young and stupid."

She swallowed hard. "And I should never
have accused you of being envious of Troy."

"You defended him so firmly. Said that he
was under a lot of strain working in the firm
with your father, that rumors of his carousing
and drinking and time with cheap women was

more my imagination than fact. I'd never seen you so angry."

"I was wrong." She clutched the sheet to her bosom. "You shocked me with the allegations. How could I believe them?"

"It's true that a young lady of your standing would never have been exposed to what goes on behind the closed doors in some men's homes. So how *could* you believe it?"

"I was livid when you confronted me. I didn't know how to react. So I pushed you away and blamed the messenger instead of—of the man I was betrothed to, who did those things."

"And I was so hurt at being cast aside that my temper got the better of me and I stormed out."

Her face was silhouetted by moonlight. He wished he could get a good look at her eyes. They always expressed so much emotion, and he was good at reading them.

Or maybe he wasn't. If he *had* been good at reading her expressions, maybe he wouldn't have left her in Chicago.

Oh, hell, he thought, knowing full well he would've left no matter if it'd been that night or three nights later. He had been mad as hell; Cassandra had been fit to be tied. Troy was lying through his teeth, denying everything, her father was adamant that she marry Troy, and Troy's parents...

"You know, I went to Troy's folks that night, too."

Her face turned. "You did?"

"After our argument. I was determined to try to help." He shook his head, knowing now there was nothing he could've done differently to help Troy with his out-of-control boozing.

"And?"

Jack pulled in a long breath. "And they told me to leave."

"What?" she said in disbelief. "But this changes everything."

"Not quite. It would be an easy answer to say I left Chicago because of them—my uncle and aunt—but I was living on my own by then, and they couldn't very well evict me from my own residence."

"They...they threatened you?"

"My uncle said my vicious rumors would damage Troy. Financially and politically. My aunt's silent disapproval was, as they say, deafening." He shrugged, thinking of how his aunt and uncle had never truly welcomed him in their home.

They'd done the right thing according to society, taking him in as a boy who'd just lost his folks in a terrible tragedy, and he'd be forever grateful for that kindness. He didn't have any-place else to go, and they were family. He'd grown to love them.

But as that boy, he hadn't understood how difficult it was for them, with the business rivalry between his uncle and father. They'd been as vicious and cruel to each other as one could imagine, each trying to outdo the other in the stockyard trades. They weren't even speaking to each other when Jack's father died, and then to suddenly have to take in the son of the brother he despised… Well, Jack had sensed the betrayal, but never understood it until he'd grown older and started asking discreet questions to those who knew the family.

"I tried to help Troy by myself," said Jack.

"How did you do that?"

"I told him I would accompany him on his outings. To gaming clubs and—" Jack noted the innocent expression in her blue eyes and decided she didn't need to know all the sordid details "—and all the places he used to frequent. I tried to make it lighthearted, as though I was acting like his bodyguard. But he grew to resent me on those outings. Every time I reminded him he'd already had too much to drink and should cut back, it made him drink more, telling me I was goading him into it. I made it worse, not better."

"He made it worse, not you. And you kept this all to yourself?"

"Until I couldn't anymore."

"You tried so hard to save him. In retrospect, it doesn't seem as though I did nearly as much."

"Troy was the only one who could save himself, and he didn't want to."

"Have you heard from him, or your aunt and uncle?"

Jack shook his head. "Not since that night. There was the letter I wrote that was returned, address unknown. I sent a few letters to my aunt and uncle, but they never replied."

"Maybe they didn't get them. Lots of mail was lost during the Great Fire."

"Oh, they got them." He blinked. He'd never told her everything that had happened, everything he'd done to get through that awful period, including hiring an investigator. The detective had told him that the letters had been received by Troy's family. But hiring someone to snoop didn't feel terribly honorable, looking at it now from a distance.

Yet there was something else he *did* need to tell her. "Cassandra…about the wedding ceremony…"

She seemed to know exactly what he was referring to. Her voice became strained. "Yes, Jack, I've been meaning to ask. Who is she?"

He tried to control the flare of his temper when he thought of what Elise had done. The embarrassment to Cassandra, the wagging tongues in town the scene had undoubtedly caused, being forced to explain himself in front of the minister.

And how on earth did it get to the point where Jack was talking in his marital bed, on his wedding night, about another woman? To blazes with Elise!

"Her name is Elise Beacon. Daughter of Wilfred Beacon, who owns one of the largest vineyards around. Except that right now, he's in South America somewhere with his latest fling. Elise has had a hard time of it. She's very good with animals—very skilled, seems to have an instinct for it. Anyway, she and I...well, I courted her for two months."

"How long ago?"

"It ended way back in January. Five months ago, for crying out loud."

Cassandra frowned. "And you proposed marriage to me in February?" Her expression grew incredulous. "Just one month later?"

"Well, I..." He'd never thought of that.

He ran a hand through his hair, determined to explain fully so there'd be no misunderstanding. "There was nothing serious—ever—between us. She was being courted by someone else at the same time, in fact, and as soon as I heard about that, I broke off with her. As for you and me, I've known you since you were fourteen. There's no comparison between how I feel for you and what I felt for her."

Cassandra drew her lips together, as though weighing the situation. Pensive, she gazed over to the red glow of flames in the fireplace, her blond lashes silhouetted by the golden light. "She's still hurt."

He rubbed a hand over the bristles on his jaw and shrugged a shoulder, so much wider and bigger than Cassandra's on the pillow. "She's overblown everything she thinks happened between us. That's the only way I can rationalize her behavior. And I'm sorry for what happened today. I can't apologize enough."

Cassandra, though, grew agitated. She tucked her tongue into her cheek and batted her lashes. "Would have been nice if I had received some warning."

He sputtered. "Well, surely you don't think I could've guessed what she might do?"

"She saw us yesterday when I arrived." Cassandra lifted her arm for emphasis, her long sleeve swirling. "I'm sure you saw her, too, coming out of the hat shop. You could've told me then who she was."

"But she's nothing to me," he insisted.

"She doesn't seem to think so," Cassandra said with a heated snap. "Neither do some of the other folks in town. I saw their faces in church. I think a few extra people showed up today just to see what would happen!"

"How am I supposed to agree or disagree with that statement?" he asked indignantly. "I can't read the minds of others."

"You should've warned me," she said with accusation. She grew still, except for her fingers flicking at the stitching on the covers. "Are there any other women you need to tell me about?"

"Oh, hell," he said, exasperated by the scrutiny. "I'm not about to provide a list, in the event any other woman holds a grudge."

Aghast, Cassandra clutched the blanket to her chin. "Are there that many?" she whispered.

"No!" Flabbergasted, he sat up, bare-chested and pulling at the sheets. What he'd done or not done before she'd become his wife was irrelevant. "There were *some* women. I haven't been an angel here on my own, but I didn't expect that I'd be getting married anytime soon."

Cassandra's eyes widened. She looked hurt, and now he felt guilty all over again.

"Come now, Cassandra, you know what I mean. It has nothing to do with you. I'm happy we got married." His anger flared at being judged and assessed and ranked and rated, and he spoke recklessly. "I'm damn ecstatic."

"Well, me too," she retorted. "I couldn't be more elated. I'm so filled with joy, I feel like shouting it from the rooftops!" With that, she grabbed the covers and turned away from him, slamming her shoulder into the mattress.

He flipped onto his side, too, and stared at the moonlit window, perturbed as hell.

Well, wasn't this just great? He and his new wife falling asleep on their first night together with their backs turned.

Chapter Six

The silence continued the next morning at breakfast. Jack had slept in past his usual time on Cassandra's account, not wanting to rush her out of bed the day after their wedding.

Sunlight poured into the kitchen from the terrace, and one would think, looking in the French doors, that things were almost normal inside this house.

Jack knew better.

He looked up from his plate of eggs to Cassandra, who was poking at her sliced fruit and biscuits.

Stubborn, the both of them, he thought.

Today she wore a peach-colored blouse and long gray skirt, soft colors that brought out the freshness in her cheeks. But for some reason, today the ragged scar was a barrier between them, and accentuated how out of reach she seemed, and what a failure he'd been by leaving Chicago when she and her family needed him most. He averted his gaze, but perhaps not before she saw his slight withdrawal.

Mrs. Dunleigh chirped around them as if they were newly hatched chicks and she'd done all the work of delivering them.

"My dear, it's simply wonderful to have another woman in the house. If there's anything you should need, please don't hesitate to inquire."

"I better run." Jack rose from the table, in leather vest and denim jeans. "My schedule's hectic today."

"You scheduled today?" Mrs. Dunleigh glanced from his face to Cassandra's, then seemed to catch herself. "Why, of course, I— I've forgotten how busy the only veterinarian in the valley can be. There's always someone who needs your services."

"I'd like to show you around the stables, Cassandra, when you're done here," Jack told her.

"Indeed, you must go have a peek, Mrs. McColton." Mrs. Dunleigh wiped her hands on her apron and peered with concern at the new mistress of the house. "Sunshine and fresh air will do you good."

Cassandra attempted a smile. "Sounds promising. I'll be right along."

"I'd like that," he said with sincerity. He hoped to make her comfortable here, to ease her transition to ranch living. "You didn't get much sleep, did you?"

Mrs. Dunleigh's eyes opened wide, as if she'd overheard them talking about something very intimate. He hadn't meant it that way. The housekeeper rushed away to the counter, where she fussed over the leftover fruit.

"I guess the long train ride is catching up to me." Cassandra gave him a pleasant look that indicated a truce. "I'll be out shortly."

He put on his black Stetson. "Good. See you then."

The truth was Cassandra could hardly move after the strain of last night. Losing her virginity had made her sore. That was one reason for her sluggishness. The other was that, quite frankly, she was still troubled by their argument. She had every right to have been forewarned about Elise Beacon and the possibility of brewing trouble.

Cassandra rose. Moving helped her physical discomfort. After spending a pleasant hour with

Mrs. Dunleigh, cleaning the kitchen, airing out the bedroom and being marched through the house to get a feel for where the bed linens and other essentials were kept, Cassandra was feeling more herself.

They were outside hanging laundry on the back line when the dogs ran over. Cassandra bent down and patted Queenie. "Hi, girl."

She found a stick and threw it for the sheepdogs. Queenie and Caesar tore off to retrieve it, bounding through the long grasses.

"Grandma!" a child's voice shouted. Cassandra whirled around to see a boy around eight or nine and a girl in her early teens approaching. They had to be brother and sister because they had the same red hair, wide nose and massive freckles.

"Hello!" Mrs. Dunleigh finished pegging a towel to the line, then embraced the children. "Come meet the new lady of the house, Mrs. McColton. Ma'am," the housekeeper said in her formal British accent, "these are my grandchildren, Julia and Ronald."

"Pleased to meet you," said the boy, his own accent strictly American. He stared boldly at her scarred face.

The girl turned a friendly smile to Cassandra, but was much quieter and withdrawn than her brother. She settled behind her grandmother, almost totally shielded from view, but peeking around at Cassandra's scar, as well.

"Now, children," Mrs. Dunleigh said curtly, obviously willing them not to stare.

"Hello," said Cassandra, glad to be among young people. "Can you show me any tricks with the dogs?" she asked Julia.

The adolescent instantly brightened. "They can jump over that stick, if you hold it steady." She proceeded to show her how Queenie did it, while her brother rolled on the grass with Caesar.

"Ronald," called Mrs. Dunleigh. "You'll stain your pants. What on earth will your mother think of me? Get up this instant!"

He jumped up and started playing tag with the dog. "Did it hurt?" he asked Cassandra. "When you got burned?"

"Ronald!" said his grandmother.

"It's all right, Mrs. Dunleigh." Obviously, thought Cassandra, they'd been forewarned about her injury. "I don't remember," she told the boy. "I don't remember anything about that day. When I woke up, the doctor gave me something for the pain and then it didn't hurt too much."

The children seemed satisfied with the answer.

"See?" Julia held a stick a foot off the ground.

Queenie made a dash for it, looking as if she'd run straight into it, then at the last minute lifted her legs and cleared the hurdle. Julia and Cassandra chuckled.

"The laundry's finished, Mrs. McColton," said the housekeeper. "If you'd like to join your husband now, I'm sure he'd be pleased to show you the horses."

Cassandra couldn't see the stables from where they stood, but figured Jack and his men would see her as she approached. She didn't relish making a grand entrance, for she'd never enjoyed being the center of attention. But if she stayed away any longer the men might consider her rude. She wanted to meet them, she truly did, but so many people all at once in the last twenty-four hours was intimidating.

Julia must've noticed her deliberating, for she offered, "I can go with you. It's easier with two."

Cassandra turned in mild surprise. "I imagine you know the stables much better than I do, since you spend so much time with your grandmother. Would you like to be my guide?"

Julia shrugged as if she didn't truly care one way or another, in true adolescent fashion, but then came readily. They left the housekeeper, and her grandson and the dogs near the laundry lines, and proceeded around the ranch house.

"We came on our own in the buggy. Father lets me drive it in the daytime. Mother's getting more used to seeing me with the reins, but she won't allow Ronald yet. She said he has to be able to see over the horses first."

"How lovely that you live so close to your grandparents. What does your father do in town?"

"Works on the railway. He's been away since Tuesday. Supposed to come home tomorrow."

"Ah, I see."

They turned the corner of the house and noticed a commotion. People were running from all directions. There was a buggy and horse tied to the hitching post, which had to be Julia's, but there was also another horse, a very large dapple-gray mare, still saddled, and drinking from the water trough. A rugged Winchester rifle was strapped to its back. Who had just arrived?

Men were dashing toward the stables from all sides, coming out of the toolsheds, from the fields, jumping off horses.

Alarmed that someone might be injured, Cassandra sprinted toward the chaos. Julia followed at her heels.

"What is it?" Cassandra asked an older ranch hand, her long skirts swinging about her legs.

"Fight!" the man hollered.

Fight? Who on earth was fighting? Jack would most certainly put a stop to it, whoever it was.

Cassandra raced through the open doors of the stables, then past the stalls and horses toward the back. She and Julia stepped out into the sunshine, where a dozen men crowded around the corral.

Cassandra had a bad feeling. She wrangled her way quietly among the shirts and Stetsons to see what was happening. "Excuse me, pardon me, excuse me."

She made it to the front, to find two men circling each other.

One of them was Jack.

Good Lord, he wasn't stopping the brawl, he was in it!

She looked around wildly—wasn't anyone going to put a halt to this?

A brute as tall and muscled as Jack dashed at him, his large fist raised, but Jack stopped it midair. The man swung again, this time punching him in the stomach. Cassandra winced. Jack doubled over, recovered quickly and retaliated with a slug to the man's ribs.

"Had enough, Thornley?" Jack cussed.

The man growled. "Stay away from Elise!"

Elise again?

The man took a flying leap and toppled Jack to the ground. They rolled like barbarians.

"Sir," Cassandra pleaded to the man standing next to her. "Can't you stop this? This is mad!"

"It's Jack's call, ma'am. No one interferes unless he says."

"Jack!" she shouted, stepping forward. "Stop it! Jack!"

He turned his head momentarily toward her and was rewarded with a right fist to his temple.

She covered her mouth in horror.

"If I hear you ever going near her again," the stranger yelled, "I'll rip your heart out!"

Jack rose to his feet, circled, blocked another swing, and this time hit the man's jaw full force. A tooth went flying. His opponent thumped onto his back, knocked out cold.

Jack swore. Then he went to the water trough, filled a tin cup, walked over to the fallen man and splashed water onto his bloody face.

The man came to, shuddered, then lay there catching his breath. Cassandra tried to step in front of Julia to shield the girl from the violence.

Unfortunately, the brute on the ground seemed to have worse intentions, for he lunged menacingly toward Jack, who was unaware and making his way toward her.

In a flash, Cassandra reached down to the holster of the nearest man, smoothly withdrew his Smith & Wesson, held it up in the air and expertly fired.

The bang startled everyone, including the man about to attack. Jack followed her gaze and sprang around to confront him. Two ranch hands were faster and were already subduing him.

All eyes turned toward Cassandra. She slowly lowered the revolver and passed it back with ease to the dismayed owner.

"I believe this is yours," she said. "Sorry to take it without permission."

The man, wearing a plaid shirt and sporting a wide black mustache, shook his head in disapproval. Then perhaps he realized there was no harm done, for a glimmer of amusement entered his eyes. "I trust it won't happen again."

Jack wobbled over to her, blood dribbling from his split lip, red lump on his temple, and pulled her out in front of the crowd. "Gentlemen," he announced in a slur, "I'd like you to meet my wife, Cassandra. And son of a gun, she knows how to shoot."

Men removed their hats and offered various pleasantries, as if this moment was nothing out of the ordinary.

"Ma'am."

"Pleased to meet you."

"Welcome to Napa."

Two of them went to help the fallen man to his feet, and the rest dispersed, returning to their tasks.

Cassandra, still reeling from the stupid display of brutality, shook her head at her husband.

"Derik Thornley," he said to her, nodding at the fellow as a means of introduction. "Excuse me for a moment." Jack turned and inhaled a few breaths to recover.

Two of Jack's men escorted Thornley off the premises.

"You'll pay, McColton!" he shouted as he was dragged out. "For everything you did to her!"

"Don't bring your sorry ass around here again!" Jack responded.

Obviously, thought Cassandra, Derik Thornley had come onto Jack's property and attacked him. Jack had every right to defend himself. But wasn't there a way to do it without the use of fists? And it seemed everyone in town had an opinion about Jack and Elise.

She swung around and noticed Julia still standing there, gaping openmouthed. Cassandra reached over and hugged the girl to her side. "Let's go find your grandmother."

They headed off, with Cassandra trying to come to grips with all the facets of her husband's character.

Hours later, when things had calmed down and Jack had collected his composure, he found Cassandra again and hauled her out of the house for a walk.

His jaw was mighty sore from his fight with Thornley, but he tried to ignore the throbbing. They stopped in the stables, next to a broodmare who'd be delivering in three months. He gave the horse a pat over the stall boards.

"This one's real gentle."

Cassandra fed her some oats.

"How is it that you know how to handle a gun?"

Her mouth puckered in sudden strain, as if she wasn't quite sure how to answer. But hell, he had a right to know why it was that his wife could handle a firearm.

"Mrs. Pepik at the boardinghouse taught anyone who wanted to learn. Her late husband had been a policeman and had taught her how to defend herself."

It wasn't something that the private detective Jack had hired had uncovered. But then again, Jack hadn't hired him for long, and had been very specific about what he wished to know about Cassandra, focusing on her broken engagement with Troy and what sort of circumstances she'd been living in at the boardinghouse.

"I—I've got a derringer pistol that I'm pretty good with."

He grinned. "Do you now? Do you keep it under your side of the mattress?"

"You might say that."

"Well, thanks for the fair warning."

"You don't mind?" Her lashes fluttered with some hesitation.

"I think Mr. Pepik had the right idea, teaching his wife self-defense."

Cassandra seemed buoyed by his answer. Her smile widened and her eyes sparkled. Was there something more to this conversation that he was missing? Her silence about the derringer was a bit odd. But before he could think more on that, her demeanor shifted. She frowned and blurted out another question. "Why didn't you have your men escort Derik Thornley off the ranch as soon as you saw him coming?"

"I didn't know his intentions. Then he took a swing at me, and I couldn't just stand there and take it."

She patted the broodmare. "I wish you would've

remembered that you have a wife living with you now, and children within earshot."

"I didn't know Julia was there."

"She told me she's never seen a fight between two men before."

"Well, it's not like she's a kid. She is fifteen." He didn't mean to sound harsh. "Is she all right?"

Cassandra relented. "She's fine. Please explain to me what this man Thornley wants."

Jack led her through a side door to the outer buildings, so he could show her those, too. They left the stalls and the men pitching straw, stepping out into the corral, close to where he and Thornley had fought that morning.

"Thornley's the one I told you about who was seeing Elise the same time I was. Except that he's still seeing her. Apparently he heard about the words between us in church yesterday, and didn't like the way I treated her. Neither did she."

"She's the one who interrupted our ceremony, and *she* was offended by *us*?"

"Apparently."

"Listen, Jack…please tell me the truth about something." Cassandra watched two men trying to saddle a wild mustang. Jack knew from experience it would take days of practice before the horse would allow anyone near her.

He squinted into the sunshine. "Go ahead. Whatever you want to know."

"Have you ever…did you ever…sleep with this woman?"

Jack swallowed hard at the question. Normally, he'd never let anyone ask him something so personal. Hell, they could ask, but he'd never say. In this case, though, he wanted to ease Cassandra's concern.

"No, I never did."

The tense muscles in her shoulders eased. She blinked, didn't say anything more, but seemed satisfied by his answer. Even so, as they finished the tour and he pointed out the bunkhouse, he wasn't so sure they were back on solid footing.

Jack introduced her to his foreman, Russell Crawford, a short bulky man in a plaid shirt with a wide black mustache and solid handshake.

"We stood next to each other," Cassandra reminded him, "earlier today. I—I borrowed your gun."

"I don't know how you managed that," said Jack with a chuckle. Hell, if she wasn't impressive. Surviving the Great Fire had made her more resourceful and self-reliant than he'd originally considered. A pretty woman with a pistol was intriguing. As long as she was using it for self-defense and nothing more. He frowned, wondering why that thought had popped into his head.

"Don't let Jack's easygoing nature fool you," Russell said with a chuckle. "He and I actually met in a boxing ring when he first got here."

"Boxing?" Cassandra glanced at Jack in fresh alarm.

"Something I used to do. I don't anymore." He shot Russell a pointed glance, and the man seemed to get the meaning.

He tipped his hat. "Got lots to do, ma'am. Nice to have met you."

It was awkward again between them, so as a means of distraction, Jack walked her through his veterinary office in the stables. "This is where I keep some of my supplies. I've got another office inside the house."

She strolled past the medicine cabinets, peered through the slatted windows above the wide pine desk into the corral, then back to some of his veterinary books. Unexpectedly, Jack was called away on an urgent matter about a wagon delivery, apologizing again to Cassandra for leaving her.

"It's all right. I'll help Mrs. Dunleigh in the kitchen."

He didn't get back to her till dinnertime, but it was not a private event. Mrs. Dunleigh served them, chatting about her grandchildren and what shops Cassandra should and shouldn't visit when she got the opportunity, while Jack wished... Ah, hell, he wasn't sure what he wished.

Dinner was over and he withdrew to his office to finish some paperwork. When he retired to bed he was hoping to spend some time with Cassandra, but she was already asleep. With a mumble, he punched his pillow and turned over in the darkness.

It was another night of cold shoulders. He went to sleep wondering where she kept her derringer, precisely, and what else there was about her that he didn't know. He had a gut feeling she was hiding something. Maybe a lunch date in town tomorrow was just the thing that would help him pry the information out of her.

Chapter Seven

⟨⟨⟨⟨⟨⟨⟨⟨⟨❦⟩⟩⟩⟩⟩⟩⟩⟩⟩

Shaded by redwoods and Douglas fir, Cassandra stood at the edge of the narrow river in Sundial the next day and worried how to make things right with Jack. Neither of them were sleeping properly or could seem to drop their guard around the other, and both were avoiding even the simplest touch.

"Watch your step. The stones can be slippery." Jack led the way along the bank, his husky figure in shadows from overhead branches. He had a bruised left jaw this morning, a remnant of his altercation with Thornley, yet it didn't stop him from going out in public.

"There's a pretty café ahead where we can have lunch." He pointed to a busy place on the corner street overlooking the river, where several customers were going in and out. A cluster of palm trees shaded the porch. "I thought we might discuss what you have planned for your days."

"It looks inviting," she said.

Perhaps they could bury their differences over the way he had handled Thornley yesterday. She'd come awfully close to revealing her interest in gaining employment in the investigation field, but had stopped short of telling him she wanted to work as a detective. However, she had to tell him sometime. He was her husband. The optimistic part of her hoped that perhaps he'd be as understanding about her wish for employment as he was about her ability with guns.

Because her father had been a criminal attorney, she'd been surrounded her entire life by conversations about law and procedures. She'd met judges and bailiffs and policemen, and felt comfortable conversing with them. How many times had she sat at the dinner table with men from her father's field, discussing the latest news in Chicago? Troy had also been an attorney. Some of their conversations about his work had been lively and riveting. She'd discovered she had a burning interest in piecing together clues in the latest burglary she'd read about in the papers, and being fascinated when women were involved, either as perpetrators or victims who

needed assistance. In cases her father wasn't involved with, she'd even made suggestions on
clues, and sometimes she'd been proved right.

Mary would always tease about Cassandra's
obsession, in a loving way, but surely Jack would
understand when she explained it to him. They
were grown now; they weren't children.

"Mind if we stop at the feed and supply shop
before lunch?" Jack asked, maneuvering across
some flat rocks. "I've got an order to place."

"Lead the way." Cassandra followed him,
stepping onto one boulder, then leaping to the
next. Her skirts swirled around her, revealing
her well-worn, brown leather boots, and cool
air played over her skin.

Jumping to a spot beside him on the grass,
she inhaled a deep breath that raised her breasts
beneath the pleats of her high-collared blouse.

In quick response, his gaze fell and lingered
there, and she felt herself flush with thoughts
of their wedding night, how he'd swept her up
in his arms in the tub and kissed every inch of
her nipples. She wondered if he might ever do
that again, and if she might have the opportunity to stare at his physique as long and hard as
she truly desired.

Jack tore his gaze away from her soft cotton
blouse, which had been washed so many times it

was threadbare in spots. Awkwardly, she pulled at one dangling gold earring and assured herself that this marriage could work.

It *would* work.

They simply needed time to reacquaint themselves and grow into the roles and duties of husband and wife. Their argument yesterday had been silly, and there was no need to prolong it.

They approached the main street. A team of thundering horses raced by pulling a wagon. Jack took her elbow protectively and led the way across the dry ruts.

She was ever so conscious of the length of his legs in his casual jeans, the wide silver buckle at his waist, the strength in his torso beneath his black shirt, and heated looks of secret approval he was getting from young ladies they passed on the boardwalk.

The shiny tips of his black cowboy boots reflected the glare of the hot California sun. When they crossed into the town square, he splayed one callused hand at the back of her waist, sending more shivers coursing through her skin.

"Let's have a look at that sundial you saw on your first day," he said. "It was put here a hundred years ago by the Spanish."

They stopped at the marble column, which

was etched with a large circle and had numbers around its face.

"How does it work?" she asked.

"That part sticking out, the pointer, is called the gnomon." He pronounced it nom-on. "When the sun hits, it casts a shadow here." He pointed to the marker, indicating it was almost high noon.

"So at different times of the day," she mused, "the shadow is in different positions, with different lengths. Shortest at noon."

"Exactly. And since the earth rotates on its axis fifteen degrees an hour—"

"In twenty-four hours, it moves three hundred sixty degrees," she finished. "Then starts all over again."

"You always were fast with numbers."

"How did they know how and where to position the sundial, to read the sun accurately?"

"It's adjusted somehow, according to the latitude."

"Ah, so that's the trick. They line it up with the latitude. So what happens when—"

He raised a palm in the air and interjected, "Don't ask me anything more. I don't know. We should share a tequila, though, and discuss it."

At his comment, she glanced up in surprise, then smiled at his teasing expression. They were a couple getting to know each other, she thought. Their marriage was unusual, with the mail-order aspect, but they were like any other lovers who might dream of a future together.

The tender moment didn't last long.

An elderly couple strolled by, the woman dressed in a fancy bonnet and suit, the gent in top hat and gloves. Cassandra heard the woman whisper, "...shame about her face. He could've made a better pick, and you'd think he could afford to put her in decent clothes...."

Cassandra looked quickly to the ground, turning her rough cheek away from them. Suddenly, she was ever so conscious of every repair she'd ever made to the hem of her skirts, and the worn darts in her blouse.

Jack didn't appear to hear the comment. He raised a muscled arm to tip his hat. "Fine day."

They nodded back. "Hello, Doctor."

For a moment, Cassandra, still mortified, wasn't sure if he was going to introduce them. However, they were quite a ways away and it would've been awkward to step out and pursue them when they were already past, so he left it at that. She recognized them as two of the witnesses inside the church who'd seen the whole debacle with Elise.

"They own a dress shop," Jack explained. "The Velvet Touch."

"I see."

"This way." Jack was about to turn left toward a laneway filled with saloons and gun shops, then must've thought better of it and steered her right, toward a more upstanding portion of town, past a handful of clothing shops, two jewelry stores and a sweets shop.

When they entered the Feed and Supply Depot, the man behind the counter raised a hand in a friendly salute. "Jack! Congratulations. This must be your lovely wife."

She was touched by his cheerfulness. It was comforting to know that not all the town residents reacted the same way to her burn injury. Some hardly seemed to notice. Jack led her past an aisle filled with sacks of oats and feed to the tall man wearing a blue apron. The air was stuffy and hot.

"Wonderful to meet you, Mrs. McColton."

"Cassandra, please."

Jack tapped a hand protectively on her shoulder blade. "Meet Mr. Alan Barnum."

"How do you do, Mr. Barnum?"

The man took her hand. "The pleasure's all mine. How is this husband of yours treating you?

Nice to see him takin' some time out from his busy days."

"He's showing me around your pretty town."

The man took a second look at Jack's bruised jaw. "Hmm. I heard about that. Heard you won, too."

Cassandra dropped her gaze in a moment of embarrassment. Knowing that he'd used his fists to settle a dispute was disquieting. He'd always been a fighter in Chicago, but that was when he had been an adolescent.

"It's over." Jack leaned across the counter, maneuvering his wide shoulders around the equipment hanging on the wall. His hair was coal-black, as were his eyes and eyebrows and the dark shadow of growth beneath his jawline. A sheen of sweat dampened his brow, and she found her pulse thrum in response to the picture of raw masculinity he made. "Can you deliver some medicines today?"

"Sure. What do you need?"

Jack explained his order in detail, while Cassandra inhaled the husky scents of grains and hay. She peered at the new hoses, shiny hoes and balls of twine—anything to stop herself from gazing at Jack and imagining him in bed.

Mr. Barnum addressed her again. "So I imagine you two will be joining us for the big celebrations on the Fourth of July?"

Jack turned abruptly toward her. Judging by his furrowed brow, he'd been caught off guard by the question.

What big celebrations? she thought. "Beg your pardon?"

"This Friday, the Fourth. The town always does it up real nice. You'll be coming, won't you?"

"I—I haven't suggested it yet," said Jack, stumbling through his words.

Mr. Barnum eyed him. "Don't you be skippin' out, Jack, like you usually do. I'm sure your young bride would enjoy an evening of music and dancing."

She wouldn't mind it, thought Cassandra.

Jack cocked his head and rubbed his jaw with long lean fingers. After a nod of approval from her, he replied, "We'll be there, Alan. Thanks." He led her back down the aisle.

"Save me a dance, Cassandra!" Mr. Barnum said boldly, to her pleasant surprise, when they neared the door.

"Will do!" she replied with a wave of her hand.

When they stepped back out the door, Jack tugged at the brim of his black Stetson and spoke

without looking at her. "I'll set up an account at
a few of the women's shops in town. You might
like a new dress for the party. And more clothes
for the ranch. Don't worry what you spend. I
can afford it."

Normally, she would've felt honored that he'd
be so generous. In fact, she was appreciative.
Except now she knew for certain that he *had*
overheard the older couple, the owners of The
Velvet Touch, talking about her scar and her
ragged clothes.

It was humiliating to know that other people didn't think she was good enough for Jack.
It was even more humiliating that her husband
had noticed it.

Jack damn well knew what everyone was saying about them while they shared a meal at Pe-
nelope's Café. Hell, if they'd only say it directly
to him, he could respond in the straightforward
manner he'd prefer. But all the whispering and
staring and sly half smiles made his skin crawl,
and wouldn't allow him to sit in peace with his
new wife. He'd removed his Stetson and placed it
on the outer edge of the table. Now he ran a hand
through his hair to settle it. Cassandra sipped
her tea and mentioned how much she was enjoying the turkey casserole. But even she couldn't

hide the bruising to her pride when Elise Beacon strolled by the café's front window, not quite as dolled up as usual, but still wearing a fashionable working skirt and blouse. Heads turned.

"There she is," someone whispered.

"Why would he pick *her* over Elise?" said another.

"Shame what he did to the Beacon girl. She was expectin' to be the bride herself."

"Why would any man find the need to mail away for a wife? Why, we've got plenty right here in this…"

"…and did you hear about yesterday? Look, his jaw is still bruised."

Jack listened, embarrassed, as Cassandra toyed with her food. Her hair was slightly untidy in a loose braid, but it fell over her lace collar and the rise of her breasts in such an attractive fashion, it made his skin heat. It was already warm enough in here for a bead of perspiration to slip down his temple. She was adding another five or ten degrees to his temperature.

Jack tried to divert her attention from the crass words of others. There was no damn way anyone's ill manners would drive him out of the café. Besides, he wanted to broach the subject of what she might possibly be hiding from him. "Are you settling in at the house?"

"Yes. Mrs. Dunleigh's been a godsend. She's showing me how she manages things at the house, and we're getting along quite well."

"And you're finding enough to do? I recall in your letters you mentioning that you'd like to occupy your time with something meaningful. There's lots to do on the ranch. I could show you more when you're ready."

Her eyes seemed to spark at the comment. She leaned forward with an enthusiasm that was captivating to him. Her skin glowed with it. "There is something I would like to discuss, now that you mention it."

That sounded promising, as though she wished to confide in him. "What's that?"

"Well…something I saw in the newspapers on the journey here. About the Pinkerton Agency."

"Ah, yes," he said lightly. "Entertaining reading, isn't it? Those detectives are always in the news. I think the stories get quite embellished in the Eastern papers, though. Readers seem to enjoy the thrill of reading about the Wild West, and newspapers are only too pleased to give it to them. Whether it's fabricated or not."

She nodded. "Yes, but there was a story about a female detective—"

"Female? You sure you got that right?"

"They've hired several of them, apparently,

dating back seventeen years. The agency doesn't speak of it much, obviously to protect the identity of the women involved."

"Why on earth would Mr. Pinkerton and his agency hire females?"

"It's said that…that women are very good observers of people, pay attention to minute details, clues that men might not notice. That women can infiltrate gangs by befriending the wives or lovers of some of the men. That criminals rarely suspect a woman of being a detective, so she has the element of surprise in her corner. Some women are quite fit, physically. They can outrun some men."

Jack whistled in disbelief. He leaned back in his chair and studied his wife. This was the sort of thing she'd been reading about? Did she find it adventurous, or the jeopardy just plain shocking, as he did?

"I imagine their husbands are none too pleased."

Cassandra's forehead grew pinched. "In this particular article, the lady detective was widowed. Young, in her early twenties, but widowed."

"Well, that explains that. What man in his right mind would allow his wife to step into that sort of danger?"

"Not all detective work has to be filled with the most dangerous—"

"And it's this sort of reading material that you might be interested in, in proposing a library?"

She blinked. "Library?"

He smiled, trying to set her at ease. "You used to do a lot of reading, as I recall. Your hands were always filled with books—law books from your father's den, the newspapers, dime novels. Usually adventure stories, just like the ones about the Pinkerton Agency."

"Doesn't the town have a library?"

"No."

"That is indeed a shame." Her pretty blond lashes fluttered and he felt a tug in his chest. "So, Jack, you wouldn't mind me working?"

Was that what she'd been hiding from him? That she wished to work outside the home, earn an income for herself independent from his?

"Some men would mind," he said honestly. "Some men think a woman shouldn't hire herself out. Think it's beneath them, and somehow injures the strength of the family if a woman should want an independent means of support."

"That's not you, Jack."

"What makes you so sure?" He eyed her from across the table. She had a sudden self-confidence about her that attracted his attention.

Her cream-colored blouse shifted as she drew a deep breath, and he noticed her throat was nicely framed by the puckered holes in the lace collar. Some scent she was wearing, a derivative of roses, heightened, then retreated, depending how close she came into his space.

"Because back in Chicago, your head would always turn at the women who *did* work. You'd spend hours in conversation with the one who sometimes assisted my father with his legal papers, remember? Then there was the merchant's wife you'd engage with about rising and falling stocks on the New York Stock Exchange. Not to mention the deep and heated conversations you had with the Latin teacher across the street when she came home from a tour of Rome."

What had come over Cassandra? Her initial shyness was fading, replaced with something much more striking and self-assured. Whatever it was, he found the change fascinating.

"My, you have been paying attention. I'm flattered."

"Don't be flattered," she said with new heat. "It just so happens I like my men intelligent, too."

He cocked his head in amusement and took a long look at her.

She raised her slender eyebrows in response,

as if amused by his reaction. "To twist oneself up in the brains of another, that's a steamy proposition, isn't it? I know you enjoy a good conversation. A good argument about world issues. It's deeply sensual and invigorating, never knowing if you're stepping on someone's toes or invading their thoughts in some devilish way."

A prickle of heat ran down the back of his neck. "You get all that from reading the paper?"

"I like to keep my mind active. It's the hopes and dreams of people that I enjoy reading about, Jack. Don't you think it's important to dream big?"

"Well, it is for a man. That is, of course, the only perspective I have of dreaming."

She smiled at his teasing.

"A library would be fine with me," he said, trying to be generous. It would be a nice distraction, and something valuable for the community. Maybe some of the judgmental folks in town would get to know her that way, and she could build friendships.

Her smile wavered. "What if it was something more I wanted?"

He frowned. "Such as?"

She lifted her water glass, pressed her lush pink lips to the rim and sipped. "Did you know Mary always wanted to open a jewelry shop?"

"Little Mary?" He grinned at the image of the adolescent girl she'd been when he'd last seen her, slender and soft-spoken and hardly one to open a business. "That must've been impressive to all."

A fleeting look of anguish passed through Cassandra's blue eyes, as if she was pained at the thought that Mary would never fulfill that dream. Then it was gone, replaced by something gentler. "If she were here right now, she would be nudging me to stop beating around the bush and to—"

"Doc!" someone called from across the room, interrupting them. "There you are!"

Jack and Cassandra both wheeled around in their chairs to see Charlie Van Horn rush over, dressed in his work overalls from the vineyards, hat in hand. Lines of concern etched his weather-beaten face. "Alan Barnum said he saw you come in, said I might find you here."

Jack sensed trouble. "What is it, Charlie?"

"Old man Finley is having trouble with his cows. Two of 'em are sick, one pretty bad off. Lyin' down on her side for the last hour."

Jack glanced at Cassandra, but she was already collecting her satchel and shawl. This was supposed to be their time together for a few days after their wedding, uninterrupted by his work.

Yet he appreciated her unquestioning response to the emergency.

"We'll follow you, Charlie." Jack rose, tossed a generous amount of coins on the table and scooped up his Stetson. He didn't look back to check what the gossips might or might not be saying as he escorted his wife out of the café.

Charlie's horse was tethered to the hitching post in the next block.

"My buggy's around the side," Jack told him, then strode past with Cassandra.

"Jack!" Charlie hollered after them.

They swung around again.

"One more thing you should know." The man hesitated, then glanced with a worrisome expression at Cassandra. "I passed Elise Beacon twenty minutes ago, and asked her to check on the cows, too. I heard about your situation…but when I saw her, I had to think real quick on my feet. I had to ask her to come because I wasn't sure if I'd find you."

Elise again, thought Jack. And everyone seemed to know about his fight yesterday with Thornley. Well, it was what it was, and he couldn't change the past. "She knows a lot about animals, Charlie. It's understandable you asked her."

Jack's hand spanned the back of Cassandra's

waist as he urged her along the boardwalk. "Sorry, this can't be helped," he explained. "Elise lived with her uncle in San Francisco for a spell while she was growing up. Her uncle was a vet, and passed down a lot of his knowledge to her. She doesn't have formal training, but lots of folks depend on her for the care of their animals."

It had been one of the things she and Jack had in common, that had drawn them together in the first place, but he didn't wish to hurt Cassandra by saying so.

She probably sensed it, anyway.

She puzzled over his comments briefly, but said nothing as they rushed to the buggy. Once seated, he flicked the reins and they rumbled out of town. Horses and cattle he could handle.

Women were another matter.

Chapter Eight

~~~~~~~~~~~~~~~~~~~~~~~~~~~~

They reached the Finley cattle ranch within a half hour. Cassandra watched Jack with a mesmerizing sense that she'd never seen her husband in action before as a full-fledged veterinarian. She shouldn't have been surprised when he parked the buggy next to a spiffy red leather one already there and reached behind the seat beneath a blanket to find his medical bag. Of course he traveled with his supplies; it was only natural he'd be prepared. He'd always been prepared when it came to matters such as business and animals.

It was she who was unprepared for the jolt to her heart when he murmured, "That's her buggy."

Miss Beacon's, of course. Who else could he mean?

No other people were in sight. They had to be preoccupied with the cattle inside the buildings that sat atop the green hill.

"Should I wait here?" Cassandra eyed the conveyance that belonged to the other woman, the polished red leather and oiled black rims glinting in the bright sun.

"It's up to you," he said, his smoky eyes watching her from beneath the brim of his dark Stetson. "But I would enjoy your company."

Her pulse did strange things when he spoke to her like that. She was further unprepared that he'd be so forthright in saying how he felt. She was disappointed that she'd been unable to tell him about her goal in working as a detective, back at the café, and that he'd misconstrued that she was speaking about a library. But the animals were her priority now.

She quickly slid off the seat and came to join him as he walked toward the stables. He led the way down the grassy path as if he'd been here a hundred times before. His muscles flexed beneath his dark shirt and perspiration mottled the cloth at his spine. She tried not to notice how his thighs tugged at the worn denim, or how his tanned forearms poked out of the rolled cuffs of his sleeves. He had a comfortable, easy way about him that Cassandra found appealing.

They soon entered the darkened building and peered over the boards, spotting a handful of ranch hands crowded around a stall in the far corner.

"Howdy!" Jack called out.

"Hey, Doc," some replied in pleasant tones.

"Is Finley here?"

"Right here, Jack," said a male voice. An elderly, whiskered man rose to his feet in the stall. "Beside the calf."

Cassandra took a deep breath, nervously patted the buttoned front of her blouse, then let her hands fall to her long, swaying skirt. She hadn't yet seen Miss Beacon, and wondered if it were possible that they'd be fortunate and escape her presence.

Jack took a few long strides toward the rancher, then turned to encircle his free arm around Cassandra. "I'd like to introduce you all to my wife."

She braced herself for the stares that would come her way, the glances at her scar and perhaps that bit of alarm that often went with it.

There were some stares, but the workers had likely already heard about the woman Jack had married, for many removed their hats in a show of respect. Some called out various friendly hellos and how-do-you-dos. Others held back, though, and looked away from her face. Trying to remain cheerful, she stepped forward and smiled. What had she been so afraid of? Once they got to know her, they'd see she was just a regular woman, no better, no worse than any other.

But with one more step, she was in view of the calf lying on the straw, and a young woman in working blouse and skirt leaning over the animal, a stethoscope attached to her ears.

Miss Beacon.

Jack didn't say anything for a moment. Men around them shuffled their feet in the straw and cleared their throats, and Cassandra felt the muscles around her own windpipe constrict with discomfort. Did everyone here know the story of what had happened on her wedding day?

Jack knelt down on the other side of the rusty-colored calf.

"Over here, my dear." Mr. Finley indicated that Cassandra might stand beside him, next to the post, as they watched the process unfold.

Miss Beacon removed her stethoscope from her ears. Her dark brown hair, braided only at the front, fell across the pressed sleeves of her rose-tinted blouse. She nodded to Jack in greeting, appeared to glance at his bruised jaw, but didn't look at Cassandra. Truth be told, perhaps the woman had, but Cassandra had been too busy saying good afternoon to Mr. Finley to notice.

"We're all neighbors." Mr. Finley pointed to Miss Beacon, by way of explanation to Cassandra. "Her father's vineyard is right next door. And Jack's is to the other side."

Cassandra nodded. "I imagine when someone's animals are ill in the valley, everyone's concerned."

Jack unbuckled his black leather bag. He removed his stethoscope, had a listen, soothed the calf with a few pats and murmurs, and then asked questions.

"How long has she been like this?"

"Last night she didn't seem herself." An older ranch hand with shaggy, windswept hair answered in a forceful tone, as if he might be the foreman. "Was slow to eat. This morning, too."

Jack peered into one of the calf's eyes. "When did she start to lose her energy?"

"This afternoon," Miss Beacon answered, "when she came in from the pastures."

Jack glanced at the woman's face, then down to her hand stroking the calf's shoulder. "Any vomiting?"

"No, sir," said Mr. Finley, crossing his arms over his tan vest.

"Is she ruminating?" asked Miss Beacon.

Cassandra wasn't familiar with the term, but no one else seemed to be confused. Serious faces peered out from beneath cowboy hats and looked to that same foreman with the shaggy hair.

"She was last night, nice and normal like, but I haven't seen her chewing her cud today."

"Something's off, then." Miss Beacon looked to Jack, her face aglow. She had such smooth skin—such a beautiful complexion—and a ready-to-please demeanor. Cassandra, unfortunately, could easily see how a man could fall for her. Not only for her looks, but her intelligence.

Jack did a careful inspection of the calf's eyes and nose.

"Let's have her stand," he said. He smoothly rose to his full height, towering over Miss Beacon and the scrawny calf, and gave a soft tug on the loose rope around the animal's neck.

The calf had difficulty rising. It got up on its rear legs, but couldn't seem to manage its front ones. Miss Beacon lunged in to try to help, but Jack held up his hand to stop her. Her arms fell back to her sides as they waited for the animal to stand on its own.

With a wobble, it finally did.

Cassandra wondered what had Jack noticed in that exercise.

"She didn't stretch her back when she got to her feet," he said with concern. "Healthy calves usually do. And she doesn't seem alert." He gave the animal another pat, looked beyond Miss Beacon's shoulder to Mr. Finley. "Do you have any other cattle down?"

"Two more over here."

Jack mumbled in disappointment as he followed the rancher to the full-grown cows lying down in nearby stalls. They seemed to have the same listless symptoms as the smaller one.

"Where have they been grazing lately?" Jack asked, after examining them. "Can you show me which pastures?"

"Certainly. Right over here." Mr. Finley led him and Miss Beacon out the back end of the barn.

Around Cassandra, the ranch hands returned to their tasks. Some picked up pitchforks, others went to attend the broken wheel of a wagon. Cassandra followed slowly behind Jack and Miss Beacon and Mr. Finley, but they didn't include her in their discussion and she felt uncomfortable tagging behind. They had work to do, and she allowed them the time and space to do it.

When she looked about, one of the ranch hands seemed to notice her predicament.

"There's a fine bench under those trees, if you'd like to sit a spell while you're waiting."

"It looks like a pretty view."

She strolled out the stable doors, yards away from Jack and the other two as they pointed and discussed. She caught snatches of their conversation.

"...to the southern fence..."

"...might be something they ate..."

Cassandra reached the bench beneath the apple trees just as Jack turned to her and called out, "Mr. Finley's going to show us the pastures! We're searching for poisonous plants! Would you like to come?"

"That's fine, go ahead without me!" she called back.

She wavered, unsure whether to change her mind and follow her husband, to keep an eye on the other woman, but it was too late. Jack took her at her word and disappeared into the meadows, with Mr. Finley hobbling on one side and Miss Beacon's fine silhouette outlined in the breeze on his other.

Despite her good looks and intelligence, something about the woman was troubling, Cassandra decided. And her beau, Derik Thornley, too. Something about Miss Beacon's demeanor and manner of addressing Jack—and ignoring

Cassandra—seemed off. Of course, there was all that sour business between them with the wedding, but was there something more? Cassandra aimed to find out. Perhaps it would be her first secret task as a detective in this town. She'd make a few discreet inquires about the pair.

Hell. How had Jack gotten trapped out here in the fields with Elise? Granted, she was behaving with professional decorum, but he would rather be spending his time with Cassandra.

Long grasses shifted about their knees.

"What're we looking for, exactly?" Mr. Finley asked as he shuffled away to the right, along the wire fence.

"Ferns. Milkweed." Jack scoured the ground, his eyes expertly going up and down the dry ridges, making out shapes of leaves and buds. "I have a suspicion of foxglove, if you see any."

"It's three to six feet tall," Elise explained to Mr. Finely, placing her hand at the height of her hip. "The stalks have rose-colored flowers."

"Or maybe it's thistles or hemlock," said Jack.

"What's that you say?" the rancher called.

"If you'd like to rest awhile, Mr. Finley, Elise and I will circle the pasture. We're more familiar with the plants, and I'd like to do a thorough search."

"Right." Finley took a breather. He removed his straw cowboy hat and swatted at the flies circling about. "That's a large field. How're you going to cover it all?"

Jack turned to Elise and told her, "I don't mind doing this on my own."

"Nonsense," she said. "We're all neighbors. Anything that affects his cattle may affect our livestock, too. Especially a trail of poisonous plants."

"I see your point." Jack's property, too, abutted the Finley ranch. "Well, then, if you'd like to follow along that other fence, the one adjacent to your land, it would be helpful to me." He found it very difficult to get the next words out. "I do appreciate your help."

She quickly worked her way to the other side of the pasture, and he was pleased—somewhat grateful—that she was taking direction so well today. Maybe the past *was* behind them, and he and Cassandra could move on with their lives without the added guilt or burden of dealing with Elise.

Thirty minutes later, they came together again near the top of the hill. He'd collected a few samples of thistles and ferns, but hadn't seen anything in large enough quantity that would be harmful.

She, too, held a batch of leaves.

"Those aren't poisonous," he told her.

"Oh, but I thought these wide leaves—"

"Harmless."

She dropped the weeds and the wind snatched them away. It also picked up a strand of her long brown hair, which she fiddled with. "Now I feel silly. I thought I was being helpful."

"You were. I'll have another look around tomorrow when I return to check on the cattle. Maybe it was moldy hay, or something else in their quarters."

They turned to head back. Finley was nowhere in sight. He must've gone back to the stables, over the rise.

"Jack, about yesterday. I heard what Derik did and I—I must apologize. He had no right to hit you."

"You didn't know he was coming out to see me?"

"I had no idea. He told me after I'd seen the bruising on his knuckles, and his split lip."

"Yeah, well…sorry about the missing tooth." Fortunately for Thornley, it wasn't a front tooth, but one on the side, so the gap wasn't visible when he talked.

"Do you think we could put this behind us?" She peered up at him, trembling in the wind.

Behind us? Well, didn't she dang well have a twisted sense of civility? She'd stepped out from the congregation in a church ceremony to which she hadn't even been invited, made a fool out of him and embarrassed his bride—and she thought an apology would suffice?

Temper, he warned himself. *Temper*.

He was trapped between his outrage and his professional role as a veterinarian, one obligated to maintain peace in the community so that he might freely roam the ranches and vineyards, without the fear of bumping into her. Without the fear that if he did still harbor a grudge against Elise and Thornley, it might be harder for Cassandra to handle as a newcomer than it would be for him.

So he took a deep breath and answered in the most gracious tone he could muster. "I would appreciate if we could all forget it and go about our business."

She smiled timidly, and seemed sincere, but he wasn't about to place one iota of trust in her. Yet when she extended her hand, he took it and shook. She seemed somehow comforted by that. Jack hoped with every breath he drew that Derik Thornley would hurry up and propose marriage to her, then whisk her out of the valley. The East Coast might be far enough away.

They reached the top of the hill and Jack searched the scene for Cassandra. She was enjoying a pitcher of what looked like lemonade with Mr. Finley beneath the apple trees. The old man was pointing to the valley below, then back up at his ranch, likely telling one of his long stories about how he was the oldest cattle rancher in Napa. Cassandra was smiling and laughing and asking animated questions.

Jack and Elise approached. He thought he heard the words *"Beacon vineyard"* and *"Thornley works there with her."* But as they got closer, he gathered he'd been mistaken, for the conversation was about the size of the town. Elise seemed absorbed in her own thoughts, and hadn't been paying attention.

Jack was about to join in the conversation about Sundial's wine-making history when he noticed a man on horseback entering the front gate, flying like a fireball out of hell. He didn't bother riding to the hitching post, but was galloping straight at them, sending dirt flying.

Finley stood up in alarm to stare at the oncoming rider.

Cassandra and Elise turned to watch, too.

"What is it?" Jack hollered when the rider got closer.

The man was one of Finley's ranch hands.

Jack had noticed the long-haired fellow earlier, while examining the calf.

Finley stepped forward. "What is it, Hank?"

The man shot off his horse. "There's trouble, sir! On Dr. McColton's ranch!" He gulped down a breath of air. "I was on my way into town to the feed and supply store, sir, when I heard. Someone's hurt on your ranch, Dr. McColton. You better go quick."

"Who's hurt?" Jack asked, stricken with concern.

"I don't know, sir. I got only half the story from a barrel salesman I passed on the road. He said someone just dropped dead on the McColton ranch."

Chapter Nine

The buggy flew around the corner on two wheels as Jack gripped the reins, in full control of the horse, but obviously desperate to get home. The wind whipped through Cassandra's hair, snatching at her skirts and making conversation impossible. Her heart beat madly, her mouth was dry and she was thunderstruck by the terrible news that someone might be dead. She prayed that the message had somehow gotten jumbled and it wasn't true.

But as they approached the top of their laneway and she saw the cluster of horses and people milling about the house, her stomach gave out.

Their horse wheeled in under the familiar trees, where the foreman, Russell Crawford, dashed out to greet them, his black mustache bristling in the wind.

"Jack!"

"Who is it?"

"Dunleigh."

"Oh, Lord." Jack jumped from the buggy and Cassandra bounded after him. "I heard you sent for a doctor. Is he here yet?"

"No, but I see him coming up the laneway now." Crawford pointed, and sure enough, the doctor's black horse and buggy were hightailing it toward them.

A gauntlet of men on the flagstone path leading to the big ranch house parted as Jack strode forward, Cassandra following.

Inside, people were gathering in the parlor. Half a dozen ranch hands encircled the long sofa where Mr. Dunleigh was lying, still as a statue with his eyes closed. His wife was kneeling on the floor beside him, alternating between sobbing and murmuring his name.

"Yule, please. Yule, wake up, it's too soon for you to go...."

Jack removed his Stetson and knelt beside her on the floor.

His gentle approach and embrace of the weeping woman touched Cassandra. She prayed Mr. Dunleigh would awaken.

"Sheila, the doctor's almost here." Jack tried to reassure her. He placed his hand on her husband's chest and tried to rouse him, but to no avail.

"He'd had his morning tea," Mrs. Dunleigh explained, rocking back and forth in anguish. Cassandra scooted in beside her for support. "We were on our private terrace and he was watching out for the delivery boy. There was a knock on the door, and he went to open it. It was Adam, with the paper. And Yule dropped. He just dropped. Halfway back to me with the *Sundial Daily News*. Just like that."

"Too sudden," Jack murmured in sympathy.

Dr. Clarkson rushed in with his medical bag, his long white hair flowing over his black suit. He did a quick examination, then turned and shook his head at the others waiting hopefully.

"His heart gave out," the doctor announced to everyone, then looked at Jack, who was now standing and supporting Mrs. Dunleigh. "I was treating him for angina. Sheila and I both knew he was ailin', but I didn't figure it would come this quick."

At this point, Mrs. Dunleigh keeled over in a faint. Jack and Cassandra dived forward and caught her before she could slide to the floor.

Embracing her on either side, they talked

to her until she came to, then led her into the kitchen and sat her gently at the table. Pulling up chairs on either side, they tried to console her.

"We came to this country together," she said with a rattling sigh. "He was seventeen, I was fifteen. I've never known a life without him."

Cassandra's sorrow for the woman's loss added to her own raw heartache for the recent loss of her sister and father. Mrs. Dunleigh searched for her handkerchief to mop up her stream of tears. It was too much sorrow. Too much pain.

"Yule was a good man," Jack told her. "I admired him for how much he went through, and how much he adored you."

This sent Mrs. Dunleigh into more tears.

"Please know you'll never want for anything. I'll make sure you're taken care of, Sheila."

"He would be appreciative, Jack," she whispered. "And so am I."

Cassandra patted the woman's shoulder. "Would you like me to send for your daughter and family?"

"Please, would you?"

Cassandra took over tending to Mrs. Dunleigh, which allowed Jack to slip back into the parlor to take care of the arrangements there. It was easier on Cassandra to have something to do rather than stand by helplessly. She sent a message with two men to fetch the family from town. She conversed with Dr. Clarkson about talking to Mrs. Dunleigh and assessing whether she needed any medical care herself. Then she started a huge pot of beef and potato stew to feed everyone.

Mrs. Dunleigh seemed out of sorts that someone else was doing the cooking when it was her duty, so Cassandra carefully allowed the woman to help in any way that might be comforting to her.

Cassandra had witnessed many folks in tragedy during the Great Fire to know that different people responded to grief in different ways. Some retreated completely, some were not themselves, and some were more vocal and finicky than usual.

Mrs. Dunleigh called out instructions on where to find things in the kitchen, reminded Cassandra to chop the onions extra fine, estimated the number of potatoes that might need to be peeled, and even at one point got up to stir the frying meat so it wouldn't stick to the bottom of the pan.

Cassandra thanked her for her lovely advice and deferred to the older woman on any matter she saw fit to discuss or criticize, no matter how trivial.

Sheila was hurting, and Cassandra understood she needed time to absorb the awful news of the death of her husband.

Others were gathering in the kitchen. The bunkhouse cook came in to help, and started getting plates to the table. He got Mrs. Dunleigh talking about how she and Yule first came to Napa Valley, and how they'd landed the job on Jack's ranch.

Stable hands gave humorous accounts of how bad a rider Mr. Dunleigh had been and how he couldn't handle a horse, which made Mrs. Dunleigh laugh and add stories of her own. Neighboring women poured in, as well as other housekeepers from adjoining ranches, each bringing a dish of something or another they'd hurriedly prepared.

Everyone wanted to envelope Sheila Dunleigh in the love they felt for her, and the evening turned out to be a comforting wake.

By the time the meal was simmering and filling up the kitchen with steam and fine aromas, there had to be over a hundred people in the house, all making their way to Mrs. Dunleigh's side to pay their respects.

Cassandra was leaning against a pillar in the kitchen, absorbing it all, when Jack came up beside her and put an arm around her shoulders.

She sighed deeply in response, for it made her feel as though she belonged here.

Then the family arrived. Mrs. Dunleigh's grandchildren, Julia and Ronald, raced in and squeezed their way to her side, giving her a big hug and sitting in her lap.

Mrs. Dunleigh's daughter, tall and thin like her mother, was sobbing, and could barely speak to Jack and Cassandra. Her husband, a bulky man in a rumpled suit, spoke on her behalf after he'd arranged for the undertaker to remove his father-in-law's body to the funeral parlor in town.

"We'd like to thank you so much for helpin' with the funeral arrangements, Jack. The undertaker and minister say they can do the burial tomorrow morning at nine."

"We'll be there," said Jack.

"And thank you kindly, ma'am," he said to Cassandra, "for all you've done in lookin' out for our ma."

"It's been my pleasure."

"We'll be takin' her back with us tonight."

"Please let her know that if she'd like to continue working here or living here," said Jack, "she may. I don't want her to feel unwelcome."

"Much obliged. We'll see how she makes out in the next few days, and what she'd like to do.

She's got a home with us, if she'd like to stay permanently."

Jack and Cassandra said their goodbyes to Mrs. Dunleigh and the family, then to the others as they left slowly in groups.

Some of the remaining few helped Cassandra scrub the kitchen, the living room, and sweep the floors after the huge volume of neighbors had come and gone. Not once did anyone mention Cassandra's marred face, and hours had gone by without her being conscious of it.

When the last ranch hand said good-night and left, it was close to midnight. Cassandra could barely keep her eyes open, yet she knew she couldn't fall asleep yet.

Jack turned to her, looming and powerful, and she could feel the burn of his dark eyes on her face.

"Let's get some air." He took her hand and led her out to the terrace. Her insides quivered at his unexpected touch.

Cassandra was still quivering when she and Jack stood outside. He dropped his hand from hers and she wished he hadn't. The lulling breeze swirled between them, stirring the heat of the day as the moon shone down. Sounds of the night echoed through the air—the call of owls, the hum of beetles, the stirring of horses in the stables, and the still, deep silence of the vineyards in the valley below.

At last, when she couldn't handle the rapid beating of her heart any longer, she peered up at Jack.

He'd changed into a white shirt, from the darker one he'd worn earlier, and she'd changed clothes, too, when she'd washed up after dinner. She was absorbed by the handsome sight of him as he stood beneath the glittering yellow ball in the dark sky, looking up at the stars spinning around them, so like the young man he'd been in his quiet rapture of the world.

She respected what he'd done tonight for the Dunleighs. He'd shown such devotion to his housekeeper, such compassion for the fallen man.

"Was tonight very difficult for you?" Jack turned his soulful eyes upon her face.

The undercurrent was so sharp between them, her breath caught in her lungs.

"For me?" she asked, startled by his question.

"It couldn't have been easy, after all the injury and trauma you witnessed firsthand in Chicago."

She peered down at the flat stones of the terrace floor. She'd tried to distract herself from the visions that kept popping into her mind all night.

Hundred-year-old homes leaping with flames. People running out of their houses screaming and crying, their clothing on fire. Children missing. She was told later that no one had been able to locate Mary. That their father had finally realized she was still trapped in the blazing kitchen, and he'd raced in to save her. Cassandra had gone in after him, apparently, but was the only one pulled out. She'd lost her memory of that awful event, and the two days that followed.

Jack stepped closer and put his warm fingers beneath her chin. He tugged gently so that she'd look up at him. Their eyes met, but he let his fingers remain.

"Tonight was difficult," she confessed. "I kept thinking about Mary's last moments and how frightened she must've been."

A multitude of feelings flickered in his eyes. "Your father being there with her...was it comforting in some way? I mean for you to know that they perished together?"

"It was," she said softly. She'd never admitted it to anyone. She was ashamed that she felt that way, for if she could've spared either one of them, she would've given her own life.

"You were the one left all alone."

She dropped her eyes to the terrace stones again, for she didn't wish to cry in front of him.

He gave her a moment to recover. Another owl hooted, and the tears in her eyes retreated. Cassandra lifted her head to watch the swaying palms in the glow of the moon.

"It's pretty here. It makes me feel peaceful. Yet other times, being surrounded by the horses and the rush of the workers...it's all so exciting sometimes, isn't it, Jack?"

For some reason, he didn't respond, just studied her with a dozen emotions rippling across his face. He reached out and put his warm hands on her arms. Then he pulled her close till their hips touched, tilted her head and kissed her.

Jack McColton finally kissed her like he should've kissed her days ago.

Her pulse raced, her stomach fluttered and her heart made such a commotion inside her chest she was sure he must hear it.

He pulled her closer and they pressed together, she so small and soft and he so strong and firm and demanding.

She had an urge to connect with him in the most meaningful way imaginable, to feel united, and to glory in the fact that they were both very much alive in a world that was so often fragile and harsh.

Perhaps he felt the same.

His kiss got deeper and harder. His lips trailed

across her cheek, down her jaw, making her skin prick with gooseflesh as he continued in a hot path down her throat.

His arm encircled her waist, his fingers digging into the waistband of her skirt, inching lower to grasp one of her buttocks and pull her toward him, their hips melding against each other in an urgent, natural need.

She felt the swell of him pressed against the thin cloth of her skirts, felt the tightening of her nipples and the soft heat of her own arousal. She flattened her palms against his rock-hard chest and felt the beating madness that lay beneath.

"Cassandra," he whispered in her ear, and to her it felt as though he was saying a prayer. "Cassandra…"

She moaned at his touch, the clever movements of his fingers unwinding her hair.

When he pulled out the hem of her blouse, she knew his intent.

Here? Right here?

"No one can see us," he murmured against her cheek, as if reading her mind, then lifted her in his strong arms and swept her down to the soft dewy grass.

Chapter Ten

Their breathing quickened, until they were panting together in anticipation.

In the dappled moonlight, Jack reached out a brawny hand and closed it upon her upper arm. Poised above Cassandra, leaning on one elbow, he gasped at her loveliness.

"Would you kiss me again, Jack? Just like before?" Her voice was mellow, like a violin resonating with some spiritual force that had the power to move mankind. She was a woman; women had been moving men with their souls and bodies for eternity.

He groaned at the rawness in her eyes, the inescapable mix of emotion that always seemed to be so close to the surface. She seemed so attentive to details around her, so aware of the sharp pain of Mrs. Dunleigh's grief. What he saw now in Cassandra's face was hope. She was so gorgeous lying beneath the stars that he devoured every inch of her flesh with his gaze.

Aroused as he'd never been before, he clawed through her braid and let the gold strands cascade over the grass. Gripping the tendrils in one hand, he swooped down to press his lips against the divine sweetness of hers.

She was an angel, come to deliver him from earth.

Her mouth responded in kind to his—the pressure gentle at first. The tiny ripples of pleasure. The growing intensity. She purred beneath him, indicating her pleasure, and he was thrilled at her reaction. It went on and on in prolonged splendor.

Unable to control himself any longer, he slid his hand beneath her blouse, over the stiff ribs of her corset, delighting in the slender proportion of her waistline, moving up to the swell of her breasts.

"Cassandra…you drive me to distraction…." Breathing heavily, he released her so he might unfasten the multitude of buttons on her blouse. The lace at her throat parted. Her loop of pearls fell against the creamy lushness of the upper rounds of her breasts.

He swallowed hard as he saturated himself with the wondrous sight of her femininity. Such a pristine, white lace corset, gently faded from obvious years of wear. She didn't need brand-new fashions to showcase her beauty. Any man within ten feet of her could well imagine her astounding figure, naked beneath his own.

Jack let his fingers trail along the valley of her cleavage, grazing the warm soft flesh. As he reached the top of her corset, he tugged on a pull-string, undid a clasp, and it opened. Then another string, another clasp, until she was bare from her throat to her rib cage to her belly, the corset concealing only the tips of her breasts. He swallowed in breathless need, and wished for a moment that their sexual time together could last much longer than he knew it would.

All night long would not be long enough.

She drove him mad.

He glanced back up to her eyes, clear blue, sparkling jewels netted by half-closed lashes. Her expression of desire was mesmerizing, as was the pout on her kiss-swollen lips and the dewy curve of her cheek.

When he turned back to her captivating body—his canvas of art—he adored how the moonlight showered her skin with flecks of gold dust.

Whatever was happening between them to-night went beyond the physical. Perhaps it was because of what they'd both witnessed this evening; the passing of a man who'd been wed for fifty-two years to the adoring woman at his side; the sorrow that was coming for her, which everyone knew would be unbearable. Or perhaps the buildup of feelings between Jack and Cassandra had started earlier that day, on Finley's ranch, with her generously allowing him to do his professional duties despite the other woman being there, and Cassandra not voicing an ounce of complaint.

And now, as he tugged away at the last remnant of her corset, his heart hammered in his chest and his blood coursed through his arteries, pounding with a fervor he'd never known.

The fabric glided away, exposing those shimmering pink peaks. A warm breeze blew over her skin and her areolas hardened. He slid a warm, tanned hand over one.

"I like the way you touch me, Jack," she whispered. "You know just what to do...."

That sent him over the edge, and he was lost.

He ravished her, kissing her full on the mouth again, while his hand explored her other breast, his knuckles brushing along her underarm, the side of her ribs, then lower.

As their mouths melted together in the riptide of desire, he tugged at the buttons of her skirt, yanked the fabric low and trailed his fingers over her curls.

"I want to make love to you, Cassandra, beyond your expectations."

She helped him tug off the last of her skirt, petticoat and pantaloons, then assisted him in sliding out of his shirt, boots and denim jeans until he, too, was fully exposed in the tranquil moonlight.

She had bunched up her skirts along one side of her as if using them for a blanket.

"Are you chilled?"

"Not anymore."

He ran his hand up her wrist, stroking the length of her arm, then reached beneath her armpit and did the same along her rib cage, hip and thigh.

He was hard, as stiff as he'd ever been, and it was torturous to try to resist her any longer.

"Cassandra, can you move on top of me?" It was a plea.

"Like this?" She rose on her knees and straddled his waist. He could feel the moist heat of her, her thighs parted on his stomach, and he wanted inside.

Yet he restrained himself. *Go slow*, he told himself.

Her breasts swayed above him, dangling orbs with pink nipples that needed to be held. He lifted his head and took one in his mouth. She fed him the other and he eagerly took it as her long hair flowed around her shoulders.

When she pulled back, nipples hardened, sensual eyes glazed with heat and lust, he grasped her upper arms and pushed upward, indicating she should lift herself up, then slide down to engulf him.

With her bare, beautiful toes pressed alongside his hips in the velvety grass, she responded. Emitting a moan, she slid her moist center along his shaft, lubricating him in a natural rhythm as she moved forward, then back. Then in a daring swoop, she rose up again and impaled herself on his large shaft.

Such rapture...

Was he in heaven?

She moved then, up and down on his erection as if Mother Nature had made her specifically for this purpose. Hell, Mother Nature *had*.

Cassandra's supple skin was illuminated by the moon's orange glow. *What a shape*. Breezes whispered around them, swaying the palms. Night animals called and sang.

She moved with more haste, more force, more raw desire. Jack could barely restrain himself; if this kept up, he would soon find release, and disappoint her.

But then he put his fingers there for her, allowing her to slide back and forth on them, at the same instance filling herself up as deeply as she wanted.

She thrust her hips harder, closed her eyes in fierce concentration, and then it happened for her. Her body quivered, her muscles squeezed in spasm, and she called out his name into the night. It was sweetness itself. "Jack…Jack…"

Loving the look of her, the feel of her, the scent of her skin and the sound of her voice, he waited until she subsided. Then in an unexpected turn, he lifted her to her side, then onto her back, until she was laid out before him on the pliant grass. He pinned her arms above her head, relishing the cascading waterfall of blond hair that spilled around her sweat-dampened face, and lowered himself, found his spot inside her and entered.

Hot flesh enveloped him, smoldering heat that felt like a river of fire. He moved up and down inside her while he devoured the side of her silky neck, sucking her flesh and cupping her full breast.

He pressed deeper and firmer and she responded by wrapping her long bare legs around his waist, taking him fully until he couldn't hold back any longer. He released inside Cassandra, calling her name softly and silently begging for more.

Jack's grip on her arms had tightened almost to the point of pain without him realizing it, Cassandra sensed. Lying beneath his flexed muscles outlined in the moonlight, she shivered with expectation about what their parting this time might bring.

He relaxed, wearing such a wicked grin he reminded her of the boy he used to be—marching out of the house he shared with Troy and his family, to see what great team of horses could be heard plodding down the cobblestone streets of Chicago.

Jack's exuberance was just as clear now, his intentions not so much.

He buried his face in her hair in a surprisingly gentle gesture, then rolled off her body to lie beside her, staring up at the half-moon. He reached for her hand and entwined his fingers with hers. She turned ever so slightly, hoping he wouldn't notice her studying him—the muscled legs, the flat abdomen, the rock-hard chest and the erection that was slowly subsiding, yet still looked so fascinating the way it fell across his thigh.

"Well, I must say," he said playfully, "that was quite a lot more than *I* had expected."

She looked up to the sleek dark lines of his cheeks and jaw. "You didn't think it could be so good between us?"

"Oh, I knew," he murmured, turning his face to stare at hers, scorching her again with that blazing hot gaze. "But it surprised me this evening...with all that happened."

She nodded in understanding.

He turned completely toward her, his dark head nestled on his propped palm, stroking her belly with delighted little circles that tempted her in many subtle ways.

How could she still be wanting more of him, when they'd both just reached their pinnacles? What was it about him that set her skin afire and her heart thrashing wildly beneath her breastbone?

She responded to his hand with a sigh.

He raised an eyebrow in amused fascination. *Again?* he seemed to say.

She smiled in response. *Of course. You do it so well.*

He ran his curled fingers along her stomach, traced the outline of her belly button, used one finger to toy with her skin, causing a mad rippling of sensations throughout her center. The swelling crescendo tugged up her body, reaching her nipples and other sensitive, urgent spots.

She brought her legs up, knees bent, the soles of her feet flat on the earth.

Inhaling sharply, Jack watched her like a mountain lion eyeing his prey, eager for just one bite. Without looking at him, she sensed his desire to watch, and she allowed it. Too timid to look at him squarely, she closed her eyes and thrilled at his tickling fingers, which seemed to know exactly how to twist and stroke and reach....

He was inside her with his beautiful fingers, wanting to please. Kissing her shoulder, her cheek, her ear, her forehead, as she swooned and rode his firm hand. The feeling built and built. Only the moon and stars were witness to Jack's charms and her glorious undoing.

With a mounting need, she took all he offered with his touches and caresses, until the night wind absorbed the sounds of her climaxing for the second dazzling time this night. Jack kissed her breast at that exact moment, and she didn't think she could ever bear to part with his hand, so strong and massive was her pleasure.

When the tremors of her body subsided, he

gently loosened his grip and she turned to look at him, flushed with lovemaking and the new-found sensations in her body.

"Aren't you a vision?" he said softly.

She sighed in utter bliss, amazed that she could lie here naked with a man and not feel any sort of shame for being so exposed. "It seems so natural with you, Jack."

"It is natural between us. Lying together like this is vital, and key to a marriage."

"Well, I think I'm ready for bed now," she said in a lighter tone.

One corner of his mouth lifted in a lazy grin. "You do tire a man out." In one sleek movement, he sat up, then rose to his feet, still as naked and handsome as nature had intended. He gathered his clothing, then held out his hand to her.

"Pick up your skirts and I'll carry you inside."

With a soft smile, she did as he asked, clasping her clothing as he swooped her up and carried her from under the stars into the house.

It was dark and tranquil inside. They were the only ones who would share it tonight. With a sliver of moonlight streaming through the windows, he carried her through the house until he reached the private bathing room nestled below their bedroom.

The door was open. He nudged it with his big

biceps, then stepped in and settled her on the plush rug by the fireplace. It didn't take him long to fan the embers, while she lit a lantern. The golden light washed over the planes and curves of his angular, massive shoulders.

Her eyes could barely stay open, she was so exhausted. But she didn't wish to go to sleep just yet, knowing that tomorrow morning would hold more sorrow.

He must've felt the same, for he continued playing with the fire, whispering softly about how he'd like to heat the water for her bath, and then watch her taking it.

When the fire was lit, the cauldrons boiling and the cold water pumped into the tub, he prepared it, pouring hot water into the cold, checking the temperature before he allowed her to step inside, and then, kneeling beside her to help wash her long hair.

When they finished, he stepped over to the hip tub, dragged it up beside her, but turned it so they'd be staring at each other face-to-face, and filled it for himself.

"Jack," she said, feeling comfortable in the warm liquid, watching his lazy eyes roving over her.

"Yes?" He leaned back in the water, but he

had to stick out one leg, for he was so tall he couldn't fit in the tub.

She gathered up her courage to discuss the one topic that had been beating in her heart for weeks.

"Jack," she said as gently as she could, "we didn't finish our discussion in the café. Remember? About what I wish to do with my life."

Chapter Eleven

"That's true." Jack leaned back in the hip tub and the steamy water splashed around his chest. "We were interrupted by the call to Finley's ranch."

Cassandra lay in her porcelain tub, naked and stunning. Her long hair was pulled back over her shoulders, and she gazed at the fieldstone fireplace several yards away, which was spitting out sparks and heat.

"Let's see…we were talking about you building a library. What more did you wish to say? I'm all ears."

She slid down lower in the water, still not looking over at him, watching the crackling red logs and concealing her body as if she were building a wall again.

Why was she feeling so awkward all of a sudden? The lovemaking they'd just shared had been monumental to him. Their intimacy seemed to bridge that gap that had been between them since she'd arrived.

Her face suddenly filled with emotion, then her lashes dropped, masking her expression. She swirled the dark liquid with her feet, and the bathwater shimmered, outlining her creamy thighs, nipped waist and those gorgeous breasts.

"It's not a library I wish to start." She finally looked his way. Her lashes were clumped with moisture. Her deep blue eyes had a way of piercing straight to his heart.

"I don't understand. We were talking about the type of books you like to read. And you mentioned the newspaper article about the Pinkerton..." His shoulders stiffened as a different thought came to him, a much more dangerous one. "Oh, no...you're not thinking of..." His voice rumbled through the air between them. "Tell me what you're thinking, Cassandra."

She inhaled and swallowed. "Being a lady detective."

His hands dropped into the water with a splash. Shocked, he glared up at the ceiling rafters. "You can't be serious."

"Why?"

He turned toward her, his face tense and knotted. "I won't allow it."

"Why not? Please, let's discuss—"

"As your husband, I say *no*."

"You don't even know what I'm thinking—"

"I know what a detective does. He chases criminals and works with bounty hunters and spies on people. I won't have you subjecting yourself to—"

"I wasn't thinking of taking the most dangerous cases—"

"What man in his right mind wants his woman subjected to that kind of terror—"

"If you'll only listen, I noticed plenty of offices in town where I might start working. I could work with lawyers and the sheriff, and help people with legal documents, or searching for missing persons—"

"A ridiculous notion—"

"You know how involved I was with my father's work, always listening and watching and reading—"

"You take me for an idiot—"

"I do *not*—"

"Everyone will think I can't control my wife. That I can't provide for you—"

"Who cares what others say—"

"Working undercover?" he snapped, unable

to control his escalating emotions. "It's a losing proposition. Because if you turn out to be a lousy detective, you put yourself at risk with any criminals you'd be trying to infiltrate. If you turn out to be an excellent detective and cause anyone to be sent to prison, they'd come after you. With your scar, you'd be noticed a mile away. You could never go undetected. Criminals could track you down easily, right to our door!"

She stopped speaking, her expression crestfallen.

He'd gone too far. He should never have mentioned the scar.

"I said that because of my concern for you, Cassandra. I can't take it back, as much as I dearly wish to. But I am sorry."

She turned away for a moment and collected her composure. "I wasn't thinking of working undercover," she said calmly and coolly. "I wasn't thinking of traveling overnight alone, or chasing any criminals on my own. I don't wish to be a Pinkerton detective. I wish to work solo, in this town and in this vicinity. And if you think my scar hampers my ability in any manner..." She looked mortally wounded as her voice trailed off.

He fought the guilt and sorrow and every other damn thing he felt every time he looked at that blasted injury to her face. By deserting her in Chicago, he was just as responsible for what had happened to her afterward as if he'd been standing as a spectator watching the burning timbers rain down on her, and doing nothing to help.

Damn that fire and damn him for leaving.

"I'm sorry, but my answer is still no." Without his agreement, no one in town would hire her. He didn't wish to use his power over her, but he was deathly afraid for her safety.

"Now, I think it's getting terribly late," he said, believing the conversation was over, "and we have the funeral tomorrow." He rose out of the cool water with a noisy splash and wrapped a towel around his waist.

But she kept talking in her tub, frighteningly calm as she watched the fading embers across the rug. Her bathwater had to be stone cold. "When I was at the boardinghouse, I did some investigation work for some of the ladies. I located a missing brother for one, found missing grandparents for another and got papers redrafted for documents lost in the fire. There were lots of missing papers. In one case, I helped the police track down a burglar who had stolen forty dollars from another woman."

"At the boardinghouse you did this?"

She nodded.

None of it had been mentioned in the report he'd been given. "But my investigator—" He stopped and quickly tried to rethink his words. "You never mentioned it before."

The ripples in the water ceased. She was as still as a piece of marble. "What investigator?"

"Cassandra, it truly is getting late. We've got to rise early. Tomorrow's going to be another tough day." He reached for her towel and offered it to her. "Shall we?"

She rose, eyes locked with his. He inhaled deeply and watched the firelight cascade over her wet shoulders, and beads of water drip off the tips of her pink nipples. Her skin was smooth and glistening, her hair golden and smooth. Her lush lips, ruby in color, pressed together as she took the towel and wrapped it around her. She used one end and rubbed it against her wet skin, then tucked it above her breasts, once more concealing her body from him.

"What investigator, Jack?"

Should he lie? How could he?

He gave her a partial truth. "I hired a private investigator to try to find you after the fire. Well, six months after, when I returned from Alaska. Remember, I said I sent the letters and they were returned? Well, the investigator couldn't find you, either. I gave him your maiden name, and what I thought was your married name, and your father's address, but there was no sign of anyone left alive."

The golden arches of her eyebrows knitted in confusion. "I'm sorry you went through that."

"Come, let's go, shall we? I'll have the cook from the bunkhouse arrange for temporary help tomorrow, to tidy this room and help around the house."

"All right." She seemed resigned to the fact that he didn't wish her to be a detective, for which he was grateful. But there was still an unsettled tension between them that had shattered the intimacy they'd shared earlier.

She peered at the fire, which was almost out. A few red embers remained, but it would be safe to leave them, and the heat would rise to warm their bedroom above. "I can certainly do all the cooking myself, though. I'd like to do that, Jack."

"Fine."

If only all her requests were that easy. He indicated that she lead the way up the stairs, then took a deep breath and tried to regain his equilibrium. He followed her up the steps, watching the twist and turn of her bottom, the slender curves of her calves, the flex of her sultry ankles.

When they reached the landing, she turned again and asked, "What else did you hire the private investigator—this detective—for?"

Her palm gripped the knot in her towel at her chest. Her hair spilled in golden rivers over her shoulders, and her face, half concealed in darkness, was silhouetted in the moonlight that trickled in the bedroom window.

Jack wished that she wasn't so aware of every nuance in his tone and every implication to what he said. How was he supposed to answer this without upsetting her further?

Cassandra knew it was late, that both she and Jack were exhausted from the day's tragic turn of events. But she had an overwhelming need to know exactly what had gone on that he wasn't telling her.

Clearly, there was something more about Chicago that was troubling him. She could see it in the tension of his massive shoulders, the rigid musculature of his chest and the tightening of his jaw.

And if he thought she was giving up on her plans to become a detective, that he could simply forbid her to do so, he was out of his mind.

She wanted to live a life filled with challenges and interesting work, helping others with troubles and problems she knew how to solve. If losing Mary in the fire meant anything at all, it was that life was short and had to be packed with love and meaning. And Cassandra could do it without bringing excessive danger to herself, if only Jack weren't too stubborn to listen.

Outlined by the moon's rays, he looked to their square canopied bed. His biceps bulged when he raised a hand and ran it through his damp black hair.

If he wasn't going to answer, she had to guess. "Did you hire the detective for *me?* To look into my personal affairs?"

"Cassandra," he moaned, "that was a painful time for you. It was awful for me, too, not knowing where you were and what had happened to you or your family. I wanted to find you and help you. I don't think bringing any of it up now helps anyone."

"But it didn't work, your hiring him," she said, feeling very exposed all of a sudden. "He searched too late after the fire, and couldn't find me. I can understand your looking, Jack. I appreciate your looking...but then why, when I was so in need of a kind word from someone...did you stay away when he finally did track me down?"

He seemed tormented by the memory. "I thought you'd left and gone with Troy to Europe somewhere."

"So then when did the search happen? Not the initial one, but the one you seem to be so determined to keep from me? You hired him twice, didn't you?"

He shook his head, more in exasperation than in answer, she thought, for he didn't deny it. He strode to the bed, found her nightshift and tossed it to her. "Let's slip under the sheets. You need a good night's sleep."

He was avoiding the question. She grappled with what he was hiding, and tried to piece it together. "The second time you hired him happened later, when you knew where I was. I gather that was after you spotted my ad in the San Francisco paper? You had me investigated after that, Jack?" she asked in disbelief.

He sighed, tightened his lips and then, broadshouldered and bare-chested, took a few steps closer till he was towering over her again.

"I was shocked to find you in that condition," he said in explanation. "Living where you were."

She sank back on her heels. "You knew. You knew I was living at a boardinghouse for desolate women." Shame, deep and fast, cut through her. She'd done what she had to do to survive, but to think his decision in marrying her might have evolved more from a state of sorrow than any real desire on his part to be with her was overwhelming.

"I don't care about where you lived."

"But don't you see? You got the luxury of deciding what you did and didn't care about in that situation. You're playing the upper hand in *every* decision. Don't I get a say?"

He stiffened. "You had the choice whether to tell me everything before we got married. You chose not to share it with me."

"For no other reason than I was embarrassed."

"I understand, I completely understand. That's why I never mentioned it. But it's what a husband and wife *should* share. We're supposed to help each other through the pain as well as the joy."

"Sharing? You tell me I can't work as a detective, but when it comes to your own personal use, you have no qualms in hiring one! How hypocritical!"

He moaned and put his hands on her shoulders, but his touch was like dousing alcohol on a burning fire. She shrugged him off and stepped back.

"And you hired him *after* you asked for my hand in marriage. When I was living in that house, aching for anyone I knew to reach out and show some little gesture of kindness, the man I thought was going to marry me relied on a paid stranger to seek the truth. And now I've got to wonder—what was it that made you so distrustful? Did you think I might come after your money? Your ranch and your horses? Was that it?"

"No. *No.*"

"And speaking of honesty, and what a man and wife should share, where was the honesty on your side?"

"Elise again? We've been through that."

"You never told me about Derik Thornley, either. But mostly what you never told me about was what happened to you, Jack. When you were younger, you used to say whatever was on your mind. Whether we were going to parties with Troy, dining with his parents or rowing on the lake with our group of friends. You'd be the most charming, the most eager to please, the first to laugh. And now what I see is someone who relies on paid messengers. And don't tell me your best man at the wedding thinks you made a wise decision in marrying me, either, Jack."

He stiffened at her appraisal.

"I'm not so thickheaded that I couldn't see how Hugh Logan was watching and judging me when he first met me. Why does he remain at a distance, Jack? He's supposed to be one of your closest friends, yet he avoids us. Everyone in town seems to know my story, and has picked their side. Should the dashing veterinarian choose the lovely local woman who shares the same love of animals? Why does he feel the need to marry a woman he sent for by mail? And what about that awful scar? Blazes, did you tell them all where I was living and how I was coping? You know what *I* think they say whenever we can't hear them? 'If she meant so much to him, he would've stayed in Chicago and fought for her!'"

They glared at each other, ever so silent and ever so threatened by each other.

All this time tonight, while they'd made love, not once had her burn injury come between them. Not once had she felt neglected or pitied. But his vocalizing that it would hamper her work as a detective made her feel inadequate. She would never again have a perfect face. Was she supposed to run from it? Hide from it? Was she supposed to beg him for the opportunity to work in a profession in which she had talent and skills?

Then when would her begging ever end?

With that outburst, she grabbed her flannel gown from his fingers, slammed the door on her way out and headed to the guest room.

Chapter Twelve

For Cassandra to storm out of the bedroom was unthinkable to Jack. How could a night filled with such pleasure and intimacy turn into such a battle?

He ate breakfast before she rose, then left to check on Finley's sick cattle, and was relieved to see they were on the mend. He returned within two hours, entering his stables to give instructions on which of his men would stay to overlook the ranch, while the rest of them went to Dunleigh's funeral. Two of the younger men who didn't know the Englishman well volunteered.

When Jack returned to the house, Cassandra had eaten, cleared the dishes and was ready to leave. She wore a black jacket and long black skirt, both threadbare along the buttons and trim, as though she'd worn them many times before. She probably had at all the funerals she'd attended in Chicago.

The two of them remained cool and cordial to each other.

"Is there anything I can get you before we leave?" he asked.

"I'm fine. I feel for poor Mrs. Dunleigh this morning, and what she must be going through."

"She's not alone today." Jack's stance softened. "Yet she will likely feel more alone than she's ever been."

He went upstairs and changed into a black suit. When his dark cowboy boots thudded on the treads of the stairs, Cassandra slipped out of the parlor and joined him at the front door.

They stepped outside into a blanket of sunshine. Jack followed her shapely form toward the swaying oaks, and the buggies that'd been spiffed up and polished for the procession. Jack had a hard time forgetting the sensual night they'd spent together. It had started out slow and steamy and irresistible. She'd given him provocative looks that could melt an iceman from ten paces. The hours of pleasure had been followed by hours of stone-cold silence.

Why couldn't she see that he was only looking out for her best interests? No man he knew would be pleased if his wife worked alongside lawmen and lawyers.

And for her to accuse him of hiring an investigator in order to guard his ranch and income from her was an insult.

He tried not to think about it as she climbed onto the front seat of the buggy—before he had an opportunity to help her. The foreman, Crawford, and the cook from the bunkhouse, Malcolm Pheebs, rode in the back. A stream of buggies—six of them—and eight more riders on horseback followed behind them, everyone dressed in their Sunday finest.

Mrs. Dunleigh was surrounded by her family when they got to the riverside ceremony. Her grandchildren, Julia and Ronald, were much quieter than usual, standing back from the newly dug gravesite and Finley's pine casket, and squinting up at Reverend Darcy when he said a few words to the family beforehand.

"Good morning, Mrs. Dunleigh." Cassandra embraced her.

The ceremony took place as the river rolled by, wide and blue and as deep as the sorrow felt by the more than one hundred people gathered. Yule had made a lot of friends in the twenty years since coming to Napa Valley, including Sheriff Leggett.

The tall lawman with the overly prominent jaw tipped his hat to Jack. His badge glinted in the morning sun. He used to be a railroad police officer, a difficult job, considering the outlaws that preyed upon the railways. Sundial was lucky to have him as a sheriff. He was tough, seasoned and fair.

With some hesitation, Jack introduced the lawman to his wife. There was no telling what she might say about possible detective work.

"How d'you do, ma'am?"

"Fine to meet you, sir," she said, and with a pointed glance at Jack, left it at that.

He and Cassandra stood beside Mrs. Dunleigh on one side, her family on the other. Jack tried not to notice that Elise had arrived—without Thornley—and was quietly keeping to herself near the rear. Jack couldn't be aggravated with her today; it would be disrespectful to the family of the deceased. So, when he was asked by the minister to say a few words on Dunleigh's behalf, Jack stepped forward in his black Stetson and black suit, and didn't meet Elise's gaze when she focused on him.

"Yule was a good man," he told the listening crowd, hat in hand. "Honest to the core. No one ever criticized him as a friend. I reckon that's about the highest compliment you can pay a man."

Dunleigh was buried beneath a big oak tree.

Jack was concerned that the funeral might bring back too many painful memories for Cassandra, but was relieved when she seemed to be handling it with no outward emotion. Yet there was a chasm between them, and he felt it now as she seemed to retreat inside herself.

All he could think of when he looked down at her blond hair pinned up beneath her black bonnet, and the dull, starched jacket, was that she was too young to be wearing black.

The ceremony drew to a close. Jack and Cassandra said their goodbyes to Mrs. Dunleigh and her family and headed toward their buggy. He placed his palm protectively against her shoulder blade and she turned her head, almost twitching at the contact. They were so aware of each other physically, and he didn't wish to make the wrong move. He dropped his hand.

Jack spotted Elise weaving her way toward them. His gut instantly tensed. Surely she wasn't going to approach. Not here. Not now.

"Jack," she called, to his disappointment.

Cassandra stiffened beside him. Her swirling black skirts came to an abrupt halt. He noticed her eyeing the buggy, as though she wasn't sure whether to stay or retreat.

Too late. Elise was beside them. She glanced at Cassandra with a tense nod, seemingly polite, then back at him. The woman was dressed in a high-fashioned black outfit as crisp and new as if it had only just arrived from one of those fancy New York dress catalogs.

It bothered him that she felt the need to get all dolled up for a funeral.

She bothered him.

"Elise," he said, edging past her with Cassandra. "Pardon us, we do have a full day ahead."

Elise raised her voice from behind him. "I simply wondered if you'd heard the bad news about Woodrow's horses."

"Woodrow?" The man was Jack's neighbor. Elise's neighbor, too. Woodrow owned a horse ranch adjacent to Jack's and Finley's properties, along the back. "What's wrong with his horses?"

"There's about five or six of them. Came down with the same sort of illness as Finley's cattle."

"When? And why didn't I hear about it?" Jack was usually one of the first to be notified.

"Well, I just heard myself, by accident, as I was leaving for the funeral. They're right behind our vineyard, and I gather one of his hands told one of our hands, and that's how I heard. They would've known you were heading here, so I imagine you'll be notified shortly."

Jack scowled. Not so much because Elise was bringing the news, but because more animals were coming down ill. What did they all have in common? It was too soon to jump to any conclusions about the illness and cause, since he hadn't seen the horses yet. "Much obliged," he said to her. "I'll head out that way."

Elise stepped back in a meek manner, and nodded politely to both him and Cassandra. But judging from her subtle smile, the slight release of tension in her pinched cheeks and the color rushing to her lips, he had an uneasy feeling he might be seeing Elise at Woodrow's ranch, too.

Jack was right. The woman was there.

He took barely an hour to return to his ranch and drop off Cassandra. There was a ranch hand from Woodrow's waiting for him, to explain that his services were requested.

"I'll be right there," Jack told the rider.

The messenger galloped away on his horse.

"Will you be long?" Cassandra asked twenty minutes later, when she'd changed into an apricot-colored dress that matched her hair, and Jack had changed into his denim pants and work shirt. She slipped an apron over her neck. "I'm preparing lunch."

"It's better if I have a look at those horses as quick as I can. The sooner they're diagnosed, the sooner I can start treatment if needed. I can't say for sure how long I'll be. An hour or two at most. You go on ahead without me."

"As you wish."

He hurried to Woodrow's ranch, and Elise was already there in her working blouse and skirt, standing on the hill at the water trough, examining a chestnut mare. Her medical bag was beside her.

Jack muttered beneath his breath, wondering why she had to be here.

Woodrow, a retired politician sporting a large belly and long mustache, was talking to her. "I'd like to thank you for coming so quick, Miss Beacon."

Oh, so she wasn't barging in; she'd been summoned, too.

Elise rubbed the horse's nose. The animal seemed a bit jittery. "Not at all, Mr. Woodrow. We're concerned this may reach our animals, too."

"Woodrow!" Jack called hello and received a friendly handshake in return.

"Jack. I'm not sure what to do."

"What's wrong, exactly?"

"Six of my horses came down with some sort of stomach ailment."

"Scours?"

"Two or three times in the past few hours," Elise explained. "Along with vomiting."

"Any blood from either end?" asked Jack.

"No." Woodrow planted his hands on his hips.

"Well, that's good." Jack moved into the shade alongside the mare and took a look at her. "Easy now, girl. This won't hurt." He pulled out his stethoscope and listened to her heartbeat. "It's fast," he told Woodrow.

"And this one's got a temperature," said Elise. "Two degrees higher than it should be."

"That's not too bad," said Jack. "Considering the heat of the day." He held the mare by her bridle and looked at her face. "Dull eyes." Jack turned to Woodrow. "Any idea why she's behaving like she is?" He preferred to ask that question directly from the owner, who often had clues about his animals that could help Jack build an illness history.

"Something they ate in the pasture last night, I believe. Miss Beacon and I were talkin' about where the horses grazed, and I was just pointin' out the southwestern slopes."

"Next to Finley's," said Jack, scanning the grassy area. "Maybe it's a patch of the same toxic weeds running through both your properties."

"That's what I was thinking," said Elise. "I was just about to have a look."

"No need to trouble yourself," Jack told her.

Alarmed, she looked up from the animal.

"I'm here," he said in a friendly tone. "I can look after it. Woodrow, would you mind showing me where? I'd also like to have a look at the other horses that have come down with it."

"Surely, Jack. Follow me." Woodrow led the way, then glanced back at Elise. "You're welcome to join us, Miss Beacon. I'm just hopin' it's not too much bother."

She smiled and followed the men. "No bother, sir. I'm glad to help."

"You always were smart as a whip. Could ride better'n any female I've ever seen."

They continued talking. Jack shook his head, determined not to be too judgmental of Elise when Woodrow seemed so grateful for her opinion. She did know an awful lot about animals, thought Jack. But she didn't know an awful lot about him, otherwise she would've picked up on the fact that he wished she'd go home.

* * *

They didn't find any poisonous weeds, which was puzzling to Jack. Unless the horses ate it all, in which case there'd be little evidence to find on the hill.

Elise didn't make a nuisance of herself. On the contrary, thought Jack, she was a help, keeping the ranch hands talking and out of his way when he examined the horses in the stable. She seemed to know when he needed equipment from his medical bag, and when he needed a hand calming one of the sicker animals when he wanted to use his stethoscope.

All in all, it took him under two hours to finish.

"Give them some of this tonic tonight. Two capfuls mixed into half a pail of water. Don't exercise them too much, but give them some air tonight. If they get any worse, send for me immediately. Otherwise I'll be back in the morning."

"Sure am glad you're my neighbor," said Woodrow. "Mighty kind of you. And you, too, Miss Beacon."

She smiled brightly and followed Jack outside into the sunshine.

His horse, River, was tethered to the hitching

rings at the far end of the corral. Elise followed him in that direction to her red buggy.

"If you need help with any of this, Jack, you can count on me."

"Good to know." He didn't plan on needing her for anything.

"I mean it. It's not like we have to keep avoiding each other."

"You're liked by an awful lot of ranchers in the area, Elise."

She beamed at that remark. It was true.

When he looked at her standing there, so proud that she'd been able to help, he wondered if maybe he was being too harsh on her. She seemed to honestly want to put the past behind them, and maybe he shouldn't hold a grudge.

In a gesture of goodwill, he stuck out his hand. "If need be, I'll call on you."

She slipped her fingers into his and radiated that same provocative warmth he remembered falling for just before Christmas. Not that he was in any way tempted now.

He slung his medical bag to the saddle, climbed up onto his horse, nodded goodbye and tore off for home. Cassandra was likely waiting for him.

He barreled over the hills, dust rising behind him, the wind billowing his shirt and the sun blazing onto his shoulders. He loved a good run. He unwound from the day's events. Dunleigh's death had taken a bigger toll than he'd realized. The man had been a close friend, and Jack hadn't truly comprehended that fact until it was too late and the friend was gone.

He came around a cluster of trees, feeling much freer than he had on Woodrow's ranch with Elise so damn close, then spotted a man on a horse on a far hill. But he was there all right, and he was watching Jack.

Jack slowed his mare to a trot. "Easy, River. Almost home."

He kept one eye on the man as an uneasy tension rolled through his body. Who was he?

As Jack got closer, he realized the man wanted him to recognize him, or else he would've galloped away.

He wore a tan Stetson and denim pants. But what gave him away was his horse. A dapple-gray mare.

Thornley.

What did he want? To intimidate Jack?

Jack shifted uneasily in his saddle and picked up speed again. Thornley turned his horse and rode down the other side of the hill, disappearing from view.

Was he warning Jack to stay away from Elise?

But it wasn't his fault, and it wasn't hers, either, that horses and cattle had taken sick. There was always some animal or another that needed Jack's attention.

A feeling, a premonition of warning, rippled through him. He pressed his thighs to his mare, which responded by leaping into a gallop. The wind whipped around them, but this time instead of enjoying the thrill, Jack found himself fighting the feeling that something was terribly wrong.

Cassandra. Was she in trouble? Had she come to harm?

He rushed over the slopes and splashed through a creek, flying like wildfire. His gut hammered the entire time.

Hurry, hurry, hurry.

All these illnesses of the past few days tied in together somehow. And he couldn't shake the ominous feeling of danger.

He had to protect Cassandra.

He galloped full-force up the laneway of his ranch, hooves thundering beneath him, his blood roaring. Two of his men spotted him and came running.

"What's wrong?" they hollered.

Jack leaped off the horse, hit the ground hard and ran like hell toward the house. "Go get the sheriff! Bring the doctor, too! *Now!*"

Chapter Thirteen

❦

"Cassandra!" Jack's shouting filled the house and startled her. "Where are you? Cassandra!"

She paused with the silver hairbrush in her hand when she heard him call, then finished pulling it through the swaying length of her hair. Standing in the hallway off the kitchen, Cassandra glanced into the wall mirror, gave her blue-buttoned collar a pat, then followed the sound of his clomping boots on the tiled floor.

They met in the kitchen.

"What is it?"

He whirled around from the windows overlooking the terrace, a wide-shouldered force to be reckoned with. "Oh," he gasped. "You're here."

"I was just about to leave. I gave up waiting on you for lunch, so I—"

"Has anyone called on you?" A swirl of black hair fell across his forehead, framing his brown eyes. Light streaming in from the window struck his white shirt, the bunched up sleeves, and the pine table he hovered over. Another slash of sunlight cut across his jaw, which flickered with intensity as he gazed at her.

She shook her head. "No one here but me. I ate alone and was just fixing my hair."

The strain in his face subsided, as though he was relieved by her answer. "I like it when you wear it down," he murmured.

"Well, I do declare. There must be some other reason you're hollering so much, other than stopping by to comment on my hair." She flushed at the manner in which he was scrutinizing her. A flash of images—appealing visions of what he'd looked like naked beneath rumpled bedsheets last night—scorched her thoughts. Followed by the recollection of how stubborn he'd been to refuse her request to work. Her palms grew moist. She knotted one hand in her skirts.

"Is everything all right at Mr. Woodrow's ranch? Did something go wrong?"

"No more so than I was informed of earlier. Six horses are down."

"Do you know why?"

"Likely something they ate."

"Seems to be something in the air."

"That's the thing. I think there *is* something in the air. Or more like some*one*."

"You're talking in riddles. What is it?"

He rubbed the back of his neck and peered around the kitchen. The pine table was still set with a plate and cutlery for his lunch. The pots were filled with potatoes and chicken. All that was missing was him.

"I've called for the sheriff and doctor."

Alarmed, she asked, "Is someone hurt?"

He shook his head. "There are some theories I'd like to discuss with them. And you."

"What kind of theories?"

He tilted his dark head, his face accentuated in shadows and light, and glanced at her blue suit, suddenly distracted. "You said you were just about to leave. Where to?"

Nervous, she grappled for an answer that wouldn't provoke more angry words. "I thought I'd go into town."

"If you don't mind me asking, for what reason?"

"I thought I might..." Blazes, there was no other way to say it except outright. "To see the sheriff."

"Sheriff? What on earth for?"

"Just some general questions, Jack, nothing for us to…to argue about."

He must've noticed the apprehension in her stance, for he took a deep breath. "Then I guess when he arrives, we'll both have something to talk to him about."

She prodded him to finish his earlier statement. "You said you had some theories?"

"Yeah. With all these sick animals, I'm beginning to wonder if someone isn't doing it on purpose."

"Making them sick deliberately?" she exclaimed in surprise.

He nodded, gauging her reaction.

"Feeding them something to make them sick?" she reiterated, making sure she understood his meaning.

"Afraid so."

"Why would they be doing that?"

"To get back at me in some way."

Her eyes roved the kitchen as her mind worked to absorb that. "You know people who'd do that?"

He shrugged. "Desperate people do desperate things."

"And in this case, the desperate people would be…?"

"I think you need to have a seat." He pulled

out a chair at the table and stood there, tall as timber, waiting for her.

She gathered her skirts and sat on the hard-backed chair, too anxious to argue. Riveted, she watched the expressions dance across his features—trepidation, concern and disbelief.

"Is this only a theory at this point, Jack, or do you have proof?"

He sat down beside her at the head of the table and shoved the cuffs of his sleeves over his sinewy forearms. "Theory."

"Then you can't be sure."

"I can't. That's why I've sent for the sheriff and doctor. I want to discuss the details and possibilities with them."

"You must be very serious in your allegations to have called for them."

"Look, Cassandra…I think it's Derik Thornley."

She settled back in her chair, not quite as stunned as perhaps he was expecting. Something odd was going on, something she was trying to piece together herself.

"I want my wife protected."

Less than an hour later, Cassandra flinched at Jack's blunt words. What sort of trouble did he think she was in? Sheriff Leggett and Dr.

Clarkson had arrived and were seated in the parlor in the upholstered chairs by the unlit fireplace. Cassandra and Jack were seated on the sofa opposite. At her insistence, he'd had some lunch while they'd waited for the men to get here. Now she fidgeted with her hands in her lap and listened to Jack explain.

Sheriff Leggett leaned forward, a thick-boned man with massive jowls and nose. "Has Derik Thornley come near you, ma'am?"

"No, sir. He attacked my husband."

The lawman swiveled toward Jack. "Just the one time you told us about, Jack?"

"Yes, on the ranch. But he followed me home about an hour ago from Woodrow's place. And something about the way Thornley was perched on that rise, sitting high in his saddle, calm as all get-out…it's the same way he was before he punched me. The same calm way a man looks at you before he pulls a trigger."

The sheriff uttered an exclamation. "I've seen that look aplenty. I know it well, Jack, but it's not enough to accuse a man of what you're saying he did to the horses and cattle."

"Dammit, he's up to something," Jack growled.

Dr. Clarkson seemed to be churning it over in

his mind. He rubbed his lower lip, his long white hair spilling over his checkered woolen suit.

Cassandra heaved her shoulders beneath the constraints of her prim blouse. Jack leaned against the sofa back, making the cushion dip beneath her, unnerving her further.

"Why would he do it, Jack?" she uttered softly. "What would he hope to gain?"

The sheriff and the doctor both grew thoughtful at the question, then riveted their somber gazes on her husband.

"That is the key question, isn't it?" Jack ran a sturdy hand along the shadow of his jawline. She could see the concern in his eyes, and the way his mouth twitched. "He's trying to get back at me for Elise." He nodded in acknowledgment to Cassandra. "Sorry, these things need to be said."

"I understand." The logical part of her *did* understand that procedures and practices of the law needed to be followed, but the emotional side of her didn't want any part of this discussion. It was hurtful and embarrassing to keep referring to the other woman.

However, if Cassandra thought about it from the point of view of a detective, it was easier to manage. She tried to separate her personal feelings from the cool, calm facts. She *would* plow through this puzzle of events.

Dr. Clarkson, who'd been sitting quietly and simply listening, finally asked a question. "How is he getting back at you, Jack? How is sickening someone else's animals getting back at you?"

"I've been asking myself that question for the last hour. And I don't have a clear answer, other than he knows it's my livelihood. He knows the animals mean something to me. If that makes any sense."

"So it's more out of spite?" asked the sheriff.

Jack shifted on the sofa, clearly uncomfortable. "Seems petty, doesn't it?" He stood up and walked to the unlit fireplace. With a hand on the mantel, he turned around to face the three of them. "Seems ridiculous and petty. And I come to you with this outlandish theory totally without proof."

Cassandra wasn't sure she could believe it herself.

The sheriff toyed with the brim of his hat. "Well, it's just…you all know that I've got to have some evidence to go on."

Jack slid his hand into his pocket. "Of course."

"What sort of toxins do you think he might've used on the animals?" Dr. Clarkson asked.

"Hard to say. Any number of plants could've done it. Nightshade, boxwood, thistles…larkspur, foxglove, clovers. The list is endless. As a general rule, those plants don't taste very good, so animals usually don't eat enough to cause any trouble. Unless maybe they're mixed with some sort of feed to mask the flavor. But the frustrating thing about this situation is that the gastric symptoms the animals are displaying— the muscle weakness and jitteriness—could be attributed to any number of causes. Including a natural illness."

"Does the man have easy access to the animals?" Cassandra asked.

Jack nodded. "Thornley works for Elise's father in the vineyard."

"So I've been told," she responded. "Mr. Finley and I had a pleasant chat about Sundial and his neighbors when you stopped in to have a look at his cattle. He told me that Miss Beacon's been handling her father's ranch for the last six months, since he's been in South America."

Jack's eyebrows shot up, as though he was surprised at how much she knew. "Correct," he said. "So it would be easy enough for Thornley to ride out to the adjoining ranches and get to the other animals when they're in the pastures. Woodrow's on one side of them, Finley on another."

"And your ranch is just as close," she reminded him.

"Our ranch," he corrected, leaving her flustered by the generous gesture. "And he hasn't attacked any of our animals."

"Yet," said the doctor, who seemed to be believing Jack's theories.

"Not to say he will," said the sheriff, who seemed to be disbelieving.

"He hasn't attacked any of Elise's animals, either," said Jack. "Which is why I tend to think he's culpable. He won't attack her animals because he cares for her—and he'd like to keep his position as Beacon's right-hand man. And he doesn't want to be so blatant to attack my animals, for that might point a finger of accusation at him."

"Then I guess we'll have to wait and see if he does," said the sheriff. "Attack yours, I mean."

Jack looked at the lawman in frustration.

Dr. Clarkson drummed the arm of his chair with impatient fingers. His shiny brocade vest tightened around his belly. "Jack, why'd you send for me? I thought when I got here it was because someone was ill. That turns out not to be the case, thank goodness," he said pointedly to Cassandra. "Then I thought it might be to discuss the types of toxins the man might've used on the animals. But you said it could be anything, and there doesn't seem to be more I could add to that discussion, either. So why exactly am I here?"

"Sorry to have bothered you, Doc. I was worried that someone might have come to harm." He glanced at Cassandra.

Her? Jack had been concerned about her safety?

She frowned, thinking on the seriousness of the situation, and decided to divulge her own concerns. "Jack, don't you think it's odd what happened earlier today, at the funeral?"

"What's that?"

"Miss Beacon attended."

He shook his head, his dark profile a striking contrast to the light-colored plaster walls. "She knew Yule."

"But then why didn't she attend the wake yesterday? Everyone came, from miles away. But not her, and not Thornley. It would've been perfectly natural for her to make a visit. She likely didn't feel welcome in my home, but then why show up at the funeral if she doesn't like the sight of me? I've been thinking about that oddity for the past three hours."

He scratched his temple. "I never thought of it. That is a bit odd."

"I'd call it suspicious," she declared.

The three men snapped to attention. Jack narrowed his eyes. The sheriff puckered his lips and the doctor shuffled his feet.

"Suspicious of what?" Jack asked, standing tall at the mantel.

"Perhaps she's involved with whatever Thornley's involved with," Cassandra said. "Could she have come to the funeral just to tell you about the ill horses?"

"I suppose...."

"And Jack, the day that you and Thornley got into the brawl," she continued, her mind racing with ideas. "Did you notice his horse?"

"What about it?"

"He had a rifle strapped to it."

The sheriff spoke up. "I don't see the significance."

All three men gazed at Cassandra, waiting for an explanation.

She cleared her throat. "If the man arrived to seriously harm Jack, he'd be carrying revolvers. Not a rifle on his horse."

"Hmm." Jack spoke again. "Interesting point."

"Your wife's got a keen eye," said the sheriff, rubbing his wide jaw.

"My father was a criminal attorney," she told him, "in Chicago. I spent a lot of time at the dinner table discussing trials."

"Ah," said the white-haired doctor, his bow tie

moving up and down as he nodded. "That would explain your noticing such details."

Shifting his weight while he stood at the fireplace, Jack shot her an inquisitive look, then glanced at the sheriff. She wondered if Jack was curious about what she had wanted to speak to the lawman about when she'd been planning her trip into town. Perhaps this was the place and time for that discussion.

"Sheriff, there was something else Mr. Finley told me about that I find fascinating. He told me you used to work for the railroad police, traveling on the passenger cars."

"That's right, ma'am."

"Did you ever happen to meet that undercover detective that used to work for them, too? Miss Abigail Pendon?"

He chuckled. "Oh, yeah, I know Abigail. Damn fine detective, that one. Pinkerton sends her out on special tasks, when they're trying to recover stolen property. No man on a passenger car ever suspects a woman in a bonnet to pull out a derringer and arrest him."

Cassandra swallowed hard and tried not to show how pleased she was at his approving summation. "I imagine it was very difficult for some of the other men to work with her. I mean, her being a woman and all."

He nodded emphatically. "Some refused. I was one of them, first time I worked with her. But she proved herself awful quick. Saved my life one time, when someone pulled a knife behind my back. She didn't hesitate to use hers."

Cassandra's mouth twitched. Well, she wasn't so pleased at the mention of the violence. She looked to Jack to see his reaction. His jaw was tense and he was glaring at her. She'd made her point.

The doctor sighed and shifted in his seat. "I've got some patients to attend to, so if you all don't mind—"

"Please," she interjected, stopping him from leaving. "I'd like your opinion on something else."

The doc leaned back and the three men waited.

She cleared her throat again, trying to get her thoughts clear. A reprehensible idea was storming through her mind, but as vile as it was, she had to lay it out as a prospect. "Since we're throwing out possibilities on crimes and suspicious behavior...why stop at the suspected poisoning of animals?"

They didn't seem to understand.

"This may seem far-fetched," she said, "but Dr. Clarkson, could you tell us, please, when you examined Yule Dunleigh the night he died…is there a chance he may have been poisoned?"

Jack sputtered, one hand on the mantel.

The doctor looked aghast.

The sheriff muttered, "Hellfire."

"Are you serious in this line of questioning?" Dr. Clarkson asked.

"Dead serious," Jack replied for her, his dark eyes acknowledging hers in sudden agreement.

"But who would want Yule dead?" asked the sheriff.

"Assuming there's logic to the killer," Jack said, gaining traction with her idea, "and not just heated rage, maybe it was someone who was trying to get back at me. Someone who wants to destroy the things that mean something to me, as I mentioned. Remember? Animals and perhaps people who are close to me."

"Your wife?" said the sheriff.

"Possibly."

"Well, now." The white-haired doctor scratched his bushy eyebrow. "Let's see if I can give you a rundown on what I observed in his final minutes. Yule's heart was racing awful fast. However, he did suffer from angina, so that would be a fitting symptom. His palms were cold and clammy. Again, symptomatic. Pale skin, then a sudden attack to the heart. It's totally inconclusive. These same symptoms could be attributed to poison, or simply that the man's heart gave out in natural circumstances."

"Same as the animals," said Jack. "It's all so cloudy, isn't it? That's why Thornley figures he can get away with it."

"Or Miss Beacon," Cassandra interjected. Her heart was racing. Could her life truly be in danger? Good Lord.

"Elise Beacon adores animals," said the sheriff. "I can't see her poisoning any."

"Truthfully, neither can I," said Jack. "I don't think she's involved."

Cassandra sighed and clamped her lips together. She didn't wish to be resentful of the fact that Jack was supportive of Miss Beacon, but for heaven's sake, the woman was acting suspicious.

The doctor nodded in agreement with the other two men. "I've seen her handle horses and kittens, Mrs. McColton. The woman's got a heart."

Cassandra wasn't convinced.

"Yule's medical condition," Jack added solemnly, "would've made him an easy target. No one would suspect poison if the man already suffered from a heart ailment. Hell, we didn't. Cassandra noted it."

"It's all very far-fetched," said the sheriff,

still disbelieving. He stretched his long legs. His cowboy boots thumped on the carpet. "Could be this. Could be that. Maybe he was poisoned. Maybe he wasn't. What the hell am I supposed to go on? Jack, I trust your judgment, but maybe you're just as riled up as Thornley is about his woman."

Jack tensed. "Now just a minute—"

"Dammit, you know what I mean. Two men fightin' over a woman. Get into a brawl and the next thing you know, one's accusin' the other of poisonin' his animals and his butler!"

The comment knocked the wind out of Cassandra. And Jack's neck turned red.

"Now, fellas," said the doctor, trying to make peace between them. He turned to Sheriff Leggett. "If the man here thinks his wife might be under attack, he's got a fair opportunity to speak up and say so." Then he turned to Jack. "I've known you long enough to know you don't jump to conclusions about matters like this. But you're an educated, logical man. You know Leggett needs proof."

"You could check Mr. Dunleigh's room." Cassandra repositioned herself on the cushion, her blue skirts shifting about her ankles and boots. "He and Mrs. Dunleigh shared one on the bottom floor," she explained to the two gentlemen. "She hasn't touched his things, as far as I know. She packed a suitcase to take with her to her daughter's home, but otherwise it's all intact."

"Good idea," growled Jack.

He led them out of the parlor, across the front hall and down the other wing of the house into the bedroom. The large double bed was immaculately made with crisp linens and pillows. The floor was spotless, the curtains dusted, the lamps polished.

"Where might he have kept his medicine?" asked the doctor.

Cassandra peered at the long chest of drawers. "In one of the drawers, perhaps?"

Jack checked one of the night tables and found women's accessories—hairbrush and writing papers. "I don't feel right rifling through their things."

"It's a lawful matter," said the sheriff. "May I look on the other side?"

Jack nodded.

The sheriff found two vials of medicines labeled with Mr. Dunleigh's name. He passed them to Jack, who removed the caps, looked inside, sniffed, and handed them to the doctor.

"You'll take them and check for accuracy of the medicine?" Jack asked.

Clarkson nodded in turn.

There was nothing more to see. As they walked out, Cassandra's gaze fell on the newspaper rolled up on the chest, the *Sundial Daily News*. It was flecked with splattered drops, as if someone had read it while sipping coffee, or in this case, knowing the Dunleighs, tea.

Jack picked it up. "Saturday's date. I never did read it. Dunleigh always read the newspapers when I was done with them." He set it back down. "I could always count on him for a good conversation afterward."

"But he wouldn't have read it, Jack," Cassandra reminded him. "This was the one he collected at the door, then immediately collapsed. That's what Mrs. Dunleigh told us."

"I guess she read it, then. It looks thumbed through. She likes to read any news she can find about England."

Sheriff Leggett returned to the parlor for his hat and the doctor for his medical bag, then rejoined Cassandra and Jack at the front door.

"I could arrest Thornley for assaulting you, Jack."

"What good would that do?" he asked.

"He'd spend the night in jail. There'd be a record of it."

"I still don't see what good it would do.

There's already a record of his assault because of the eyewitnesses, and me telling you about it now." He looked to Cassandra. "What I would appreciate you doing, Sheriff, is checking into Thornley's past. I don't know much about him. I know he came into the valley shortly after I did. From Wyoming Territory, I believe."

"I will."

"I'll speak to my lawyer about it, too," Jack told him. "I'll talk to Hugh tomorrow."

The men shook hands and tipped their hats to Cassandra.

When Jack shut the door behind them, he turned and studied her. She felt vulnerable again, beneath his scrutiny. His voice was gruff, his dark gaze intense. "I'd like to provide you with an armed guard as a precaution."

"A bodyguard? I...I suppose that's a good idea." She ran a hand along her neck. "And I'll carry my pistol from now on."

Jack shifted uneasily, but didn't object.

"Look, I'm not sure about any of this," he reminded her. "It seems unlikely someone would sicken the animals, but with Dunleigh passing... protection can't hurt. A lot of my ranch hands can shoot real well. I'll ask one of them. No one will think anything of it, if he's accompanying us."

"Us?"

"I don't wish to alarm you, Cassandra," he said, but of course he was. "However, I'm not leaving your side for the next little while."

Chapter Fourteen

It was silly to be staying in the guest room, thought Cassandra as she tossed and turned. The bed was comfortable enough and the room very quaint, but she was married, for heaven's sake, and she should be more giving to her husband.

But shouldn't he also be more understanding toward her, and what she wished to achieve with her life? He was a practicing veterinarian and rancher. Was she supposed to pretend she had no interest in law and police procedures?

Was she supposed to pretend it for the rest of her life?

Jack had shown such care toward her this afternoon with the sheriff and doctor—yet he had spent the rest of the afternoon working on the ranch while leaving her indoors, alone. They had spent a couple quiet hours in the evening reading in the parlor, but there hadn't been very much interaction. All her personal things from last night were still in the guest room, so she had headed that way when they said good-night, half expecting him to invite her back into their matrimonial bedroom, but he hadn't said a word. So she'd bathed, put on her nightgown and retreated to the guest bed.

She turned over and peered at the clock on the night table. Eleven minutes past midnight.

Go to him. Tell him you're sorry you argued about being a detective. Tell him you'd like to work things out. And please, might he only listen to what she had in mind?

She should try. Being separated from Jack and stingy with her kindness wasn't helpful to their marriage.

Feeling a sense of relief, Cassandra flung back the covers, rose in the darkness and padded across the warm plank floors to their bedroom.

The door was ajar, as if he might be expecting her. On the other hand, ever since she had arrived in Sundial, they'd slept with it open, so maybe he wasn't expecting her at all.

Taking a deep breath, she flattened a hand on her waistline and stepped into the shadowy room.

Moonlight spilled across the bed.

He was facing away from her, toward the window. His bare shoulder twitched slightly. Even alone, it appeared he slept with no clothes.

He'd tossed the blanket to one side and was lying beneath a single cotton sheet. His legs were outlined by it and she imagined what he might look like if she were to go to his other side and see the front of his body draped by the warm light of the moon. She recalled how the rays had rippled along the muscled planes of his chest and abdomen the other night....

My, it was getting steamy in here. She fanned a hand in front of her face. But they were married now, and she was allowed to fantasize in any manner she chose.

"Jack," she whispered, reaching the foot of the bed as he snored softly. "I'm sorry for everything. I know you're under a lot of strain, and it's not that I think you're badly intentioned. I only thought your intentions were misplaced, by hiring the investigator to investigate me. And then forbidding me to work as one, as though you've got veto power over me." She shifted her bare legs beneath her long flannel gown. Very quickly, she could be out of it and lying naked beside him. "I do wish we could discuss this rationally."

She slid into her side of the bed, her toes gliding over the smooth cotton sheet.

"Jack?"

His snoring grew louder, rattling through the room.

Disappointed that he hadn't heard a word she'd said, she sank onto her pillow. She was hoping for a heated rendezvous, that he might make her body and spirit feel as splendid as he had last night, but she wished to receive an invitation first.

She had half a mind to give him a good elbow in the ribs…but instead she lay there for a solid five minutes, staring up at the ceiling beams. She wondered if his hands had helped build this place, and what his hands might feel like running along her rib cage and over her breasts.

He had such a way with his hands.

Frustrated, she threw off the covers.

He was still snoring.

With a huff, she rose from bed, tucked her feet into her slippers and left the room.

She went down to the kitchen, lit a lantern and rifled through the cold pantry. She came out with some sausage, a loaf of bread and strudel.

It made a nice midnight feast.

When she finished eating, she fetched some writing paper and the large square package she'd wrapped earlier in brown paper, while Jack had been working in the stables. The package was light as she set it on the massive kitchen table.

The glow of the flickering lantern guided her hand when she sat and placed a sheet of paper before her.

The darkness around her felt suddenly lonely. There was so much darkness. The window beside her was outlined faintly by a waning quarter-moon. Outside, the blackness of the night seemed to swell.

What was she doing here? Here in California?

She was married to a man she barely knew. They were sleeping in separate beds. He was caring on the outside, and did and said all the right things in front of others, but when the doors closed and it was just the two of them this evening, he'd barely spoken to her.

And now with everything that was happening—or *perhaps* was happening with Thornley and that woman and the possible murder—Cassandra was afraid of how everything might end.

Had she been wrong to accept Jack's proposal of marriage?

Looking down at the parchment filled her with a severe bout of melancholy, missing her friends at Mrs. Pepik's boardinghouse.

She dipped the nib of her fountain pen in black ink and began writing.

Sundial, California
Monday June 30, 1873

My dear friend Natasha,
I pray this letter finds you well. Please give my regards to Mrs. Pepik and the others, and let them know I'm doing well in California. I think of you all with fondness, and eagerness to hear of any news.

Sundial is prettier than I expected. You would love it here with all the sunshine and rolling hills. My wedding to Jack McColton went as planned, and I am settling into his house on the ranch. I do wish you were close by, as I miss our coffee hours together and more importantly, our friendship.

I was grateful for the use of the wedding gown. Please let Mrs. Pepik know I am returning it, enclosed, in the hopes that another lucky bride may wear it in good health.

Natasha, please write me back at the address below. I would dearly love to hear from you.
Warmest wishes and affection,
Cassandra McColton

There was no need to tell Natasha about the death of Mr. Dunleigh, or Cassandra's problems in her marriage with Jack and their distrust of each other, or the dismal prospects of her becoming a detective. The news would only worry her friend.

Cassandra folded the letter, stuffed it into an envelope and sealed it. She was about to carry the letter and package nearer to the front door when Jack's sultry voice called, "Can't sleep?"

With a jolt, she whirred around in her high-collared flannel gown to see him standing at the kitchen doorway, barefooted and bare-chested, in nothing but his blue jeans.

The scent of the kerosene lantern filled the tense air between them, and the glow flickered over Cassandra's innocent face as Jack strained to read her. She looked so damn vulnerable in the soft flannel, even though it covered nearly every inch of her body. Even those inches it didn't hide—her face, her slender hands, her pretty ankles—made him react with something raw and intense.

God, he only wanted to protect her. He hadn't been able to in the Chicago fire, and look what had happened to her there. He couldn't let her become a detective. Never ever. The next time he let her out of his sight, it might be worse than a burn injury—she might lose her life.

He always felt as though he was on the outside, looking in. Now she collected her envelope and package as if she was hiding the world's biggest secret from him, as if he couldn't be trusted to ask his wife who she was writing to and why she was up in the middle of the night.

He cursed the fact that he felt as vulnerable as she looked, and that there wasn't a damn thing he could do about it.

"Problems sleeping?" he asked again.

"I—I found it hot and stuffy in my room."

"You could have joined me in our bedroom."

Her dark lashes fluttered over her cheeks, as if she was debating what to say.

"Cassandra?"

"I thought about it...but you were sleeping."

"So you did look in?"

She nodded very properly, adjusting her posture and pulling her feet underneath her chair.

"Was there any particular reason why you wanted me *not* to be sleeping?"

She flushed, her cheeks stained an enthralling raspberry color. He'd hit a nerve and he enjoyed seeing her wiggle. Her mouth opened slightly; her blue eyes grew wider. She shrugged a soft shoulder and even beneath the thick flannel, he could imagine her bare breasts moving up and down with that shrug.

"No particular reason," she said in a breathy voice.

She did something crazy to his stomach. It turned and flipped and tightened.

His body hardened.

He would try to resist. He would give it his best shot to resist the temptation of his wife. *She* would have to come to him. He wanted to hear her beg for his touch.

"Why won't you admit it?" he asked.

"Admit what?"

"That you wanted me to be awake because you wanted to seduce me."

That flustered her. "Well, I just…it isn't… For heaven's sake, someone does think quite a lot of himself, doesn't he?"

Jack stood there, fighting desire, fighting every impulse his brain was sending to his muscles to reach out and catch her and take her right here on the spot.

"You want me, Cassandra, admit it."

"I won't."

"You like the way I touch you."

"I don't."

"You mean it's awful for you?" He raised his eyebrows, but there was amusement in his voice.

She responded with some teasing of her own. "It's…it's all right, but I wouldn't be calling for any parades, if you know what I mean. I don't know what all the fuss is about, really."

He wasn't sure if she was kidding or being truthful, which put him off-kilter again.

"The fuss…?" He floundered, then realized she was too stubborn to even admit she enjoyed being made love to. He'd never met any woman like her. "Well, maybe I need to show you what the fuss is all about."

"No," she said, grappling for words. "No need to show me anything."

"Oh, but I must." He straightened at the door, getting ready to move toward her. "I think it's absolutely necessary when a wife tells a husband—"

"The wife didn't mean it!" Cassandra jumped up from her chair, but was a fraction too late.

He moved.

She leaped.

He grabbed her around the waist. She panted and heaved and grabbed for the back of her chair, but it tumbled over.

With ease, he scooped her into his arms, and as she tried to push with her palms against his bare chest, he laid her, struggling, across the kitchen table.

He pinned one of her hands high above her head, and found her face infused with color, the lantern light skimming across the bridge of her nose and puckered lips.

"Beg me, Cassandra," he urged.

"I won't!"

He smiled softly as she continued to struggle and gyrate beneath him on the massive slab of wood.

"I can feel every part of your body underneath mine," he said with warning, "and if you continue to squirm like this, I may need to show you right here and now what I think of your nonsensical talk."

With her turbulent gaze riveted to his face, she threw out a challenge he could not resist. "You wouldn't dare!"

Chapter Fifteen

How could Jack be such a beast?

Cassandra didn't know whether to kick him or kiss him.

Lying beneath him on the hard kitchen table, with her hands pinned above her head, she stared up into his bold brown eyes and longed greedily for his lips on the tender curves of her neck. She wanted to know how it might feel if he brazenly took what he thought was his.

On the other hand, she wanted to give him no part of herself, for he was much too arrogant for his own good. How could she go on living with him if she allowed him to believe all he had to do was snap his fingers and she'd come running, breasts bared?

He didn't wait for her approval. With a slow

grin, he slid a large hand under the hem of her flannel gown, up her calf and thigh and hip.

She squirmed, trying to get out from under him, but all that accomplished was making him grin more.

"What do you think I am?" she panted. "One of those—those saloon women you've cavorted with?"

"How do you know what type of women I've cavorted with?"

"By the way you grab me."

She jerked her hip away from his hand, so instead he ran it up the side of her stomach. His grazing touch gave her gooseflesh, and it annoyed her that she was responding to him when she truly didn't wish to.

"Do you know what saloon women like me to do to them?"

"Don't tell me." She tried to pull her hands from his grasp, but he tightened his grip as easily as if he were holding a kitten. "You're a spoiled man who always has to have his way. I bet the next thing you're going to tell me is that they dropped their knickers as soon as they saw you coming."

A short laugh escaped him. "Oh, the dream of every man."

"Being manhandled is *not* the dream of every woman."

"It's your dream. Right here, right now." Still holding her hands above her head, he pressed his mouth to her cheek, her earlobe, the tender spot on her neck, his lips so silky and soft she wanted to throttle him.

"Stop it!" she groaned.

"In a minute," he murmured, while a riptide built inside her. His lips snagged against her high flannel collar, stopping him, and she was so pleased at his inconvenience she couldn't help but smile. When he fumbled with the buttons at her chin, one-handed, and was unable to unfasten even one, she smugly watched.

"Laugh, will you?" He released her hands and in a move so quick she had no time to halt him, grasped either side of her collar and yanked hard.

Her flannel nightgown ripped wide open from top to bottom; buttons popped on the table and flew against the walls.

Shocked, Cassandra parted her lips and her mouth dropped open.

He secured her hands again, gripping them high above her messy, loose hair.

"Oops," he said sweetly, basking in the view

of her nakedness. "I guess you'll have to go shopping."

"You son of a..."

"Now, now. You wouldn't want to be sounding like a saloon girl." The beast didn't even bother looking at her face when he spoke, but focused on the sight of her breasts.

She jerked her knee up, he instinctively flinched to protect his groin, and she heaved with all her might in his weak moment to flip him over onto his back. She hadn't actually kneed him, just pretended as if she was about to, and the trick had worked.

"How do you like it when the tables are turned? How does this feel now?" She hovered over him on the table, pinning his hands above his dark hair, sitting on top of his hips, with her frayed gown and bare breasts dangling.

"It's getting better by the moment."

She growled.

"You've caught a big fish. What are you going to do to him?" Jack's dark cheeks lifted in humor. His black hair lay tousled about his face. "I think you need to bait me with something delicious." He indicated the body parts inches from his face.

She couldn't believe he was insinuating that she offer him her bosom. "If you think I'm going to fall for such a dumb…" Her blond hair swayed about her body.

"Come closer," he whispered.

"No…"

"I want you to."

"You shouldn't assume I want the same thing."

"But you do…you know you do…."

Since her gown was ripped open, it meant she was lying with her bare crotch over his denim jeans. He was hard. If she moved just slightly, like so, it hit such a pleasurable spot on her body. And if she lowered her shoulders, like this, her nipple brushed his lips.

Mmm.

The experience was mesmerizing. He took her breast ever so gently and kissed it. When she moved the other one to his lips, he did the same, closing his eyes, lost in the fever of the moment.

The heat, the need, the tempo burned within her. She rose up and down on top of him, rubbing ever so softly against his rock-hard erection, and it was his turn to moan. She wouldn't allow him to lead, he would have to follow, and he would have to be satisfied with whatever she gave him.

They dipped and sucked and she rode him at her leisure. She sensed his urgency but didn't give in to it, instead taking her time to enjoy the scent of his skin, the light tickling of the hairs on his chest against her nipples, the spilling of her breasts into his mouth. The pressure of her thighs and the moistness there soon sent her on another chase, a more desperate one.

When she released one of his wrists he promptly slid his hand along her thigh and up over her rump, clamping her body to his.

She bent lower and kissed him, as seriously and intensely as she'd ever wanted to. The heat between them built as the kiss grew into a feverish melting of lips and tongue and teasing.

"Cassandra, I've never felt such soft lips… such untouched skin…."

She didn't remember when she'd released his other wrist, but her palms were now firmly pressed on the table on either side of his head, and his hands were kneading her bottom, caressing the curves. He slid one finger to her center, and she loved the feel of the slick, hot glide as they moved together.

He reached to loosen the buttons of his trousers and claw the denim off his hips. His erection sprang to attention.

Jack's chest was tanned from working in the sun, but his hips were white and attractive. Dark hair trailing from his belly button and farther down drew her attention to an entire area that was new and fascinating to her.

She rested her weight on one knee while he kicked off his trousers, then repositioned himself beneath her, his wide hands splayed over her buttocks, guiding himself inside her.

She arched her back and loved the feel of him, so thick and large and incredibly filling. His hands slid up her rib cage and over her breasts.

"Such beauty I've never seen before," he whispered into the semidarkness. The lantern flame fluttered and illuminated their joined shapes as though they were living, breathing sculptures in some masterful artwork.

He groaned, "I'll be done so quickly. Let me move into a different position."

She allowed him, and he slid off the table and stood behind her, his feet imbedded in the soft rug. He knotted his fingers in the ropes of her hair, ran his other hand along the smooth trail of her spine, then gripped the indentation of her waistline.

"Is this all right for you, Cassandra? Are you all right?"

"Yes," she moaned, loving the feel of them together.

She felt the smooth warmth of his erection on

her rump. Then, approaching from behind, he slipped inside her again, filling her up.

"Why don't you control things?" he whispered. "However feels good to you."

"This feels good...." She rocked backward onto his hard shaft, rubbing back and forth until it hit the sweet spot, riding and riding till she crested the wave. She climaxed in a height of ecstasy, every muscle releasing, every fear erased, leaving only a burning desire to please her husband and herself.

She wasn't yet finished when he began to climax inside her. He uttered a guttural moan, his pace speeding up in a familiar frenzy, his hot fingers clenching her hips as he rocked into her with a powerful force.

She embraced the moment and basked in the sheer pleasure, feeling as though she was bound to Jack by some plan of the heavens above.

It was different this time between them, Cassandra sensed.

Moments later, they untangled their legs. She quickly slipped into the bathing room to tidy herself, then returned to the kitchen to find Jack straightening the chairs and table. He'd already tugged his denim jeans back on.

The light of the lantern danced over the ropy muscles of his back and shoulders.

"Eating dinner on this table will never be the same," he said with a wry twist to his mouth.

"I won't tell if you don't."

They were still teasing each other, but it wasn't the same. The barb in their tone had left. Feeling suddenly self-conscious, Cassandra tugged the ripped opening of her flannel gown closed.

He watched her hands.

They were more aware of each other, perhaps a bit intimidated about the intimacy they'd just shared. Before, they'd always withdrawn, but this time they seemed content to leave for the bedroom together.

Cassandra gathered her envelope and package and set them down on the crescent-shaped table in the front hall. When she turned around, Jack surprised her by sweeping her into his arms and carrying her up the stairs. He did it with such ease and grace, his long legs nimbly covering the distance. She leaned her ear and cheek against his bare chest, listening to the drumming of his heart. It was still beating fast, but his breathing had subsided to a more normal pace.

He didn't bother with the guest bedroom but strode right past it and straight to the marriage bed, where he laid her down and tucked her feet in. Just before he covered her, his eyes strayed to her ripped gown, which had slid open to reveal one rose-tipped breast. He lowered his head quickly and kissed the tip.

"Good night," he said softly to Cassandra, then went to his side, stripped and eased himself in.

It didn't take him long to fall asleep—mere seconds, in fact.

She lay awake, wondering what he'd been thinking about her after their bout of lovemaking, and where she stood with him now.

How could she not feel something for Jack? Something deep and alive, and whispering to her what a good man he was, how he was taking care of her and watching out for her.

The torment of Troy's words, *"I always found you too prim and proper,"* seemed to wash away in a river of mud when she compared them to the night she'd just spent with Jack.

Her husband had certainly found her pleasing. Why, he'd even come right out and said so. He'd made her feel womanly and wanted.

Yet he resisted her request to work. Blazes, how could she get over that? Why should she have to? And this whole business with the possible poisonings was extremely worrisome. Was someone out to harm her or Jack?

Couldn't he see how hard she'd tried tonight to help solve the puzzle of Thornley's behavior? Couldn't Jack see she had ideas of her own merit that even the sheriff and doctor acknowledged, and that she'd make a good detective? Cassandra sighed. No matter how hard she tried, perhaps she and Jack might never solve their differences. Yes, Troy had hammered her heart with his disappointing lies and dalliances with prostitutes, but hadn't Jack, as well? He'd left her once before, in Chicago, and he could do it again.

It would be much harder for him to leave her now that they were married, but a person could leave emotionally, too. He could pull away and decide he was done with her, that she was too much trouble to figure out, that he was tired of waiting to see if they could put things right between them and learn to trust each other.

It wasn't as though either one of them had declared their love to the other.

Truth be told, Cassandra was scared to love deeply; her heart was still trembling from the loss of Mary and her father. And if it was pity Jack felt for her, for having to live at the boardinghouse, how was she to tolerate that?

Turning on her pillow, she fell asleep thinking of Chicago and that last, reckless night with Jack. She didn't recall the nightmare of the burning buildings, or calling out for help before Jack gently touched her shoulder.

"Cassandra, it's just a dream. It's a dream, honey."

She awoke in the morning and he was gone.

Reaching for her robe, she pulled it over her ripped gown, slid her feet into her slippers and made her way down the stairs to find her husband.

Chapter Sixteen

Cassandra found him in his office, at his desk, concentrating on the papers in front of him. The doctor of veterinary science looked more like a well-toned ranch hand, his physique polished to a fine hue from the hours he spent riding, and attending to his horses and stables. His black hair was a touch too long and tousled for normal standards, but it made him look rough and dangerous. He wore fresh denims and a gray shirt that accentuated his tanned skin and dark features.

Maybe Jack realized he was being watched, for something made him turn in her direction. "Cassandra, good morning."

He seemed to be pleased at her appearance,

although she wasn't sure why, since she was so disheveled.

"You're up early," she said.

"I had some things to go over before we head to town."

She frowned. "We?"

"I owe you a shopping trip." He glanced down at her robe.

"You don't need to replace anything, if that's what you're concerned about. I have two more flannel gowns just like it."

"Oh," he replied with a faltering smile. "That's splendid."

She nodded. "So you needn't worry."

"But you do need ranch clothes. And a new dress for the Fourth of July."

"We're still going to the dance?"

"I assumed you wanted to?"

"In light of the troubles with Derik Thornley…I thought you might want to avoid the celebrations."

His dark eyes glimmered with marked determination. "We can't postpone living our lives, and I'll be damned if I let his presence dictate where we decide to go. We'll protect ourselves and proceed with caution. Besides, there's still a chance that I'm wrong, that there was no foul play with the sick animals, or Mr. Dunleigh."

The knot in her neck seemed to unwind at his words.

Suddenly, it was just the two of them again, and she did truly look forward to buying new clothes. "I'll be quick."

"No need to rush."

She was almost out of the room when Jack added one last comment. "Cassandra?"

"Yes?" she said, enthusiasm ringing in her voice.

When his smoky eyes roved over her, skewed robe and all, she knew he was thinking of their time together on the kitchen table, and she could barely breathe, thinking of it herself.

"I'm glad you still have two more of those granny gowns left. I look forward to removing them, too."

She gasped. "Dr. McColton, you really must learn to censor your thoughts."

Then she retreated from the room with a deliberate air of wounded dignity, followed by his laughter.

Their bodyguard was Russell Crawford, Jack's foreman. Wearing two holstered guns on his hips, the man nodded to Cassandra as he walked past her, to climb into the buggy behind her and Jack.

"Crawford used to be a bounty hunter," Jack explained as Cassandra fidgeted uneasily on her seat.

"Back in Denver," the foreman confirmed.

That was interesting news, she thought, and related to the field she wished to work in. He would be a good source of information on possible gangs who roved the area, and names of the lawmen in various districts. "Good to see you again, Mr. Crawford. I hope you never have to prove your worth as a gunslinger."

"Likely not, ma'am." His striking black mustache lifted in the wind. "Sometimes these things have a way of workin' themselves out. No need to concern yourself. I'll be here if you need me, otherwise I'm just comin' along for the ride."

His easygoing manner was reassuring to her as Jack flicked the reins and they rolled out. He, too, was wearing a holster with two guns. The mere presence of weapons made Cassandra that much more aware of the danger they were in. But no one in these parts would think it odd for a man to be wearing guns, and Jack likely wore them on many of his longer journeys to check on animals.

Cassandra was carrying her own derringer. After showing Jack the silver-handled pistol, she'd placed it and several extra bullets into her satchel. The weight of it shifted on her lap, while the wind snatched at wisps of her hair escaping from her long braid.

For this outing, Jack had harnessed two mares to the buggy, and he handled them with skill. He knew exactly when to accelerate around a corner, and maneuvered easily over ruts in the dry road.

The package containing her bridal gown shifted on the floor in front of Cassandra's long skirts. She had filled a second box filled with shortbread biscuits, honeys and jams, and intended on mailing the two boxes and the letter to Natasha today.

Cassandra stayed near the buggy with the former bounty hunter when they stopped for twenty minutes on the Woodrow ranch. The ill horses were still doing poorly. Jack gave them more medicine and promised the rancher he'd return the next day.

They continued on their way and entered Sundial.

The main road was busy with wagons and riders, and folks walking along the boardwalk, intent on their business. Jack turned right at the main square. They drove beneath a large white banner that read Independence Day Festivities—

Friday from Noon till Midnight in the Town Square.

Anticipation rolled through Cassandra at the thought that she and Jack would be attending. Maybe Friday would be the beginning of a whole new "independence" for them and their marriage. Even though he had that tough side to him, the one that didn't allow his pride to bend, he could be incredibly considerate and sensual and generous.

"Before we get to the clothing stores," said Jack, "I thought we'd drop in to see Mrs. Dunleigh."

"Lovely idea," Cassandra replied.

They pulled up beside a white house shaded by palm trees. Mrs. Dunleigh was sitting on a swing on the front porch, gray hair pinned into a bun, dabbing her eyes with a handkerchief. When she spotted the three of them, she greeted them warmly.

"Good morning," Cassandra said. "We've come to see how you are."

"Missing my husband terribly," Mrs. Dunleigh replied with a sob. "But it helps to see kind faces." She ushered the McColtons into the house. Mr. Crawford remained outside to keep a discreet watch.

They stayed for an hour, drinking tea and

listening to her stories of the early years of her marriage. Cassandra felt great sympathy for their years of hard living, and could well imagine two immigrants arriving from England with big dreams of a new life in America.

She was surprised to see Jack listening intently, too. He didn't mention anything of his suspicions about Yule's possible poisoning, much to Cassandra's relief; for it would be upsetting for the older lady. He did ask a few pointed questions as they stood by the door, preparing to leave.

"It's terrible, how sudden it all was," he said to Mrs. Dunleigh. "You say you finished eating lunch, and he went to get the newspaper at the front door. Was it your usual lunch, in your wing of the house?"

"Yes, yes, prepared in our kitchen. Yule loved to watch the birds."

"Birds?" asked Cassandra.

"We ate on the small terrace outside our quarters."

"Did you get up and leave the table for any reason?" Jack asked.

Mrs. Dunleigh frowned at the question. "Well, Yule set the table, as usual, while I prepared the sandwiches. The only time he got up was when he saw the rider approaching from the laneway. He left the table to go to the front door and collect the paper."

"I see."

So, thought Cassandra, there would've been no opportunity for a stranger to put any poison into his food, if they hadn't left the table. And since Mrs. Dunleigh hadn't suffered any poisoning symptoms herself, it meant the food in general hadn't been tampered with.

Jack scratched his temple. "What did he have to eat earlier that day? For breakfast, for example?"

"The usual. Sausage and eggs. We ate together. I always made our lunch and dinners, but he always cooked us breakfast. Said he liked serving me the morning meal. Why do you ask?"

"I'm trying to get a feel for how he spent his last few hours."

"He wasn't feeling well the night before," she said, absently shaking her head. "Came down with an awful headache. And that constriction in his chest."

"Yes, I heard you mention to Dr. Clarkson that he'd taken two pills for his angina that night."

"He had for the last several nights."

Jack's brown eyes flickered.

There didn't seem to be any indication, according to what Cassandra was hearing, of anything unusual, such as foul play.

"We'll be off," Jack said.

Mrs. Dunleigh and Cassandra embraced, and the older woman waved as the two of them headed to their buggy.

"Did you hear anything that helped you?" Cassandra asked Jack as soon as they were out of earshot. Crawford was pacing the street several yards away.

Jack tugged on the rim of his black Stetson. "Not especially. I didn't know Yule had been having heart symptoms for the last week. Everything seems to point to a natural cause of death."

The foreman once again climbed into the buggy behind them. Five minutes later, they were parking outside the shops along Sundial's main street. They went into the postal outlet and mailed Natasha's packages. Cassandra didn't mention what was inside, and Jack didn't invade her privacy by asking.

"How much does Mr. Crawford know about your suspicions?" Cassandra whispered to Jack when they were alone again.

"I didn't tell him about the potential murder of Dunleigh. Only that we want his protection because Thornley had pulled some punches at me, and I was concerned about his retaliation at you. I told Crawford to keep it to himself, and he will."

Jack nodded hello to a few people strolling by on the boardwalk as he and Cassandra made their way to the clothing shops. One store, Lucille's, had a big, beautiful sun hat in the front window. Another was called The Velvet Touch. Cassandra recognized the woman who was arranging a skirt in the display case. She was the snobby owner who'd commented on Cassandra's scar and shabby dress when Jack had been showing her the sundial last week. Now, the woman smiled and eagerly motioned for Jack to come inside her shop to look at her merchandise.

Cassandra stiffened. "I'd prefer Lucille's."

"Me, too. But before we get there, would you mind if we dropped by Hugh's office?" Jack pointed to a stone building on the corner of the next block.

"Not at all."

She turned at Jack's light touch on her spine, and stepped beside him through the crowd. She noticed that Crawford was following a few paces behind, as if casually scouting the area.

Cassandra wondered what Jack had to say to Hugh Logan, and whether this might be her opportunity to voice a few matters of her own.

* * *

Several minutes later, in Hugh's office, Jack wished that Cassandra didn't look so uncomfortable, her fingers fidgeting, while her lips twitched. He supposed she had every right to bristle in the presence of his attorney, since she'd told Jack in one of their blustery arguments that she was well aware Hugh had disapproved of her as a mail-order bride.

"Hello, Cassandra." The lawyer, with his red hair slicked back, and wearing a checkered suit, greeted her politely. "Please have a seat, both of you."

Jack held out a chair for her near the window. Her glossy braid fell over her shoulder, and she wore a simple cream-colored blouse and skirt, but the woman beneath was anything but simple. She was nuanced and complicated and the most exasperating female he had ever met.

And it was high time that she and Hugh got to know each other. Maybe then the next time they visited, she wouldn't be so ill at ease.

Hugh's gaze flicked over her worn clothing. Jack wondered if his friend could see the obvious—that if she were after Jack's perceived wealth, she wouldn't be dressing so modestly, wearing so very little jewelry except her wedding band and a thin gold locket around her neck. This woman was not after his money.

Hugh sat behind his desk. "Cassandra, tell me how you're getting on at the ranch."

"I'm finding my way," she answered.

After the pleasantries were dispensed with, Jack leaned forward on the chair, Stetson in hand, and asked outright, "What have you discovered about Thornley?"

"Jack, for heaven's sake, it's only been a day since I received your note, asking me to check into him."

"Yes, I know. That's plenty of time. So what did you learn?"

Hugh exhaled in exasperation. His suit glistened in a streak of sunlight pouring in the window when he turned to Cassandra. "Is he always this impatient at home?"

"Oh, yes, quite." A soft smile reached her lips. "You should hear him hollering for his porridge in the morning."

"Come now," Jack argued, "that's not true."

Hugh nodded in her direction. "Once when he and I were crossing the Rockies, he wouldn't go to sleep at night because he was convinced we were surrounded by rattlers."

"Hey, I saw one," said Jack.

"A baby."

"Where there's a baby, there's a thousand of them nesting."

Hugh scoffed. "If you expect me to believe something that ludicrous—"

"Maybe I exaggerated a bit 'cause I knew you were squirmy," Jack said with a chuckle, enjoying the ribbing. "But you know you can't shoot worth beans. So *I* had to stay up, because if the rattlers attacked—"

"If you hadn't been drivin' the horses as if we were in some race, I might've enjoyed a bit of that fresh air."

"Who're you kidding?" Jack retorted. "You don't like fresh air, you like city living—"

"Never thinking about anyone else's time but your own—"

"I think about your time. You charge me enough for it."

Both men turned to Cassandra and shook their heads. She appeared uncertain who to side with. "You sure you two aren't somehow related?"

"He should be so lucky," muttered Jack.

"I'm the better looking," said Hugh. "And I was hoping that marriage might mellow you, Jack."

"It's made me more aware that time is passing. Now hurry the hell up and say something intelligent. So far I've gotten five minutes of useless chatter that you'll probably add to your hefty bill."

"You didn't hold back when you charged me for that black stallion."

"It cost extra for all the hand holding I had to do, teaching you how to saddle him and ride. You're worse than a schoolkid."

"Quit your gripin'." Hugh leaned back in his leather chair. "Now then, about Thornley. What I've discovered is he moved here from San Diego—"

Jack interrupted. "I thought you never had time to look into his past?"

"I never said that." Hugh raised his sleek eyebrows in an expression of insult. "I said it's only been a day since you asked. Most lawyers wouldn't be able to get it done in that time, so I hope you appreciate it. I don't enjoy being taken for granted. Something I'm sure Cassandra can attest to, even in her short time with you."

She nodded in solemn agreement, as if the two of them were in collusion.

"You're a fool," Jack told him. "What else did you uncover?"

"He was thrown in jail there once, but the charges didn't hold up in court."

"For what?"

"Assault with a weapon."

"Aha. I knew it." Jack slapped his palm against his thigh.

"He grew up with a tough older brother. The brother's broken the law on numerous occasions for theft and assault. He's serving time in San Quentin as we speak, for train robbery."

"Oh," whispered Cassandra. Her braid shifted against her blouse.

"Watch yourself," Hugh warned Jack. "He's already come after you once."

Jack scowled at the recollection. "Anything else?"

"He was born and raised in Wyoming Territory. I sent some telegrams there this morning, but it'll take a few days to hear back."

Jack absorbed the information.

Cassandra gripped the satchel on her lap. "If you don't mind, Jack, may I ask a few questions?"

She was always surprising him with the way her mind worked. This should be interesting. "Be my guest."

"Would you mind if we told Hugh the entire story?" she gently urged Jack. "About your suspicions?"

Jack shifted his weight to the other side of his chair.

Hugh looked from one to the other, suddenly much more serious. "Please do. What's this about, Jack?"

"We think some of the animals I've been looking after these past several days may have been poisoned. And what's more, we wonder if Dunleigh was."

Hugh frowned and didn't say anything for a moment, then asked, "What makes you think so?"

Jack went into his suspicions on the timing of his vet calls, the presence of Thornley on the ridge, the fistfight, the problems with Elise and the coincidence of Dunleigh dropping dead.

"And the motivation?"

"Thornley's anger at my involvement with Elise."

Hugh shook his head slightly. "Thornley's the suspect? Seems a bit far-fetched to me."

Cassandra was straightforward. "And we have no proof, either, Mr. Logan."

"Call me Hugh, please."

"Hugh." She sighed. "No proof thus far. But I was wondering if you might tell me—either one of you—where the newspaper office is. The one that delivers the *Sundial Daily News*. I think it's worth speaking to the boy who delivered the paper that day to Mr. Dunleigh, don't you, Jack?"

He hadn't thought of that, but it was a damn good idea. "Yes, indeed it would."

"It's two streets over," Hugh told her.

"And about Elise Beacon," Cassandra continued. "Has she ever done anything that you might consider a touch unstable?"

Hugh looked to Jack. Both men took a moment to ponder the question.

"Nothing other than objecting to your wedding," said Hugh.

Jack shook his head. "Her father's the unstable one. He's a heavy drinker. Last year he tore off to South America with a questionable woman who used to drink with him. Left Elise in charge of the vineyard, but she rose to the challenge and has done a good job with it. I'm sorry to see her involved with Thornley, to tell you the truth. She could do a lot better."

Cassandra sat quietly listening. He felt guilty again for bringing up Elise's name, but Cassandra was right that it should all be brought into the open with his attorney.

Her eyes roved the stack of books and papers on Hugh's desk. "Is that the new California penal code? Released earlier this year?" she asked. "They had it at the Chicago library, but I got only three-quarters through it before I had to leave for California."

This admission caught both men by surprise. Hugh blinked at her, likely wondering why on earth a woman would be reading the penal code, and Jack found himself growing uncomfortable again. She knew too much for her own good, for her own safety.

She answered Hugh's unspoken question. "My father was a criminal attorney. I became interested in the law due to him."

"You don't say."

"And there's just one more question, Hugh," she said softly. "But this one is of a more personal nature. Please forgive me for being so frank, but you must've had some reservations about me, when you first heard Jack answered my advertisement? When you first heard that he wished to marry me? You must've been very protective, because that's how I would've reacted, if I had been as close a friend to Jack as you obviously are."

Hugh's mouth opened in obvious surprise. "I admit I was."

"I would like to invite you, sir, for dinner at our ranch sometime. I do hope that as you get to know me, your opinion might change."

Hugh's expression softened. He looked at her

with newfound respect, then glanced at Jack as if to say that perhaps he'd been wrong about Cassandra. "I would enjoy that."

Jack scratched his head. How had she sensed in such a short period of time with Hugh that what the attorney most appreciated in his friendships was straight talk with no nonsense?

Jack rose from his chair and Cassandra followed suit.

"I suspect we'll see you at the Fourth of July celebrations?" Jack asked him.

Hugh nodded. He rose in turn and shook Jack's hand, then said to Cassandra in a humorous tone, "Fair warning—most women say he's a lousy dancer."

"And Hugh can never get the same woman to accompany him more than once. What does that say about his ability to entertain a lady?"

"Lucille Anderson's coming this time," the attorney told him.

"Lucille? She's too good for you."

"I know."

Both men laughed.

Hugh opened the door for them. "Nice seeing you again, Cassandra."

"The pleasure's mine," she said, smiling and appearing much more comfortable leaving his office than when she'd entered.

She had a remarkable way with people. Jack led her out, quietly thinking about all the impressive facets of her character as they headed to Lucille Anderson's dress shop. He had an overwhelming urge to buy her the prettiest dress there, to treat her to a new wardrobe and the luxuries he could easily afford. He wondered if it was to perhaps erase his guilt for not having been there in Chicago when she'd suffered through the fire and her incredible losses.

Chapter Seventeen

Cassandra squinted in the late morning sun as she strode along the boardwalk, guarded by Jack's towering figure to her right, and Mr. Crawford up ahead, keeping a watchful eye on them as he hovered near the horses. A handful of folks passed by. She was struck by the curious relationship Jack had with Hugh. Despite the good-natured ribbing and the humorous insults flying fast between the men, she didn't for a moment doubt that their loyalty and friendship ran deep.

That must have made it all the more difficult for Jack to go against Hugh's advice concerning a mail-order bride. She had a twinge of discomfort about that. It was a raw wound that didn't need to be reopened, and so she decided to ignore it and focus instead on the more pleasurable chores ahead.

When they approached Lucille's dress shop, Jack leaned in so close that tendrils of hair at her neck tickled.

"I'd like you to go ahead and try to break my wallet in this store." His low voice held a fair amount of humor.

Cassandra smiled reassuringly. "I don't need much. I'll behave myself."

"But I like it when you misbehave." The mischievous twinkle in his brown eyes indicated that he was referring to something other than shopping. A seductive night they'd shared, perhaps.

"Then I'll be sure not to disappoint you."

"Ah," he said, the single syllable holding a wealth of meaning.

As she walked beside him, her skirts swirled about her legs. They had almost reached the shop when he suddenly looked over his shoulder. She followed his gaze, spotting only a man dressed in overalls. On the street, there was just one passing horse and rider.

What was Jack sensing? she wondered.

Had he heard a strange sound? He took particular care to look at the buildings across the street, but nothing seemed out of the ordinary. She noticed the office for the *Sundial Daily News*.

"How about I drop you off at the shop," he said, "while I go poke around the newspaper office? It'll be less noticeable if I go alone."

"Good plan."

"Any particular questions you'd like me to ask?"

She stifled a smile of victory at his implication that she had some talent in questioning, and in her observation skills. "Only the obvious ones. Who was the delivery person? What did the person witness? Where, when, why and how?"

"Right." Jack pushed open the door to Lucille's. Bells above the door tinkled when they entered.

The sun's rays lit the open space. Racks of colorful dresses, blouses and skirts lined the walls. Hats and bonnets hung on display hooks. Satchels, handbags, belts and shoes filled a cabinet.

A most unusual collection in the far corner caught Cassandra's eye. It was an assortment of women's work clothes. There were garden gloves, hats with wide straw brims to shade the sun, overalls in slender sizes, denim jeans, work shirts and rubber boots in female sizes. She'd always heard there was more freedom for women here in the West, with more ladies owning shops of their own, or panning for gold, or making business deals with bankers. Goodness, it was pleasing to her.

"Howdy, Lucille," Jack said.

Cassandra turned to see a pretty red-haired woman with clear fair skin and green eyes stepping out from a display of high-heeled boots she'd been arranging. She had a wide, affectionate smile. "It's a pleasure to see you, Jack."

"I'd like to introduce my wife, Cassandra."

"It's lovely to meet you. I hope you're enjoying California."

"Indeed, I am. I'm also enjoying your shop."

Lucille beamed. "Is there something in particular I can help you with this morning?"

"I'd like you to outfit her from head to toe," Jack said generously. "What she'll need on the ranch, both in the house and when she's out riding. And something special for the Fourth of July. I hear you'll be attending, by the way. Cassandra and I would be honored if you and Hugh sat with us."

"I'd like that," Lucille replied promptly.

Cassandra liked her. They'd only just met, but Cassandra had a good feeling about the friendly young woman, who was not much older than her. And she operated a shop. Cassandra had never met a woman who'd owned her own business. How intriguing.

"All right, then," said Jack. "I'll leave you two. Let me know when you're finished, darlin'. I'm going to the newspaper office, then I'll wait for you by the buggy."

"I'll try not to be too long," she told him, flustered at the affectionate reference.

"Take your time." And away he went.

Cassandra was distracted when Lucille held up two long skirts, one golden in color, the other a deep coffee.

"These would go well with your hair," urged Lucille. "Match them up with a pretty blue blouse the color of your eyes...see? How do you like that?" She held them up in front of Cassandra, before a full-length wall mirror.

Lucille certainly had a keen sense of style.

"If I may try them on...I'd love to take them."

The seamstress smiled. "Hugh told me you're from Chicago. Sorry to hear about...about your family not surviving the Great Fire."

Cassandra was a little taken aback by the forthright statement. What else had Hugh mentioned? "Thank you," she replied.

"I had an uncle who also perished in the

fire," Lucille said gently. "He was one of my favorite relations." Her eyes welled up. Then she blinked the tears away and reached for a pretty dress on a rack.

Cassandra was still trying to digest what she'd just said. "You lost an uncle. How awful. Where did he live?"

"On the outskirts, far from the fire, but he was trapped that day in the middle of it, on a business errand. It was pure bad luck."

"I'm sorry to hear that."

Lucille turned her focus back to the shapely red dress with daring straps.

Cassandra hesitated. "It's a little too bold for me."

"Jack would like it."

Cassandra turned back to have another look. "I suppose you're right. Do you have something in a different color?"

"I do. There's one here that's even lower cut, but Jack would surely adore you in it."

"You seem to know him well."

"I suspect he and Hugh are the same in that regard."

Their eyes caught in the mirror and both smiled.

Men.

"Cassandra, if I may be so forward to suggest…my sister is a theater actress in New York, and the last time she came to visit, she left me something. I liked it so much I ordered some for my customers." Lucille reached behind the counter and came out with a small jar of powder. "They wear heavy cosmetics beneath the stage lights, and this is wonderful for masking blemishes. I thought that you might…well, maybe it's a bit presumptuous of me to…"

"I'd love to try it." No one had ever suggested anything like this to Cassandra. She powdered her injured cheek. The heavy scar was still visible, but the mottling had disappeared and somehow her skin color looked better. "Oh, I do like that."

Lucille was gracious and didn't dwell on it.

Cassandra truly enjoyed spending the next hour with her. She discovered that the Fourth of July celebrations would be the first time Lucille and Hugh would be courting. That Jack had been considered the bachelor catch of the town, and that's why some folks might not be warming up to Cassandra, for she'd stolen the town treasure. That Jack's favorite meal at the steakhouse was medium rare steak with a glass of red sauvignon.

And that Elise Beacon and Derik Thornley

had had a big argument this morning outside the jewelry shop, and that Elise had left in tears.

Jack had the eerie feeling he was being watched. He'd taken ten minutes to check in with Sheriff Leggett, who'd reported some interesting news about an argument that had taken place between Elise and Thornley. Then half an hour later, as he stepped out of the newspaper office, after speaking with the publisher, Jack instinctively held his hands near his guns and looked sharply from left to right. He recognized the folks walking by, nodded in greeting, then watched a team of horses pull a wagon loaded with wine barrels. He waved hello to the driver, as well.

Nothing looked out of place, it just felt out of place.

He knew better than to ignore his premonition.

Still, there was nothing to react to on the street, so he headed toward Crawford, who was leaning against a post near the buggy.

En route, Jack noticed a strange woman exit Lucille's dress shop. Her wide straw hat concealed her face. She was smartly dressed.

He peered past her through the windows, wondering where Cassandra was, as he stepped aside to let the other customer by. "Ma'am," he said, touching the brim of his black Stetson.

"Jack, it's me." Her hat brim shot up, revealing Cassandra's pretty face.

"Well, look at you." He marveled at the transformation.

She wore an enticing, silky cream blouse. A long brown skirt hugged her hips and fell to the tips of her fashionable, high-heeled shoes. The skirt had a pleat down the center, and he noticed that it was actually a pair of riding pants that some women were wearing now, concealed as a skirt. Cassandra wore leather riding gloves that molded to her fingers and matched her knotted belt.

"Very nice," he murmured. "Very, very nice."

A smile danced along her lips in appreciation. Her blond hair had been newly braided, and curled over her bosom like a shiny rope.

"The packages are still inside, on the counter, if you don't mind helping me put them into the buggy."

"Not at all."

He went in, offered his thanks to Lucille, then loaded up the boxes and brown-paper-wrapped parcels and headed toward the ranch.

When they were back in open country, with the noonday sun blazing down on the buggy's rooftop, Cassandra leaned over and asked, "What did you discover at the newspaper?"

"Not much. The delivery boy, Adam, was the same one who always delivers the paper, twice a week—every Wednesday and Saturday. I know him. He's a good kid, sixteen, son of the publisher. Adam said he didn't notice anything unusual on Saturday with Mr. Dunleigh. My paper was labeled with my name, as it always is. He reached into his sack, removed it from the top and handed it to Mr. Dunleigh. He said the front door closed behind him, so the boy didn't see or hear Yule collapse."

"Oh, the poor lad."

"He said he felt bad when he heard." Jack was well aware that Crawford could hear their discussion from the backseat, but there wasn't any news from the publisher to conceal. Jack would keep to himself the information the sheriff had relayed, until he could speak with Cassandra in private. If they were wrong about Dunleigh being murdered, it would be a horrible rumor that might reach Mrs. Dunleigh's ears and cause her more grief. The only thing Crawford had to know was that Cassandra needed bodyguard protection, and to be especially alert for Thornley.

It seemed as though Cassandra wanted to

add something, but then her eyes shifted in the foreman's direction and she must've thought better of it. She pressed her lips together and peered ahead as they rolled up the familiar laneway home.

After they alighted from the buggy, Crawford asked, "Anything else, boss?"

Jack peered at the stables, the horses being led out to pasture and various ranch hands going about their everyday tasks. "You can get back to your regular duties. I'll let you know when I need you again. Thanks, Crawford."

They were back inside the house when Cassandra told Jack what was on her mind. "I heard about an argument between Thornley and Miss Beacon."

"I heard it, too, from the sheriff. He said he didn't know what it was about, but was trying to find out. He's also keeping an eye out for Elise's safety, but so far there's no evidence that Thornley is a violent type with women."

"I never thought of it…that she might be in danger."

"She knows he came after me on the ranch, but a lot of men are hotheaded when it comes to standing up for their women. So his behavior isn't necessarily that unusual. I can't tell you the number of fistfights I was in when I was young and hot-tempered myself. Stupid fights over the years. It doesn't mean Thornley would hit a woman, though."

"Do you think Miss Beacon and he are still together? After their fight?"

"I don't know." Talk of those two made Jack uneasy. And incensed.

How dare Thornley interfere with his marriage to Cassandra? How dare he make Jack worry about her safety? And dammit, if Thornley had anything to do with Dunleigh's death...

Jack's heart pounded in outrage.

Murder. He was dealing with the possible murder of a good friend.

"Jack?" Cassandra was staring at him. "Are you all right?"

He kept his voice cool and calm, but his heart was pounding like a trapped bear's. "I'm going to get to the bottom of this. Mark my words."

Cassandra was worried about Jack. For the next four days, he seemed a man obsessed. She had been hoping, now that they'd found some shared moments of intimacy in bed, that the heated nights might continue. Perhaps he wanted them to, but he was pulled away by his work.

On Monday, no sooner had they arrived home

than an adolescent boy knocked on the door, indicating Jack was needed for an injured horse.

"Johnny," Jack asked, "you're saying he's lame?"

"Yes, sir," said the trembling young cowboy, one she didn't recognize. "He stumbled when my father was riding through the creek. There were some rocks there, and Pa didn't see them, and now he's feelin' sick to his stomach that something might happen to the animal. Please say you won't shoot the horse, Dr. McColton. Please say it."

"Let me have a look at him."

Jack looked at Cassandra, and she knew by his expression that they were both thinking the same thing. This was a physical injury to the stallion and had nothing to do with Thornley, nor did there seem to be any suggestion of possible foul play. It seemed to be an honest accident.

Jack didn't return till after midnight. He'd sent word to Mr. Crawford to stay in the house and guard Cassandra, and Jack must've stumbled to bed sometime in the wee hours, after she'd finally closed her eyes.

On Tuesday he left before she rose. He'd written a hurried note telling her the stallion seemed to have an open hairline fracture, but there was a possibility no infection would set in if Jack applied poultices and helped calm the animal.

He came in for a rushed dinner. She was relieved to see him, but he had to hasten out again to check on Finley's cattle, then go sit with the stallion with the hairline fracture.

On Wednesday, they shared breakfast, but Jack kept looking out the front door, waiting for the newspaper to be delivered. When it arrived, Cassandra rushed outside with him, to see the paper boy adjust his leather gloves and hand it over like he always did. Adam held it out nervously, likely because he knew he was being closely observed.

"I didn't do nothin' wrong, did I, Dr. Mc-Colton?"

"No, Adam, nothing at all. I just wanted to see for myself how the paper was delivered. Mr. Dunleigh always took it in the three years since I've been living here."

"Yes, sir. Good day, sir. Ma'am."

Jack took it, retrieved the one from Saturday afternoon that Mr. Dunleigh had handled, brought both papers into the kitchen and scrutinized every page, side by side.

"Something's here," he said. "A message of some sort, staring me right in the face. You know when you're trying to search for a word in your head? It's the perfect word for what you want to say. You know it's there in the back of your brain, but you just can't think of it? That's how I feel when I hold this paper. Something's here, just beyond my reach, if I could only see it."

Jack pored over the pages for the umpteenth time, while Cassandra sipped her coffee and peered over his shoulder.

"Let's see," he mumbled to himself, "there's an ad for the livestock auction, vineyard wines, guns and holsters.... What am I missing?"

Cassandra pointed to an interview the paper had done with Sheriff Leggett about a recent bout of thefts on trains coming in from San Francisco. "Could there be something here? The article mentions one of the Beacon ranch hands getting his pockets picked two weeks ago when he traveled to San Francisco."

"Two weeks ago," Jack muttered. "I don't see the connection...." He flipped the pages and came to an advertisement for California Jewelers, the shop Thornley and Miss Beacon had had their argument in front of. "Sometimes the correct answer is the one staring you right in the face. Were they arguing over a piece of jewelry? A necklace? A wedding band?"

"Could've been anything, Jack. Maybe it had nothing to do with jewelry."

"Did he want to buy her a wedding band and she said no? Or maybe she wanted the wedding band and he said no?"

Jack was beginning to look haggard. His eyes were rimmed in dark circles, and Cassandra was concerned about where this obsession of his was going to end.

He tapped his finger on his chin as he thought some more. "And these tea stains here on the paper... I know he didn't get a chance to read it, so where did the stains come from? Dunleigh took his tea with honey, but Mrs. Dunleigh always drinks hers black. Do these tea stains have milk in them or not? If Dunleigh was poisoned, maybe it happened at lunch, just before he got the paper. Maybe his tea was poisoned." Jack sprang out of his chair and headed down the hall.

"Let me guess." Cassandra followed him to the Dunleighs' wing. "You're going to get their tea caddy."

"Blazes, you're sharp."

"You're going to find their tea leaves and their jar of honey. Maybe even their milk pitcher."

"That's right. I'll take the items and these

newspapers to Dr. Clarkson, to explain my theory. He can test them all for traces of poison."

"God, I hope he doesn't find anything." She offered a suggestion, hoping to relieve some of the strain and worry he was under. "Jack, let's go out riding today. You promised you'd let me ride River."

"All right, I'll be only a moment."

He collected the specimens, put them in a pillowcase with a note to Dr. Clarkson, and handed them to Mr. Crawford to deliver. Cassandra quickly changed into her riding clothes, and was heading to the stables with Jack when one of Woodrow's hands came galloping up.

"The horses took a turn for the worst," he panted. "Come quick, Doc."

Jack turned to her apologetically, but he didn't need to apologize for sick animals.

"Make them well, Jack," she told him. "I'll prepare us a private dinner."

But she didn't think he heard her. He was already turned away and asking more questions of the messenger.

Well, she thought, walking back into the empty house yet again, at least no new animals had fallen sick this week. That was a blessing. Only Finley's and Woodrow's from last week remained ill. If someone had indeed fed the animals something unsavory, that person was lying low.

Maybe none of the illnesses had been orchestrated. There were always sick animals cropping up, and who could tell if Finley's and Woodrow's were simply a coincidence? None of Jack's animals were affected, thank goodness, and if Thornley had wanted to retaliate against Jack, wouldn't he start with them?

And as far as poisoning Mr. Dunleigh...

Cassandra shuddered at how her mind had twisted to the point that she was trying to think like a supposed killer.

Mr. Crawford soon came galloping back up the laneway, returning from his delivery to Dr. Clarkson, ready to guard her again.

She prepared dinner—medium rare steak with red sauvignon—but Jack didn't return home. He sent word that he had to tend to the stallion with the hairline fracture and might be all night.

She went to bed without her husband. It was the same the following night. Sighing, she turned to the wall and watched the play of cold shadows from the curtains ripple along the beams.

Tomorrow was the Fourth of July, with the accompanying celebrations. She didn't know if Jack would have time to take her. She didn't know if he truly even cared. She wondered what her friends in Chicago were doing, and longed to see a friendly face. She realized with a painful thud of her heart that instead of growing closer to each other, she and Jack were pulling away.

Chapter Eighteen

It was finally Friday.

When Cassandra came down for breakfast, Jack had left another hasty note saying that he'd be back for four o'clock, if she could please be dressed and ready for the Independence Day celebrations.

She was relieved that he still planned on escorting her.

Then she reprimanded herself for being selfish. She hoped the animals he was caring for pulled through with healthy vigor, that Jack didn't work himself too hard, and that all their worries about possible poisonings and murder would prove baseless.

There wasn't anything more she could think of doing to investigate the possible crimes; no other witnesses to talk to, no further evidence to collect. They had to sit tight and wait for Dr. Clarkson's results on the testing.

She hadn't spoken to anyone at length for days, and couldn't seem to stifle her lonely feelings of how large and expansive this house was, and how solitary it all seemed.

She had hours to prepare, and did so at her leisure. In the privacy of their bathing room, she filled the tub. She dropped in a few beads of scented oil that she'd bought at Lucille's shop, stepped into the heated water to soak, and savored the fragrance and the silky feeling.

When she was finished scrubbing her skin with an oatmeal paste, she washed her hair and wrapped it in a towel. She tidied the room, then called to Mr. Crawford through the door, asking him to kindly seek help from the ranch hands to drain the water.

She climbed the private stairwell up to her bedroom and took her time deciding how she'd wear her hair tonight. She selected her jewelry— not that she had many pieces—and laid out her new dress.

Lord, was she actually going to wear it? Why had she let Lucille convince her to buy something so revealing and unlike anything she'd ever worn before?

Cassandra looked to the clock on her dresser. It was half past three and Jack would be home soon. In fact, she heard the soft thud of the front door opening and closing below, the exchange of mumbled words between Jack and Mr. Crawford, then Jack's boots on the tiled floor as he stepped into the bathing room to wash up.

Her nerves fluttered as if she were preparing for her first courtship with a boy.

Jack was her husband now. For heaven's sake, they shared a bed. Why was she so nervous?

With a towel wrapped around his waist, Jack peered into the wall mirror in the bathing room and combed his wet hair. Droplets of water fell onto his bare shoulders. He was late, he knew, and rushed up the private stairs to the bedroom so he could dress. Cassandra was likely already waiting for him in the parlor.

When his bare feet hit the plush Persian carpet on the upstairs landing of their dressing room, he swiveled, ripped the towel off his hips, hurled it to the wooden counter, then rifled through the hanging shirts to choose one. He shouldn't have left his choices till the end like this, but he'd been so damn busy running to various ranches and vineyards that he was lucky to be going with Cassandra *anywhere*.

He grabbed his newest white shirt and a black suede vest, and strode naked into the bedroom, to toss them onto the bed. Except when he crossed through the doorway, he found he wasn't alone.

Startled by the sound of clothes hitting the mattress, Cassandra swiveled around from the full-length mirror by the window.

Hot damn.

She was fully dressed, and he was buck naked.

A provocative gown in the same gorgeous color as her light golden hair shimmered over the curves of her body. It was almost strapless; slender sleeve cuffs slid off her glistening bare shoulders to midarm. The neckline swooped low between her plump breasts, and the corset beneath seemed to push up her cleavage in a stunning silhouette. A red velvet ribbon trimmed the upper edges of the golden fabric, the ruby color enhancing the pink hue of her cheeks and lips, and doing something amazing to her skin tone. A string of warm white pearls graced her throat.

She'd left her hair down, the way he adored it, but had used a sparkling blue barrette to clasp one side over her ear, matching the blue of her eyes and framing her beautiful face to perfection. Her golden eyebrows arched at the sight of him, her shapely lips turned upward.

His pulse kicked and he swallowed hard at the vision in front of him.

He nodded in pleasure. "I like."

Her eyelashes flickered. They were glossy and darker than usual. Had she added some sort of polish to them?

He sensed a standoffishness, an invisible barrier between the two of them. Dammit, it was still there. When would that protective shell of hers crumble?

"Sorry about the time," he said. "I know I'm late, and I apologize."

Her gaze dropped over his body, raking him from top to bottom, then back up again. Lord, he'd never felt so exposed in front of a female.

Her gaze came back to meet his. "Apology accepted."

Was this how women felt when men raked them over? Jack felt like a bull at an auction, waiting for his number to be called, but hell, he wasn't complaining. In fact, she might have noticed he was aroused. He stepped forward to kiss her, but stopped when he suddenly heard a knock at the front door.

He muttered in frustration. "That'll be Crawford and Giller. I asked them to come with us."

Cassandra scooped up her white lace shawl from one of the upholstered chairs. "I'll let them in."

"Check to see it's them before you open the door," he said, exasperated that the sexual moment between them, and his opportunity, had been thwarted.

Cassandra was looking forward to an evening out.

They took the smaller, two-seater buggy. She sat alongside Jack, while two of his men, with holstered guns, rode on either side. One of them was Mr. Crawford, the other a younger, clean-shaven man called Mr. Giller.

Jack, too, wore holsters. He'd taken to wearing guns lately, so she was growing accustomed to seeing him with the weapons at his hips. Surely some other men in town would likely be wearing theirs tonight, too, although she had a feeling Jack wouldn't care what anyone said or thought about his.

"They're necessary," he'd told her when she'd watched him slip them on. She, too, had her derringer in her drawstring purse, and prayed she would never need it.

He'd tossed his medical bag into the rear of the buggy as he always did. He was tall and impressive in his sleek white shirt beside her, while she squirmed at the thought of his nakedness earlier. He'd looked like a caveman to her, primitive and lustful and so clearly wanting to snatch her and have his way with her on the spot. He likely would have, if it hadn't been for that blasted knock on the door.

They got into town on the late side of five and stopped in first to check on Mrs. Dunleigh.

Cassandra pulled her lacy shawl over her shoulders and hid her dress from view as much as she could. It didn't seem appropriate to be so exposed here.

She was pleased to see the familiar faces of Mrs. Dunleigh's family, including Julia and Ronald, and that the kind woman herself appeared in good health. None of them would be attending the Independence Day celebrations, since they were all in mourning.

In a sign of respect, Cassandra and Jack wouldn't be dancing tonight, either. As Mr. Dunleigh's former employer and the head of the household where the man had lived, Jack had consulted with Cassandra, and both had decided it wouldn't be appropriate to be too festive.

It was after six when Jack parked the buggy by the water troughs set up for the animals. He tipped one of the boys hired to take care of them this evening while everyone else celebrated.

"Thanks, mister," said the black-haired lad. "Awful generous of you."

Mr. Crawford and Mr. Giller dismounted and discreetly followed Jack and Cassandra.

She loosened the shawl about her shoulders and it dipped along her arms. Her drawstring purse dangled off her wrist, a bit heavy.

A boisterous crowd was milling about the lawn of the community center. On a stage beside the white clapboard building that served not only as the entertainment center for the town, but also the courthouse and town hall, a band was playing.

Lively music filled the air from accordions, fiddles, guitars and banjos.

"How is your work progressing?" Cassandra asked as Jack motioned toward the crowd, and the barbecue pit where men were roasting a steer. Jack's gaze wandered down her throat to her pearls, then farther.

"Finley's cattle finally seem to be all clear of whatever was ailing them."

"Thank goodness. And Woodrow's horses? They were the sickest."

"On the mend, but not completely healed. And as for that stallion with the hairline fracture, it's still up in the air whether he'll have to be put down or not. The skin closed nicely, but we'll have to wait and see if there is indeed a break in the bone, and if he can bear any weight."

"If you need to go, Jack, at any time, please let me know. I'd much rather we left early and you tended to the stallion if necessary."

"I don't think there'll be any need. I left someone else in charge tonight."

Cassandra didn't want to ask, but it came out anyway. "Was Miss Beacon helping you?"

Jack jerked in her direction, as if surprised by the question. He shook his head, so handsome in his white shirt and black suede vest.

She wished that they could somehow overcome this rift between them, but every time they got closer, Elise Beacon's name came up.

"No, she wasn't there."

Cassandra breathed out a sigh of relief. However, it came a bit too soon, for as they approached the crowd, and the admiring glances of some men sweeping over her and her dress, she looked straight over at the profile of Derik Thornley.

Cassandra almost let out an audible gasp.

Where had the man come from? He slid into view out of nowhere. He was holding a whiskey and standing beside Miss Beacon, who was drinking wine, both apparently in good spirits.

So they hadn't broken off their courtship.

Thornley turned and glared in Jack's direction; the cold, menacing look made Cassandra shudder. Miss Beacon glanced at her then hastily looked away. She was coifed and polished and downright stunning in a green satin gown. Her brunette hair was pulled back in tiny braids knotted at the nape of her neck.

"Don't make a stir," Jack whispered to Cassandra. He raised an arm and cupped her shoulder blade, the warmth of his palm reassuring on her skin as he guided her in another direction. "We'll avoid them."

Cassandra noticed a slender red-haired woman up ahead. It was Lucille, chatting with Hugh.

The seamstress turned and smiled when she saw them. She wore a stunning brown dress that hugged her bosom and flared out at her hips. "Lovely to see you again, Cassandra. We were looking for you two."

"We only just got here."

"Good to see you," said Hugh.

Jack nodded to Lucille. "I'm much obliged to you for my wife's pretty dress."

Cassandra flushed, and the other woman's eyes twinkled.

"We're both lucky tonight," Hugh said to Jack, glancing with appreciation at Lucille.

"You look wonderful," Cassandra told her.

Hugh discreetly leaned toward Jack and whispered, loud enough for Cassandra to hear, "Nothing new to report on that person." She knew he meant Derik Thornley. His telegrams to Wyoming Territory inquiring about Thornley's past had either gone unanswered thus far, or been answered in the negative.

"Are you two ready for a drink?" Lucille held up her glass, half filled with white wine.

"I'd love some wine," Cassandra agreed. "What do you recommend?"

"I'll get us something. Do you trust my taste?" Jack teased.

"I imagine you might know something about grapes and bouquets," Cassandra replied in good humor.

The next three hours went remarkably quickly. The two couples sat down at one of the picnic tables for dinner, she and Jack on one side—a fair distance apart, to her disappointment—with Hugh and Lucille on the other.

They enjoyed a rambunctious discussion on the prettiest seaside resorts to visit along the California coast.

Every so often, another townsperson would walk by, say hello to Jack and join in the discussion about the health of their animals and the state of the weather.

Cassandra was almost able to ignore Thornley and Miss Beacon altogether, except when they occasionally came into view, dancing the waltz with the rest of the crowd, or laughing together at some remark he'd whispered in her ear. They were both drinking an awful lot, Cassandra noticed, for neither seemed to be without a filled glass.

Jack only had one drink with dinner, for he said he wished to remain clearheaded in case he was called for the stallion later. And that he had to rise clearheaded in the morning to check on all his animals. He encouraged Cassandra to have another, but she insisted on drinking non-alcoholic punch along with him.

They were almost a normal couple, she thought. If only she didn't wish to be a detective, and if only he would compromise.

Throughout all of it, she was ever so conscious that she was being watched. Most of the time when she'd glance around, she saw no eyes upon her. Thornley and Miss Beacon were always caught up in each other's attention. To any other observer, it would appear they weren't even aware Cassandra and Jack were present.

Cassandra, though, was skeptical.

Once in a while, she'd catch the eye of Mr. Crawford or Mr. Giller eating a cob of corn or glancing in her and Jack's direction from over someone's shoulder. Maybe that's why she felt she was being watched. Because she was—by the two bodyguards.

Close to eleven, long after the sun had gone down and the lanterns were lit, the fireworks started.

Cassandra leaned back and arched her neck, gazing up in wonder at the blackness that suddenly burst with a sunflower of crackling lights.

"Jack. There you are!" Sheriff Leggett tapped him on the shoulder. "Can I speak to you in private, please?"

Taking their punch glasses with them, Jack and Cassandra excused themselves from Hugh and Lucille and found a quiet corner beyond the crowds.

There was a slight chill in the air now that the sun had disappeared, so Cassandra pulled her lacy shawl over her bare shoulders.

A big bang of fireworks exploded above their heads. She jolted in surprise.

"What is it?" Jack said to the sheriff.

The lawman tilted the brim of his hat and spoke in a low voice. "I just got word by telegram that Thornley had a charge of horse theft placed against him in Cheyenne, ten years ago."

"How much time did he serve?"

"None. He settled the dispute with the rancher, so the charges were dropped. That's when he left town for San Diego, with his brother."

"Tells you what sort of man he is," Jack muttered.

"None too good," said the sheriff. "But it doesn't mean he hasn't changed. I've seen several men straighten their ways, Jack. Especially if they were young like he was when he made the original offense."

"Still, I don't trust him."

"Can't say I blame you, seein' how he came after you. But it's no cause for a war."

Jack inhaled and looked at Cassandra. The news made her bristle, too, but there didn't seem to be much either one of them could do.

Another crack of fireworks above startled her. Then Dr. Clarkson appeared, his long white hair floating behind his shoulders as he hailed them. "Young 'uns! I thought I'd find you here."

"Did you just arrive?" Cassandra asked, as she, Jack and the sheriff shifted slightly to widen their circle, allowing the old doctor to join them.

"Yes, I'm late because I had a babe to deliver.

It was a false alarm, though. The contractions waned."

"What's the word?" Sheriff Leggett asked.

"Those pills you gave me, Jack? The medicine Dunleigh was taking? I tested them and they're all clear."

"Nothing in them? No poison of any kind?"

The doc shook his head. "I checked 'em for a few things. Nothing there."

"But you can't be sure. We don't have testing for every poison under the sun."

"Oh, I'm sure."

"How can you be?"

"I consumed one of the pills myself. It wasn't poisonous."

Cassandra gasped in dismay.

"You crazy old-timer," said the sheriff. "Why'd you go and do that?"

"I just took one that was labeled for angina."

"I have to agree with the sheriff here," said Jack. "Can't say that was using your good judgment."

"Don't go all fuzzy on me. They're the same pills I take for *my* angina."

"Oh." Jack took a long hard look at him. "I'm sorry to hear that."

"Ah, don't be. Mine isn't nearly so bad as Yule's was. And I was so certain the pills weren't tampered with, I had to prove it to you. I knew you wouldn't believe me."

Jack stared from one face to another. "Have I been that stubborn about suspecting foul play?"

"You sure have."

"What about the tea leaves? And the honey and the milk pitcher?"

"All three negative," said the doctor.

Cassandra was so relieved to hear it, she took a step back and sighed.

The doctor nodded his regards. "Now if you'll excuse me, I've got a bed to catch. Blazes, my feet are sore."

The sheriff tipped his hat, too, and they left.

Cassandra crossed her arms over her shawl, still holding her punch and her drawstring purse, and studied Jack's brooding face. His jaw was set in a stubborn line, then flickered at another sudden blast of fireworks. His wide shoulders remained tense, his eyebrows furrowed in concentration.

"You're not letting this go, are you?" she said with some regret. She sipped her punch, trying to sort out what this meant. There was no evidence of any poisoning, so shouldn't Jack be more content?

He swigged his drink. "Anytime in the past when I've ignored my gut, I've lived to regret it. We'll continue doing what we're doing, with Crawford watching over you."

She quivered with mixed feelings. "It can't hurt, Jack, but for how long?"

"Until we both feel comfortable. What do you think about the doctor's announcement? Do you think we should lower our guard against Thornley?"

"I don't think I'll ever trust him," she whispered. "Or Elise Beacon."

Jack tilted his head with a sober expression. He was about to reply when the sound of galloping hooves thundered up behind them. They turned to see a young ranch hand fly off his horse.

Heads swiveled as he spotted Jack and came running.

"Dr. McColton!" the young man panted. "Have you seen Miss Beacon? Some horses on her ranch just came down awful sick."

An anxious flutter became trapped in Cassandra's throat. She assumed this young man was a ranch hand who worked on the Beacon estate, for Jack nodded in recognition.

The messenger kept talking in nervous gulps as he peered through the crowd. "Have you seen her? Or Mr. Thornley?"

Jack stiffened and pivoted to look for them.

"Not lately. But you need to tell me about those horses."

Fireworks burst overhead, soaring and crackling, making Cassandra's heart skitter as she, too, turned with a shudder and searched the faces for the man and woman she most wanted to avoid.

Chapter Nineteen

"There she is," Jack appeared to say calmly, still holding his drink. "Miss Beacon."

Cassandra followed the direction of his gaze to the left side of the dancing area, where Thornley stood with his arm around her waist. They were both sipping their drinks and smiling about something. Her green satin gown shimmered in the golden glow of a lantern that was hung on a post above them. Her brown hair, with its elegant braids and knots, shone, too.

The messenger ran to them. Jack followed and so did Cassandra. She knew Jack had to go, being the only veterinarian in the valley, yet she was exasperated that he had to deal with such an inflammatory couple.

On the other hand, didn't horses falling ill on

Beacon property dispute Jack's theory of Thornley being the perpetrator? Logically, he wouldn't harm any animals on his lover's estate if he truly cared for her and was fighting for her honor, as he'd indicated when he'd brawled with Jack.

Unless the man himself was cruel or twisted in some way. Studying him now, Cassandra saw no evidence of that. He seemed appreciative of Miss Beacon as he conversed with her.

Several yards away, to Cassandra's left and right, she saw Mr. Crawford and Mr. Giller walking along the outskirts of the crowd in the same general direction, keeping a watchful eye on her and Jack.

The messenger was just telling the couple the news when Jack and Cassandra arrived. Jack set down his drink on the empty table near Thornley, but Cassandra held on to hers as she slid in next to Miss Beacon.

The woman was visibly shaken by the news. "Which horses, Ben?" she asked, her forehead ruffled in concern.

The messenger gulped. "Three palominos."

"Oh," she said softly. "They're such gentle animals."

Cassandra kept up her guard, yet couldn't help but feel sympathetic. The woman obviously cared for the horses a great deal and had to handle this crisis on her own, since her father was out of town.

Thornley had gritted his teeth at Jack's arrival. He shifted his dark eyes to glare at Cassandra, which appalled her, then he snarled at Jack, "I think we can handle this. There's no need for you—"

"Jack's a doctor of animals," Miss Beacon interjected. "His opinion is always welcome." She sighed as she turned toward them. "Hello, Jack. Cassandra."

Thornley shifted his weight from one boot to the other, his dark features lost in the black shadows of the night.

Cassandra nodded, but clutched her punch glass. She was grateful she had something to do with her hands so no one could tell she was uncomfortable standing here. It irked her that Miss Beacon had used her first name so casually, as if they were great friends. Cassandra still couldn't—and wouldn't—refer to the woman by her Christian name. She preferred to keep a formal distance.

Miss Beacon glanced down at Cassandra's drink and nervously slid one hand into her skirt pocket. Perhaps she wasn't comfortable here, either. Her tone was urgent. "Who's there with the horses, Ben? Tell us what's happening."

All eyes turned to the young man as he described the scene. "Dickson's there with them, ma'am. You know how good he is with horses. They were shaky about two hours ago. First we thought it had to be something minor, or maybe they got too much exercise today. We used them for riding through the vineyards, pruning and cutting the weeds. Settin' up the scarecrows to keep the birds away. We hitched the horses to one of the smaller wagons, you know, 'cause our palominos are a perfect size to squeeze through the rows."

Jack crossed his arms. "What are the symptoms, Ben? What do you see?"

"Like I said, shakiness was what we first noticed. Then runny noses. One's got a puffy face, on the left side. Dickson said the heartbeats are running fast. One's got a fever now, and that's when he sent me to get you, ma'am." The sweaty ranch hand looked from Miss Beacon to Jack. "And you, sir. He said to get you, too, if you were here."

Jack glanced over at Miss Beacon. "Let's go, then. I've got my medicine bag in the buggy."

The woman peered at Cassandra. "You don't mind that he's leaving?"

"I admire that he's doing what's best for the animals," said Cassandra. "He wouldn't be the man I know if he let sick horses fend for themselves." He truly had no choice but to go. "Besides, I'm going with him." She nodded at Jack to confirm it, and he silently agreed. He searched the area and caught the eyes of Crawford and Giller.

They were in this together, thought Cassandra, and the bodyguards would be coming along, too. Safety in numbers. Although at this point, both the sheriff and the doctor didn't think they had anything to guard against. It was simply one man, Thornley, angry and jealous at another for having courted the same woman. Cassandra was beginning to agree. Perhaps she and Jack were both too involved in the relationship to see it for what it was.

Miss Beacon's cheeks flushed and she lowered her lashes at Cassandra's statement that she was coming, too, but didn't have anything to say about it.

Jack conferred with Ben about more details regarding the animals, Thornley interrupting with questions.

While the men talked, Cassandra returned her gaze to Miss Beacon. The woman tilted her head, her expression demure and yielding. "I appreciate your kindness, Cassandra." Raising her glass, she softly clinked it against

Cassandra's, then took a sip and set her empty glass on the table. She lifted her large beaded handbag, opened the wooden handles and removed her gloves.

The toast seemed to be a gesture of goodwill, thought Cassandra, as the other woman walked away. Yet as she clutched the dangling purse that held her derringer, she vowed to remain careful. She finished her punch, set down her glass, then hastened to Jack's side to find their buggy.

"Thanks for being understanding, Cassandra," Jack told her. "Sorry it's interrupted our evening."

"Please let me know when we get there if there's anything I can do to assist. I'd much rather get involved than stand by and watch."

The empathetic glimmer in his eyes indicated he appreciated her offer. Jack instructed Crawford and Giller, then added, "Thanks for coming. It shouldn't take too long."

"Sure, boss." Mr. Crawford swung up on his horse and they all rode out.

Miss Beacon's red leather buggy flew ahead of them. They rode a little too fast and a little too rough to be able to talk much. Cassandra held on to her seat and wondered what they'd find when they got to the Beacon estate.

As their buggy pulled into the laneway of

the property, she was mesmerized by its beauty. She'd never been at a vineyard before, and could truly feel in this moment why Jack was smitten with California.

Moonlight glimmered on the still slopes. Acres of green vines clung to wooden stakes, their tendrils woven through gentle ropes that supported the weight of ripening white and burgundy clusters of grapes.

She inhaled the earthy scent of loam and silt clay. A refreshing breeze kissed her bare arms, causing her to pull her shawl tighter. The orchard held trees she wasn't sure she recognized—apples, pears, cherries.

They raced along the laneway, leaving ample room behind the red buggy to avoid its swirling dust. As the road narrowed at the top of the hill, a cliff appeared beside them.

"Look." Jack pointed, equally enthralled.

They were riding along a stony ridge with a breathtaking view of the valley and the town of Sundial below. Cassandra embraced the beauty, the silence and the wonder of being a part of it, at an hour when only night birds and animals were awake. It was all so calm and peaceful.

Fifteen minutes after they arrived, Jack removed his stethoscope from his ears. His guns shifted around his hips. He gave the weak palomino mare a pat on her golden coat. Her white mane and tail stood out in contrast beneath the orange glow of the lanterns they'd set up around the stall. The stable was a large one and held half a dozen horses, a milking cow and several goats.

Cassandra leaned back on her hands, standing at the stall boards immediately beside him. Both women looked odd, thought Jack, all dressed up and awkwardly out of place.

Elise stood across from him, patting the animal and doing her own visual examination, although he could sense she'd consumed a fair amount of wine this evening. For some reason, she'd always had the ability to drink a lot but not show it. Thornley stood beside her with his arms crossed. Crawford and Giller watched from a distance. As did young Ben, the messenger.

The mare coughed.

"That doesn't sound good," Jack said to Elise. "She's got a respiratory illness."

"I think it's gastrointestinal."

"It's a combination of both."

"It's got to be something they're eating out there," she said. "But what?"

"We can check the slopes tomorrow. For now, you should segregate the sick horses."

"Segregate?" Elise looked alarmed. "You think that's necessary?"

"Only for the respiratory part. You don't want your other animals coming down with it." Jack looked around, hoping to make this visit a quick one. He appreciated Cassandra coming with him, but he didn't wish to prolong their stay.

Thornley was getting twitchy, watching. Jack could smell the whiskey on his breath from ten paces.

But the annoying thing was that every time Jack spoke to Elise, Thornley's face twisted in misery, his eyes narrowed, his mouth thinned, and he leaped to hear every word Jack said to her. As if Jack would somehow overstep his bounds and say something inappropriate!

Never.

Whatever he'd once felt for Elise sure as hell was over.

"There's no other barn to put them in," Thornley snapped. "Did you think of that?"

Jack was jarred by the mean-spirited words, but deliberately kept calm and avoided saying or doing anything that might provoke him. "There's the corral out there. I had a good look at it as we rode in. All you need to do is pitch some straw in one of the corners and the animals would have a clean place to rest. You could keep them there

for as long as it takes the illness to pass. I don't
expect it's going to rain anytime soon, so it'll
likely be a good spot for a few days."

Elise brightened. "You don't think it's a serious condition, then?"

"You never know, but I think it's going to
pass."

He heard the straw crunch behind him, and
then Cassandra was at his side, raising her arm,
her white shawl floating over her formal dress
as she stroked the golden mare.

Elise inhaled sharply when Cassandra
touched her horse, and Jack had another sudden urge to hurry and leave.

"Crawford! Giller!" he called out to his men.
"See if you can pitch some straw outside. Let's
speed things up and we can all be out of here
in good time."

"Yes, sir," they replied, already scouring the
stables for pitchforks and talking to each other
about who was going to do what.

Ben ran for the cart.

Elise turned and looked at Thornley expec-
tantly.

"Me?" He raised a hand to his chest, almost
incredulous that she was asking him to help.
"You want me to do it?"

"You are my foreman, are you not?" Elise

bristled and shot him a look of disbelief. "Or shall I wake some of the laborers in the bunk-house?"

Thornley scoffed. "Is that what you think of me? A laborer?"

"No, I simply—"

"All you have to do is ask nicely, for hell's sake."

Elise winced. She looked away, embarrassed.

"Easy," Jack warned him. He didn't like when men picked on women.

Thornley snarled. "Mind your own business, you son of a bitch."

Everyone froze. Boots stopped shuffling. The men stopped talking. Cassandra seemed to stop breathing.

Jack's pulse bounced inside his chest as he told himself to go easy. "If you ever speak to me like that again," he said with cold calculation, trying to maintain his equilibrium as his arteries drummed, "I'll take you outside. It'll be like it was before. Just you against me. And I don't need to remind you who won last time. Now if you don't want to help, step aside."

Jack led the horse out of the stall and signaled for Crawford and Giller to keep their eyes on Thornley. A storm was brewing inside that man, and he'd been drinking all night.

Jack was relieved to see that the animals weren't in serious danger, but the only way he could've known that for sure was to examine them, and so he had to come. But twenty more minutes and they'd get the hell out of here.

Cassandra was appalled at Thornley's behavior. For a grown man to snap at a woman the way he had was indefensible.

With a curse and a mutter, Thornley did what was asked of him and looked for a pitchfork.

Jack handled the horses while the other men went to prepare the corral outside. They were going to pitch a pile of fresh straw in the far corner onto the open bed of a wooden cart, then wheel it outside to unload. They'd need to make a few trips.

Miss Beacon had withdrawn into herself after Thornley yelled at her, and Cassandra couldn't help but feel sorry for her. The woman rubbed her bare arms, then walked over to an old plaid shirt hanging on a nail, and put it on. Much too large, it spilled over her body and her beautiful gown.

She picked up her beaded handbag off the boards and tucked her leather gloves inside. Her posture was bent slightly, as if in defeat, and Cassandra went to stand beside her, holding her drawstring purse. The other woman smelled like stale red wine. Cassandra took a breath, but it made her head spin. Her eyes began to sting, too, from the late night.

"They'll get this done as quickly as they can, Miss Beacon," she said, hoping to lighten the woman's concerns. From the tenseness around her eyes and lips, she seemed terribly upset.

"Elise," she corrected. "My name is Elise and you never say it."

Somewhat startled, Cassandra couldn't argue. She was not comfortable being on a first-name basis. Perhaps it was simply that she'd never liked her enough to want to be familiar.

"Elise," Cassandra said, realizing the woman was feeling hurt because Thornley had mistreated her, and had done so in public. Cassandra got the eerie feeling that perhaps Elise needed protection from him, too. That it wasn't just she and Jack who should watch their backs.

"Are you all right?" Cassandra asked gently.

Elise crossed her arms in those bulky shirt-sleeves. "He's not easy to be around."

"I—I noticed the way he talks to you."

"I'm talking about *Jack*. Jack is not easy to be around."

That was more surprising than anything Elise could've said.

She explained. "I've tried to make peace with him. I've tried to apologize on numerous occasions for upsetting you in the church.... He says he's fine by it all, but I can see in his eyes he doesn't forgive me."

Cassandra frowned, and standing in the stables, looked from Elise through the doors to Jack and his men working hard outside in the moonlight.

"Sorry," Elise said suddenly. "I hadn't intended to bring it up."

Cassandra nodded, feeling stifled from being indoors. She needed fresh air, and indicated they should go outside after the men. A wave of deep concern flowed through her, yet she didn't quite know how to broach the subject. She spoke carefully.

"When I was in Chicago, I stayed at a boardinghouse for women. You'd be surprised how much you learn about people there. A few of the women had been through some terrible times with men. Some of those men were sometimes... sometimes violent with them."

Elise gasped and drew to a halt.

"Has Derik—Mr. Thornley—ever been violent with you, Elise? Do you need help?"

She snapped her head up, in shock and surprise. Her gaze widened, and she started panting,

as if on the verge of confessing something—
something awful. "I'm not really sure who to
talk to about it," she said quietly.

A lump of cold misery settled in Cassandra's
throat. What she'd sensed in Elise this whole
time was fear and loneliness. But the woman
didn't need to take abuse from any man. Cassandra motioned that they should keep walking on
past the corral, so they wouldn't be within earshot of the men. Imagining Elise's problems and
what they might be made Cassandra squeamish.
In fact, she didn't know when it had started, but
she also had a searing headache.

Glancing over her shoulder, she noticed Jack
in the moonlight, leading the first palomino into
the corral. The other four men finished unload-
ing one cartful of straw and went back inside to
get another. Jack settled the first horse inside the
wooden fence, then turned to search for Cassandra. Waving a hand in the air to acknowledge
her, he, too, disappeared inside the stables.

It was precisely at that moment that a fearful
premonition slithered through Cassandra like a
snake through the grass. She felt and heard and
smelled everything around her as though it were
happening at half speed. The smell of the grapevines, the shuffle of hooves in the distant stalls,
an unexpected pain in her stomach.

She stumbled, trying to call out for help, but unable to in her weakness. It was Elise. She was the evil one, and she was trying to trick Cassandra now. With her derringer so close, yet tucked out of reach inside her purse, Cassandra swung around in a daze, grasping her temple and trying to focus on this monster.

In the semidarkness, Cassandra no longer saw a frightened, timid woman ready to seek help. Instead, Elise looked haughty and menacing. She'd removed a revolver from her beaded handbag and was pointing it straight at Cassandra.

Chapter Twenty

Cassandra's heart pounded in her chest as if the devil himself were beating it. "No," she mumbled to the woman holding the Colt revolver. "No, no, no."

Elise's eyes were crazed and diabolical. "Do you damn well think you can just stroll in here and take everything I want?" She snapped her head from side to side. "Jack? His ranch? His babies?"

Cassandra tried to focus in the dim moonlight, but spasms of pain clenched her stomach. What was wrong with her? Had she eaten something spoiled? "You've been drinking," she moaned. "You don't know what you're doing."

"I know exactly what I'm doing."

Cassandra turned to look for the men who'd

just disappeared into the stables, but a stab of pain struck her temple and she nearly fell. She tried to scream, but it came out as a mild whimper.

The sound of someone chuckling echoed in her ears.

"It was you. It was you all along," Cassandra whispered.

"This way." The woman grabbed her wrist and yanked so hard Cassandra saw a flash of rainbow colors. She was pulled by her arm, dragged down a very steep slope with grapevines on either side. When they reached the ridge, Elise shoved her aside.

What was wrong with her? Cassandra tried to scream again, but couldn't. She rasped, "What are you going to do? Shoot me? They'll hear you...you won't get away with it."

"I don't have to shoot you, you stupid thing. I just have to wait this out."

Cassandra forced herself to focus. Her eyesight sharpened, although the headache was almost unbearable. She stumbled weakly, but Elise stepped behind her and jabbed her with the gun, forcing her to move along the stony edge. The sharp cliff veered off to their right and disappeared a hundred yards below, somewhere in the darkness.

The woman was leering. Her braided hair had come free of its ties and perspiration slicked her temples. She was obviously crazed, fearful, and therefore capable of anything.

"What do you mean, you have to wait?" Cassandra groaned between spasms. She still had her gun. If only she could reach her purse and yank at the drawstring. "What are you going to do?"

Elise smirked. "I've already done it. I just have to wait for it to take effect."

Cassandra's mind swirled again in kaleidoscopic colors. She saw jewels and blasts of light and pulsating orbs, and in the haze, she suddenly knew. "You poisoned me...."

Elise let out a snicker of mocking laughter. "A toast to your kindness."

"Back in town," Cassandra mumbled in horror. She would not let this female beast win. And so she kept talking, aiming for distraction as she walked two paces ahead and clasped her purse in both hands. "You put something in my punch. Right there, when the messenger was telling you your horses were sick. You put your hand in your pocket and you took out a vial. You're the one who was watching me all night. I felt the heat of your eyes..."

"You're an empty-headed, witless bitch. I

don't know what he sees in you when he can have someone more his equal. No one will be able to trace the toxin back to me. They'll think you died of some mysterious illness. When you're dead and buried, I'll spit on your grave."

Cassandra held fast to the blurry outline of her pistol and discreetly tried to locate one of the drawstrings of her bag. "Did you poison your own animals, too?"

Behind her, Elise stomped harder in the dirt and she called out viciously, "What the hell are you saying? What kind of a person do you think I am? I'd never harm an animal!"

With that, she thrust the barrel of her gun into Cassandra's spine.

Cassandra groaned at this new stab of pain and stumbled forward, losing her grip on the strings. The bag swung from her wrist. Even in her dazed state, she comprehended that no animals had been sickened on purpose...and was so very grateful for that. Jack's theory on that point, at least, had been wrong.

Hatred oozed in the woman's voice. "Before you came along, I was always at Jack's side, helping him care for any animals in the valley that needed us. Woodrow's and Finley's were no exception. Last week I was blissfully happy to spend time with Jack, but you…you always had to come running, like some forlorn filly."

Cassandra struggled to comprehend. "What did you expect? He married me. Were you hoping we'd divorce?"

She scoffed. "I would have gladly been his mistress." She smirked. "Now I'll be his wife."

"Ugh…" Nausea gripped Cassandra. "And Mr. Dunleigh?"

"Ha!" The lunatic chuckled in mocking tones. "Would you look at that? Maybe you do have a pea brain, after all. But no one's going to pin anything on me. And you're about to die."

"I don't know how you did it, but Mr. Dunleigh's poisoning…it was meant for me, wasn't it?"

More chuckling.

"To think I felt sorry for you with Thornley." Cassandra regained her footing and reached for her dangling bag again. There. She had it gripped between her fingers.

"Shut up!"

"You and Mr. Thornley, I thought. Such a miserable couple."

"Shut up!"

"Is he involved with Mr. Dunleigh's death? What did you argue about at the jeweler's?"

"I said shut up!"

The woman cuffed the back of her head, and in the darkness, Cassandra lurched forward. Her shoe hit a vine and she stumbled. Her face hit the dirt. She was about to lose everything she'd ever cared for.

Jack, she thought. He'd be gone, just like Mary and Father had disappeared so suddenly one fiery October day. Young Jack studying so hard in Chicago to be a vet. Young Jack so caring and loving that he dared speak up to tell her Troy wasn't worthy of her love. Young Jack who ran thousands of miles away from her because... because he loved her, she realized. He'd moved because he loved her, and there was no time left to tell him she felt the same.

Jack coaxed another sick horse from its stall. "Come on, girl, you'll feel better outside." The mare took her time walking down the aisle, so he drew a deep breath and remained patient.

With a quick look at the four men who were pitching straw in the corner, to ensure that Thornley was behaving himself, which he was, Jack turned back to the mare and thought about the evening. He'd been so sure that Dunleigh had been poisoned. But now that Jack observed Thornley, it didn't seem probable that the man paid that much attention to detail that he could have carried out such an intricate plot. Thornley was a clumsy oaf who gave little thought to his actions. He was aggressive with his fists, not his mind. Although with his volatile temper, Jack believed him capable of anything.

And then the doctor's assertion that the medicines weren't tampered with. He'd gone so far as to ingest one himself.

But still…there was one remaining piece of the puzzle. Saturday's newspaper. Dr. Clarkson hadn't said that he'd tested the paper for poison, had he? He'd said all three items had tested negative—the tea leaves, the honey and the pitcher.

Jack came to a halt with the horse. *Oh, no.*

Maybe the drops on the newspaper weren't tea. Maybe *those* were the drops of poison he was looking for all this time.

If someone had sprinkled the paper with toxins…

The delivery boy wore gloves, thus any toxins wouldn't penetrate his skin, but they may have penetrated Dunleigh's. Maybe just enough to get into his bloodstream and push his angina into a full-fledge heart attack.

Hellfire. Who was the newspaper poison meant for?

Dunleigh? Jack? Maybe even Cassandra?

Cassandra! Where was she? He wheeled

around, panicked that he couldn't see her, or Elise.

His heart seemed to rip. "Ben, look after this horse! Crawford, Giller, come with me!"

Elise was smart enough to work out such an intricate plan. And she had the brains to carry it through.

Jack cursed and ran, bolting through the stables into the moonlit field. He didn't see them. He pivoted. Nobody.

He pulled out his Smith & Wessons. "Cassandra!"

His voice echoed into the night.

"Cassandra!"

He cursed himself for being so stupid. For taking his eyes off her and leading her straight into this damn ambush. He was going to lose her and all the plans they had together. She needed protecting, and he'd failed her. He'd brought her to California and had been too damn stubborn to let her know how much she meant to him. He'd been too weak to be the man he should have been.

Hell!

Crawford and Giller ran up beside him.

So did Thornley, reaching for his guns.

But Jack already had his revolvers trained on Thornley's brawny figure.

"You're going to tell me where she is. And if she's not there, I'm going to blow your face off."

Thornley's hands froze in midair. He swallowed hard and his chest heaved. He blinked and Jack could smell the whiskey on his breath.

"I don't know what you're talkin' about."

"Drop your guns."

Thornley tossed them to the dry ground. They thudded.

Jack heard a faint call from the slopes below. Was it Cassandra? An owl hooting? He listened, but heard nothing more.

Desperate, he reached for the back of Thornley's shirt and hauled him into the vineyards. "Start running," Jack growled. "And it better be in the right direction."

"What did you give me?" Cassandra's skull felt heavy, as though someone had filled it with liquid and the muscles of her neck weren't strong enough to hold it up. Her head wobbled, dizziness overcame her and nausea started in. She reached for the grapevines to stabilize her as Elise held the gun to her back. "Was it arsenic? Hemlock?"

"Only something to make you sleep forever." Elise butted the barrel into her ribs. "Hurry up and die, would you? I'm on a schedule."

"Sadly for you…I had a full meal. It's likely slowing the poison."

"You make me yawn. I bet you bore him, too. How can he stand to look at your ugly face?" Then she got vicious and thrust the barrel so hard that Cassandra felt a pop in her ribs. The pain was excruciating and she doubled over, breathless.

She toppled to the ground. The blackness of the cliff drop-off was a yard away. Petrified, Cassandra yelped and sucked in a mouthful of air.

"Good. That's it. Take your last breath."

For a moment, the world stopped spinning. Everything went black from the pain. Then rage overtook her. On the ground, Cassandra clamped a fist around a rock and in one jerky motion rolled over and whipped it at Elise.

Cassandra heard the crack of bones, and the gun fell to the ground with a clunk.

"Ahh!" Elise screamed and grabbed her injured hand. She kicked hard and hit her victim in the hip, but Cassandra grabbed more rocks and threw them, then clawed her way toward the fallen revolver.

She swooped it up and pointed it at Elise just as the woman was about to kick her a second time.

Panting and heaving, Cassandra held on to her sore ribs and rose slowly to her feet. Her derringer was still in her purse, swinging from her wrist, but this gun was better. It had six bullets, while her derringer had only one.

Elise, terrified, held her palms up in the air in a signal of surrender, her injured fingers slightly curled, and pleaded, "Don't do that, Cassandra. You're not the type. Let's talk about this."

"You'd like…to keep me talking, wouldn't you?" she moaned. "Just long enough for the poison to set in, then you'd be free. Is that right?"

Elise blinked and pursed her lips in fear.

"I said is that right?" Cassandra raised her voice and tried to shout, but couldn't manage it. So to alert Jack and the others as to where she was—if they were looking for her—she held the gun in the air and pulled the trigger. The bang echoed along the ridge and made Elise jump. Cassandra quickly aimed the pistol at the other woman again.

Elise nodded softly in answer to her question. "Yes, yes, that's right."

"Now I'm going to ask again. What did you give me?"

"Horse medicine. A muscle relaxant."

Cassandra stumbled to one knee. Elise jumped for the revolver, kicked it from her hand,

and as it landed somewhere beneath the shadow of the grapevines, well out of view and reach, the hag laughed.

When she turned back to gloat, Cassandra had already dug into her purse and pulled out her derringer. Still on one knee, she cocked the trigger.

The other woman gasped as she looked down the barrel.

"One bullet is all I need."

In the darkness around them, Jack's voice rang out. "Cassandra!"

On her knees, but still keeping the other woman at bay with her pointed pistol, Cassandra looked up, blurry-eyed. She saw shapes and figures. Jack was running toward her, one of his men beside him, but then...

Then Thornley ran at the other bodyguard and pulled a weapon from the man's holster.

Thornley shot at Jack, who rolled over, hit in the lower leg.

Cassandra screamed, "No...!" Colorful lights whirled before her eyes.

Jack shot back at Thornley and struck him in the arm. Their two bodyguards, Crawford and Giller, jumped on the man and pinned him to the ground.

Limping, Jack approached the women. So

there they were, staring at each other. Jack and Elise Beacon, both standing, and Cassandra swaying on her knees with her gun still pointed.

"Jack," Cassandra mumbled. "You've been hit."

"I'm all right." He held his weapon straight at Elise. "I know you planted poison on that paper."

The woman, quiet until now, sobbed at his words.

Cassandra tried to make sense of it. It wasn't paper, it was the punch…. Didn't he know?

"Run away with me, Jack," Elise pleaded. "We could conquer the world together."

He was heaving and out of breath, clearly outraged. "I'm taking you in."

"I just want you to love me, Jack," she murmured in a frail voice. "Can't you please do that?"

"I'm taking you in!"

"No," she sobbed, stepping backward, closer to the ridge.

"Don't do that, Elise, there's a cliff behind you. Don't do that." He stepped back to show her he was giving her a wide berth, and that she could step forward.

"Tell me you won't take me in."

"You murdered Dunleigh. How can I—"

That was as far as he got. With a shuddering scream, and the moon shining down on her braided hair and the wrinkled plaid shirt covering her green satin dress, Elise Beacon jumped off the ridge.

Her death was as silent as snow in the night.

Jack let out a gasp of pain and then fell to the ground beside Cassandra.

"You had your gun, Cassandra. I'm so glad you had your gun. Can you stand up? Let me help you up, darlin'. What is it?" Her mind fell in and out of darkness as he continued talking and trying to rouse her. His deep familiar voice grew more and more urgent until desperation hit him. "God, what is it? No, don't tell me. Please don't tell me she gave you something."

Cassandra tried to fill her lungs with as much air as she could to call out the words, but they came out barely a whisper. "Horse medicine... muscle relaxant..."

She heard shouting in the distance. Men from the bunkhouse being led by Ben came charging down the moonlit vineyard slopes to help.

And then her world, and everything she knew, faded out.

Chapter Twenty-One

~~~~~~~~~~~~~

"Jack, you're bleeding!" his friend Crawford yelled from the vineyards.

"Jack, you're hurt," Giller shouted, too. "Stop!"

When Jack looked down at his trouser leg, he saw the hole rimmed with gunpowder, the frayed denim, the shredded black cowboy boot and the pouring blood, but the pain was obliterated by his rage at what Elise had done to Cassandra.

Ignoring the warnings to stop, Jack scooped her unconscious body into his arms and raced up the moonlight-bathed slopes, panting, heaving, flexing all his muscles till he felt they might snap.

He had to get her to his medical bag. He didn't care about his leg. He didn't care about his bleeding.

Gasping for air, he ran through the rows of

sauvignon blanc and Riesling red, alarming even the nighttime rodents weaving along the paths. Scarecrows on crosses seemed to be watching him in the yellow glow of the moon.

He rushed into the stables, his boots slapping on the stonework, and laid her gently on the straw. His fingers flew through his medical bag till he found the brown bottle labeled with the proper tonic, uncapped it and poured it into her mouth.

Eyes closed, she fought him—a good reaction —swallowed, and then within seconds, her guts came heaving up. He tilted her face and swept her blond tendrils away from the mess as she vomited into the straw.

"That's it," he coaxed. "Keep going."

He poured more into her mouth to get the same wonderful reaction.

When she seemed to be finished, he moved her to a fresh spot, wiped her face with a clean towel and whispered words of love.

She did not regain consciousness.

"Cassandra…please….you can't go…we've only just found each other."

His hands trembled. He was getting weaker, and had forgotten about his own injury. Looking down in annoyance, he noticed how much bloodier his pants seemed. They were now soaked all the way up to his knee. Blinking, shaking, he reached for a fresh towel inside his medical bag to tie it up and stop the bleeding, but didn't quite make it in time.... He slumped over beside her and his troubles about his injury were forgotten.

"You've got to take care of yourself," Dr. Clarkson told Jack. "It might only be a flesh wound, but dammit, Jack, you lost some blood and you don't want to wind up with a permanent limp."

It was fifteen hours later, the following day, and the good doctor was making his second house call to Jack's ranch.

Jack, dressed in a black robe that barely stretched over his shoulders, was out of his mind with concern for Cassandra. She was lying in bed beside him. She'd regained consciousness on and off for the past few hours, enough to drink some water and open her eyes, but she kept falling back into that frightening stupor. Jack wasn't the praying kind, but he'd been praying an awful lot in the last twelve hours.

The doctor had seen a lifetime of misery and all sorts of illness—and even a few poisonings in his time, he'd told Jack when he'd arrived at two in the morning.

Now both men turned from where Dr. Clarkson was bandaging Jack's ankle, to study Cassandra's face.

Her blond lashes quivered in the late afternoon sun streaming in the windows. Her cheeks were pale and wan, her lips bloodless and still. Her hair fell in tangles about the open collar of the white robe Jack had put her in when he'd brought her home. Her chest moved up and down slightly with her light breathing.

How could Jack ever have thought that he didn't trust this woman? He trusted her with his whole heart. Hadn't she proved she was willing to face death for him? And he now realized that if it hadn't been Cassandra advertising as a mail-order bride, he never would've married anyone.

"I don't think she broke any ribs, Jack. I think they're just bruised. There's no indentation and she didn't fight me hard when I wrapped them. Luckily, the bruising isn't affecting her breathing."

Jack moaned with relief. "Do you think the poison got to her?"

"You're a medical man, Jack, so I'll speak to you point-blank. She's not having any convulsions. No seizures or eye rolling or uncontrollable tremors. Her color's been pale, but good. There's been no blue or green or yellow shade to her skin. Her posture's not stiff—it's fairly relaxed. And she was able to drink water from a cup several times. So my frank opinion is that if she can wake up out of this stupor, that's most of the battle. I don't foresee any long-term effects, but we can't be sure of that until she wakes up and starts movin' and talkin'."

Jack pressed forward to have a look at her.

"Would you stop your shiftin'?" grumbled the man. "There now, knotted and finished. Continue to keep your weight off of it for another week at least. Use the cane I gave you."

"Hello?" said a female voice from beyond the doorway. "Jack, are you up there?" It was Mrs. Dunleigh calling from the stairwell. Crawford must've let her in.

"I'm not fit for company," Jack told her, snatching at the ties to his robe. He lowered his bandaged foot, hitting the carpet with his bare feet.

"Nonsense, it's only me."

But it wasn't. Her young grandson, Ronald, came running in, along with Queenie and Caesar, who were wagging their tails so hard they nearly knocked over a lamp. Julia followed beside her grandmother, carrying a tray of fresh-baked cookies.

Jack swung himself up, supported by his cane. He towered over everyone.

"How is she doing?" Mrs. Dunleigh took an apron out of her handbag and looped it around her neck, as if she was about to go to work. She was frowning in concern, but seemed calm and stoic in light of her own grief at losing her husband.

"Better than before," said Dr. Clarkson, rising from his chair, with his long white hair swinging about his suit collar. "Are those oatmeal and honey?"

"Yes, sir," Mrs. Dunleigh replied. "I hope you'll take a few off my hands."

"Howdy!" called another voice from the hallway, then Hugh entered, along with Lucille. The seamstress handed Jack a package. "New nightgown. I thought she might like it."

"She's not awake yet to see it."

"Then she'll see it when she does," Lucille said optimistically.

"Yes," he said, buoyed by the care and love he saw here.

"Her eyes are flickering," young Ronald declared.

With exuberance, Jack turned and saw that indeed they were. He watched for a moment, but to his disappointment, they didn't open.

"Come along, children," said Mrs. Dunleigh. "Let's go downstairs and do something useful.

I was going to suggest we bring in some roses
from the garden, but I see Jack's already taken
care of it."

She looked toward the bouquet of pink wild
roses sitting in a vase at the window, cut from
the same bush as the ones he'd given Cassandra the day of her arrival. Then Mrs. Dunleigh
looked at the ones on the dresser. Then the ones
on her night table. Then the white ones on the
armoire, and the yellow ones on the other side.

"A woman can never have too many flowers," she said with a gentle smile. "Julia, Ronald, bring the dogs and the cookies, and off we
go to start on dinner."

Dr. Clarkson reached into his medical bag
and handed Jack a vial of pills. "Something she
can take for those sore ribs when she wakes up."

As quickly as they'd all come into the bedroom, they left for the kitchen.

Jack used his cane and hobbled behind them,
locked the bedroom door and got in under the
covers with Cassandra.

He was hoping she'd come to, but the flutter of her eyes didn't result in her awakening.
However, when he hugged her from behind,
loving the soft warm feel of her body, she reacted to his touch by running her hand over his
and whispering, "Jack."

He buried his face in the warm crook of her neck, kissing softly, praying again that she'd find the strength to wake up and be his wife. He fell into a slumber, on and off for hours, to the comforting hum of voices downstairs, the soft thud of the front door as it opened and closed, the playful barking of the dogs outside.

Many hours later, after he'd gone downstairs and, at Mrs. Dunleigh's insistence, had a light dinner, Jack returned to the bedroom with a dinner plate for Cassandra. Perhaps it was the delicious scent of the housekeeper's cooking, but Cassandra's eyes finally opened.

"Umm…" she whispered. "That smells good."

His heart gave a start, his pulse flashed, every cell jolted to attention. He cautiously set down the platter on the large ottoman beside the bed. His hands went to her shoulders. "You're awake. You're truly truly awake," he murmured, so softly he could barely be heard. "Don't slip away again, Cassandra. I couldn't bear it…."

"Jack…how did I get here?"

She looked around in the semidarkness, for the night sky was deepening.

"I brought you. Do you remember what happened?"

Her lips trembled; her hand rose to clutch at the white lapels of her soft robe. Her eyes slid closed and she faltered over the words. "We went to the Beacon ranch…yes, I remember. She poured something into my punch, Jack. Poison. Oh…poison."

"Dr. Clarkson has seen you several times, and he doesn't think you'll suffer any damage. How do you feel?"

She glanced at the plate filled with roast beef and fresh-baked rolls and vegetables. She went to swing her legs over the side of the bed, and his heart quivered with joy at how good it was to see her move. She groaned then and held on to her ribs with one hand.

"Bruised ribs," he said, at her look of alarm. "Not broken. Here, let me help you up."

"Just a bite, Jack."

"Take it slow." There was so much he wanted to say to her, to explain about himself and Chicago, but he had to allow her time to gain her strength.

He helped anchor her upright, smoothing out her silky blond hair, reaching to encircle her slender waist. Her robe parted over one leg, exposing the shimmer of a golden thigh and beautiful skin. She let the robe lie open, and they both sat in semidarkness, neither one wishing to disperse the sensual shadows forming over them and the soft angles of the furniture. A dreamy light streamed through the white drapes.

Her eyes fell to his wrapped ankle.

"Oh," she said in sympathy. "Jack, you're hurt."

"We're a fine couple, aren't we?" he asked gently, not too serious because he didn't wish to scare her. "Both injured?"

"There was a bang. I remember you were shot."

"It's just a flesh wound."

"Thornley did it," she gasped, as if remembering it only now. "What happened to him?"

"He was hauled away to jail. He's been charged with attempted murder on my life. He didn't have anything to do with Dunleigh's demise. Elise worked alone on that."

"And what about…about Elise Beacon? What happened to her?"

Jack didn't have the heart to say the awful words, but then Cassandra seemed to recall that, too. "Oh," she said with an agonizing realization. "The cliff."

"It's all my fault," he whispered. "For putting you through this. For bringing you to California."

"I wanted to come, Jack. It was me who chose to come."

"Life here has been the opposite of everything I've wanted to give you. How can you ever forgive me for that? I can't forgive myself—"

"You mustn't say that. You had no control over what those two did to us, no ability to foresee the future and what sort of people they'd turn out to be."

"I should have protected you. Even right up till the end, I didn't realize you'd been poisoned, and when I did I wished I could drink the elixir myself—"

"God, I'm so glad you didn't. It's over now, isn't it? And I'm not leaving this bed for as long as you'll have me."

"Cassandra," he murmured, placing his hand on the patch of soft skin above her knee. He restrained himself from touching her further. What he wished to do was take her into his arms and kiss her everywhere imaginable, to show her how much he wanted her. Instead, he swallowed hard and tried to remember that she was still recuperating and he was here to help her, not tax her strength.

"Take some food, Cassandra. Eat something and get your strength and then…"

Someone knocked on the door and he rose to open it.

Mrs. Dunleigh stood there, without her apron

and all tidied up to leave. "I've come to say good-night, Jack." Her eyes slid to Cassandra, perched on the edge of the mattress. "My dear! How wonderful!" She rushed to help her.

Cassandra smiled timidly, overwhelmed by the woman's care. "Are you coming to stay with us, Mrs. Dunleigh?" she asked.

"I would indeed very much like to." Mrs. Dunleigh peered from Cassandra to Jack. "I do enjoy living with my daughter and her family, but I feel rather useless there. They won't let me do much, thinking I'm too frail, and Yule and I shared so many happy memories here."

"We've missed you," Jack told her. He had shared the other horrible news earlier, when the sheriff had come calling and joined them for dinner downstairs. That Yule had been poisoned by Elise Beacon—poison that had been intended for Cassandra. Dr. Clarkson had checked the newspaper drops and had found a homemade brew of toxins that included a combination of different substances. It had infiltrated Dunleigh's skin and caused his death. Mrs. Dunleigh had been devastated and horrified at the traumatic news, like everyone else in the house.

Jack had yet to tell Cassandra, but it could wait a couple days, till she regained her health.

"My dear, would you like some help to rise

and wash your face?" Mrs. Dunleigh sighed with satisfaction when she noticed that Cassandra had eaten her roast beef.

"That would be nice. I could use refreshing."

But as she rose to her feet and braced herself for a moment, assisted by the housekeeper, Jack thought Cassandra had never looked more beautiful. Her blond hair shifted over her shoulder, her robe opening slightly to reveal the creamy cleavage of her bare breasts before she noticed and tucked it closed again. Her ties had loosened and the white fabric spilled open at her leg again, arousing him to distraction.

"What's that?" Cassandra pointed to the package Lucille had brought.

"A gift from Lucille," he told her.

Cassandra lifted it and took it with her to the dressing room.

From behind the closed door, she insisted she had the strength to prepare for bed on her own, so Mrs. Dunleigh left for the evening, promising to come back in the morning with her luggage packed. Jack went downstairs with her briefly to say good-night. Crawford told him to go back upstairs, that he'd see to everyone else as they left. Within half an hour, all the noises down below ceased, and Crawford locked the front door as he hollered good-night up the stairs and left, too.

Jack removed his robe and settled onto his side of the mattress, naked between the cool fresh sheets.

He and Cassandra had things to say.

There was a rustle behind the dressing room door, he saw the light of the lantern snuffed out, and then Cassandra entered the moonlit bedroom in a swirl of lace and satin.

Chapter Twenty-Two

Rich, golden streams of light from the California moon danced over his naked shoulders. Cassandra hesitated at the doorway, as though pausing at the lair of a big grizzly too dangerous to approach, so entranced was she by the vision of Jack and all that made him the man he was. From the stubborn lilt of the jaw, the ache she saw buried in his eyes, the curl of his tender lips, to the faint throbbing of the artery at his throat that told her how affected he was by this moment.

His heated gaze slipped over her face, down the see-through red lace that clung to her breasts, the satin tucked at her waistline—the bandaged, tender ribs—and the long slit exposing her thigh.

"I thought I lost you, Cassandra," he said in a

deep, husky voice. "I thought I lost you on that ridge, and my life was about to end."

"Jack," she breathed, her chest tightening with all the unexpressed emotions of the last twenty-four hours. "I was so careless with how I felt... taking for granted that you'd be here and that we'd have all the time in the world to piece together our marriage."

He inhaled a breath of air and she noticed a steamy mixture of feelings in his eyes.

"I swore to myself I was going to wait. I watched the shadows under the door and told myself that when you came out I'd be a good boy...that I'd keep my hands off you...I'd let you sleep all night and tomorrow, too, if you needed it. And now all I can say when I see you standing there, so beautiful in your lace trappings, is that I would like to guzzle you whole...." The muscles in his jaw flickered. "Are you going to come here so I can kiss you, or do I have to get up on this sore foot?"

He sprang forward like that dangerous grizzly and she readily sank to his side.

"Be careful," he said. "I don't want you to hurt your ribs."

"I took one of those pain pills the doctor left behind. I'm fine."

She eased herself on top of Jack. He grasped

her by the wrists, their faces mere inches apart. She felt the warm heat of his breath on her neck, on her earlobe, then on her mouth. His kiss was needy and urgent, and filled her with such raw desire she felt drunk.

"I'm afraid I'll hurt you tonight," he said in a strained voice. "I want you so much, but I'm so afraid if I unleash everything I feel, I'm going to crush you...."

"Do it, Jack...please do it."

She was giddy and crazy and recklessly head-over-heels as she kissed him with as much heat as he offered. She matched the movements of his lips with her own, the teasing dance, the sweet caress, the flick of his hot tongue on hers.

He yanked off his covers and gently helped her move forward over his bare legs till she was seated near the apex of his thighs, facing him. Her slippery satin gown rode up and anchored at her waist. Hungrily, he slid a large tanned hand over the strap on one side, coaxed it down her arm and let his fingers grip her naked breast.

She moaned and reveled in his touch. He cupped her possessively, bending his head and his soft black hair closer to her body, working his hot mouth on her nipple, then the other.

She abandoned her constraints, allowed him to kiss and suck and lick, letting him press her backward over the bed till they were upside down and she was on the lower end. It was a very comfortable position for her. He kissed along her breastbone, the seam of her body, dragging his lips lower still till he met that mound that was so sensitive and responsive to his tongue....

He brought her to the brink, and she found herself lost in the heat of sexual battle, her bare legs entwined over his shoulders. Found herself lost in the sweet exuberance of his embrace.

Then she halted him, to his groan of complaint, and pulled him upward. He hungrily kissed his way up her body. She danced her fingers upon his belly, grazed his inner thigh and felt him grow rock-hard beneath her touch.

He uttered another eager moan. "Cassandra..."

He lowered his face and kissed her throat, the heat searing through her flesh. Naked, they lay together in yet another position on the bed, limbs sprawled over each other.

"I love you, Cassandra," he murmured, with lids half-closed. Yet he was very much aware of her, gauging her, watching her. "I fell in love with you in Chicago, and that's why I had to leave."

Was he truly saying it? Saying it to her, after all these years?

Her heart trembled and soared like an eagle taking flight.

"I think somewhere deep inside I knew that," she whispered. "My gorgeous Jack...I love you, too."

His breath was quick and warm on her cheek, then on her mouth as he claimed it again. His hands—those heavenly hands—slid gently up her arms, then he turned himself so that he was poised above her.

She felt an undeniable rush of heat to that part of her that only Jack had ever touched, and welcomed him when he gently came to her. Her breasts strained forward through the slippery satin and her body trembled with sensations.

It was a month later when she received the letter.

Cassandra was in the stables shortly after lunch, talking to Jack in his office there, when it arrived. They had just finished an hour-long ride on the ranch. He had generously given her his gentle horse River as a gift, which Cassandra adored, while he handled a more spirited mustang.

Jack's sexual appetite certainly hadn't been affected by his injury, and his leg was almost completely healed. She, too, was feeling fine.

They hadn't spoken much of that horrible night, or all that had led up to it, but privately, Cassandra still continued to read her law books. She practiced target shooting in the pastures, she read the newspapers, she wondered how on earth to approach Jack with the subject of working in the field of investigation again. And while she thought of all that, she got to know her neighbors.

It turned out that most of them were rather charming. Some of them came right out and apologized to her for what Elise Beacon had attempted to do. They'd asked Cassandra not to judge the town by the behavior of a few.

Thornley had been arrested for Jack's shooting and attempted murder. Since there were so many witnesses, he'd already been sentenced and taken away to state prison.

Hugh and Lucille were becoming good friends with Cassandra and Jack, dropping by for dinner and arranging swimming dates and dancing nights as couples. Cassandra found their friendship invigorating.

All the horses and cattle that had been affected by poor health a month ago had fully recovered. Jack had discovered a small strain of suspicious wildflowers in the pastures that he suspected was the cause, and he'd since had them destroyed. The stallion with the possible hairline fracture had fully recovered, too. They would never know for certain if it had been a fracture or a very bad sprain, but Cassandra knew it had healed only because of the caring patience of her husband.

Now, she tossed the new cowboy hat he'd bought her, tan in color and a special order from Lucille's dress shop, onto his desk and smoothed back the hair from her face.

Jack was leaning in the doorway, watching her in that lazy, sexy way of his.

"Jack? Is your wife here?" Mr. Crawford, with his wide black mustache, inched around Jack's bulky shoulders. "There you are, ma'am. Mrs. Dunleigh says you might be waiting for this."

Jack stepped aside while the foreman handed her the cream envelope.

"Much obliged," she told him as he left. She rubbed her palm on her skirts, and looked down at the return address. *Mrs. Pepik's Boarding-house.* A tremor of anticipation fluttered to her throat.

Jack seemed to know what she was waiting for. "A letter from your friends?"

She stared at the pretty, cursive writing. *To Mrs. Jack McColton.*

Would she ever get enough of looking at that name?

"I recognize the writing," Cassandra said as she ripped the envelope open. "It's from Natasha."

"What does she say?"

Cassandra skimmed the lines, eager to hear news of her friends and her former home. "Mrs. Pepik recently acquired three new boarders. She appreciates the wedding gown I returned.... two more ladies have happily gotten married as mail-order brides. The timing doesn't work out for Natasha to use the same gown I wore, so she's borrowing another. She's next to be wed!" Breathless, Cassandra read on, so very delighted for her friend. "Oh, Jack, could we please send a new gown? We could have it delivered by express train, straight from Lucille's dress shop."

"Absolutely. Who is she going to marry?"

"She's deciding right now. She said she received over twenty offers and doesn't want to make the wrong choice."

"I can understand that."

Cassandra was involved in reading the last bit of the letter, and didn't see Jack reaching behind his desk for a large wooden plaque, until he was holding it in his hands. "Cassandra, when you write your friends back, you'll have to tell them about this."

It looked like a flat, varnished board. Perplexed, she smiled quizzically. "What is it?"

"Well, something I've been giving an awful lot of thought to. Something that I think you'll enjoy…and that you're good at. Something that Hugh and I were talking about a few days ago."

"Hugh?" The curiosity was getting to her.

"He came to me and asked if you might be available for an important job he needs done."

"What type of job?"

"He's working on a case that involves an elderly woman in San Francisco. She inherited a small fortune years ago, and now she'd like Hugh to draw up a will. But the thing is, she doesn't trust him. She says she doesn't trust any man with her money. So Hugh thought it might be something that requires a woman's touch. He was wondering if you might like to help him discuss the documents with her, and search for her long-lost son. Apparently, they had a terrible row years ago and he moved away. She'd like to make amends with him."

Cassandra was so wrought with emotion, she could scarcely speak. She swallowed past it all and tried to convey how much this meant to her.

Jack turned the plaque around. It was a small, burnished sign saying Mrs. Cassandra McColton, Private Detective.

"I think you can handle yourself quite well, Cassandra. You proved it to me that night with Elise. I didn't realize how good you are with a gun. And, hell, everyone in town—the sheriff, the doctor, Hugh, not to mention me—is impressed with how you pieced together the clues involving Dunleigh. You were the first to rightfully suspect murder. You even said you suspected Elise Beacon's involvement, but we tried to convince you otherwise."

He *had* given it a lot of thought. He truly had.

"But please, Cassandra…could we go slow with this? It's going to take me some time…"

"We'll take it real slow, Jack. I'll be careful."

"I objected before only because I wanted to protect you. I couldn't bear the thought of…of anything. Not after we finally found each other. Not after what you went through with losing Mary and your father."

"I know," she said softly. "I know now how much pain and sorrow you felt, too, at their passing."

He placed the sign in front of her on the desk.

"It's beautiful," she whispered.

"You can set up an office in the house, next

to mine. That way, when people call on you, they'll know if they mess with you, my guns will come blazing."

He rested his palms on her shoulders, swooped down and nuzzled her neck. With an insistent hand, he tugged the letter out of her pinched fingers and set it on the desk. Then he lowered his hands over her arms and pulled her to her feet.

He turned her around and kissed her on the lips, a slow soft burn between them. His deep brown eyes took her in. She never felt as beautiful as she did when she was in his arms.

"Now don't you think, since I've been such a good boy, that I deserve a reward?"

"Oh, a very special one," she teased. "All day and all night long."

He kissed her neck and she loved the thrill he gave her.

She inhaled long and deep, feeling so content with Jack staring at her like this that she didn't ever want to break the spell. "It's you, Jack McColton. It was always you I was wishing for, ever since Chicago."

* * * * *

A sneaky peek at next month...

HISTORICAL

IGNITE YOUR IMAGINATION, STEP INTO THE PAST...

My wish list for next month's titles...

In stores from 7th February 2014:

- ☐ Portrait of a Scandal — Annie Burrows
- ☐ Drawn to Lord Ravenscar — Anne Herries
- ☐ Lady Beneath the Veil — Sarah Mallory
- ☐ To Tempt a Viking — Michelle Willingham
- ☐ Mistress Masquerade — Juliet Landon
- ☐ The Major's Wife — Lauri Robinson

Available at WHSmith, Tesco, Asda, Eason, Amazon and Apple

Just can't wait?

The Regency Ballroom Collection

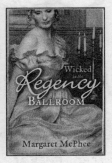

A twelve-book collection led by Louise Allen
and written by the top authors and rising
stars of historical romance!

Classic tales of scandal and seduction in
the Regency ballroom

**Take your place on the ballroom floor now, at:
www.millsandboon.co.uk**

Discover more romance at

www.millsandboon.co.uk

- ❤ WIN great prizes in our exclusive competitions
- ❤ BUY new titles before they hit the shops
- ❤ BROWSE new books and REVIEW your favourites
- ❤ SAVE on new books with the Mills & Boon® Bookclub™
- ❤ DISCOVER new authors

PLUS, to chat about your favourite reads, get the latest news and find special offers:

- 🔲 Find us on facebook.com/millsandboon
- 🐦 Follow us on twitter.com/millsandboonuk
- ❤ Sign up to our newsletter at millsandboon.co.uk

The World of Mills & Boon®

There's a Mills & Boon® series that's perfect for you. We publish ten series and, with new titles every month, you never have to wait long for your favourite to come along.

Blaze®

Scorching hot, sexy reads
4 new stories every month

By Request

Relive the romance with the best of the best
9 new stories every month

Cherish™

Romance to melt the heart every time
12 new stories every month

Desire

Passionate and dramatic love stories
8 new stories every month

Visit us Online

Try something new with our Book Club offer
www.millsandboon.co.uk/freebookoffer

M&B/WORLD